I0754858

SHARDS OF SILENCE

ALSO BY BRIAN YOUNG

Healer of the Water Monster

Heroes of the Water Monster

SHARDS OF SILENCE

BRIAN LEE YOUNG

Heartdrum
An Imprint of HarperCollinsPublishers

HarperCollins Children's Books, a division of HarperCollins Publishers,
195 Broadway, New York, NY 10007

HarperCollins Publishers, Macken House, 39/40 Mayor Street Upper,
Dublin 1, D01 C9W8, Ireland

Heartdrum is an imprint of HarperCollins Publishers.

Shards of Silence

harpercollins.com

Library of Congress Control Number: 2025947093
ISBN 978-0-06-322908-2

Typography by Laura Mock
26 27 28 29 30 LBC 5 4 3 2 1
First Edition

Díí shicheii John Williams Sr. dóó shimásání Jessie Williams ba'

For shicheii John Williams Sr. and shimásání Jessie Williams of Sawmill, Arizona

1

Dimóo dóó dį́ʼíjį́, Biniʼ Anitʼą́ą́ Tsʼósí 29

Thursday, August 29

I hold on to Másání Mildred's wrinkled hand while we wait for her primary care physician to come into the bright, sterile room. She squeezes my thumb. The round, dark grease burns on her hands, from years of making meals for our entire family, stretch and distort. A warm feeling of being loved fills me as I squeeze her hand back. For a ninety-three-year-old, she's still got a strong grip. She tugs her light jacket tighter around her neck. It's hard to believe that she's cold, given that it's eighty-seven degrees outside and the dinky air-conditioning unit is barely working.

Feeling a little restless, I ask my great-grandma, "Másání, do you want some chips?" Should I be offering to get her chips? We are, after all, at the hospital for her heart condition. Whatever. As far as I'm concerned, she's earned all the bags of chips. And it's getting close to one o'clock, well past time for lunch.

"Huh? Oh, okay, sha'awéé'," she responds. There's a gentleness to her breath and words, like a breeze flowing through a cornfield.

She pushes up her thick glasses that have transition lenses. I can barely see her pearlescent eyes behind their darkness.

"Derrick," Grandma Rosie says to me on the other side of Másání Mildred's wheelchair. "Here." From her bulbous tan purse, Grandma Rosie pulls out a five-dollar bill. She stands up and walks with me to the door. Even with the added height of her perm, she's still three inches shorter than I. Being five-eleven and a solid 190 with plenty more room to grow as a fifteen-year-old, I stand tall over her and can see some of her gray roots underneath her inky-black curls.

"I can get it," I say, releasing Másání Mildred's hand. There aren't any Diné words for a great-grandparent, so I just use the word for maternal grandma. I'm told I started calling her másání because my mom was calling her that.

"No," Grandma Rosie responds. "You'll need your money in Connecticut."

"Okay," I relent. I'm glad that my mom is at work and not here right now. Otherwise, she would have gotten all pissy with me for accepting money. Especially since I worked with Grandpa Dominic cutting and hauling firewood to earn a few bucks. Her pride makes her touchy about things like money.

"Where is that doctor at?" I hear Grandma Rosie ask herself as I walk down the hallway. "Mom? What was your doctor's name?"

"Huh?" Másání Mildred responds.

Out in the quiet hallway of the Tséhootsooí Medical Center, I navigate to the area where the vending machines are. My phone vibrates in my pocket. I stick close to the wall as I walk and read the text in the group chat with my two best friends, Chris and Jayden.

Chris writes, Still down for That's-A-Burger tomorrow?

Jayden emphasizes it. The whole text bubble shakes and expands.

I respond, Hella down.

Both Chris and Jayden respond with a thumbs-up.

They are in school at Navajo, New Mexico, a few miles north of Fort Defiance, Arizona. I approach the vending machines and pay for two small bags of chips.

Five minutes later, I'm back in the hospital room, and the doctor stands in front of Másání Mildred. The doctor is more than likely Diné, because she wears a turquoise necklace and has her hair in a tsiiyéél. She looks young for a doctor, probably fresh out of medical school. The stethoscope that rests around her neck has elaborate beaded designs in red, white, and blue.

"That makes you my daughter," Másání Mildred says. I gather that they must have exchanged clans. So, through the clans, this doctor is my grandma.

"Yá'át'ééh, shimá," the doctor says with a wide grin. Másání holds her right hand, and with her left hand, she reaches up and pulls their foreheads together.

"'Aoo', shich'é'é, my daughter, how are you?" Másání Mildred says.

My chest warms. I absolutely love my great-grandma. She's so full of warmth and compassion.

The doctor turns to Grandma Rosie and says, "That makes you my older sister." They shake hands. "I like your hair, shádí."

"Oh." Grandma Rosie blushes and smiles. "Thanks."

Then the doctor turns to me and says, "That makes you my grandson."

"Yup," I say. Her name tag reads *Dr. Naomi Platero*.

"So, grandson," Dr. Platero starts. There is a playfulness to her voice. "What are you doing out of school? It's the middle of a school day. Ha'at'iilah?"

I smirk. I like her. A lot of Diné do this when we learn we are someone's grandparents through the clans—take on a playful disciplinary tone. It always makes me feel all connected to the community when we uphold our traditions like this. "I'm actually not going to school on the rez." I don't tell her the whole bit. Not yet.

But before she can ask, Grandma Rosie adds, "He's going to the East Coast next week for school."

Dr. Platero's eyebrows raise. "Really?"

Proudly, Grandma Rosie explains, "He got a full-ride scholarship to go to Sagefield Academy in Connecticut."

Dr. Platero's eyes fully widen, and she nearly screams, "No way! I went to Van Doren."

"Van Doren?" I ask. That doesn't mean anything to me.

"It's another college preparatory boarding school. We're actually rivals, and we're not supposed to be hanging out. But I'll let it slide because you're my grandson. So are you doing senior year, a post-grad year?"

"Oh, I'm a sophomore," I respond. A lot of people assume I'm older because of my height.

"Wow! You're so tall and big!" Dr. Platero says.

"Thanks," I say with a forced grin. I'm never certain how to respond to people saying I'm tall. It's beyond my control. And I'm not going to thank my dad for my height.

"All righty, then," Dr. Platero says. She leans against the examining table in the center of the warm, bright room. The stethoscope around her neck sparkles in the midday sunlight. "I've reviewed your file and notes from your previous primary care physician. Can you tell me when you have these dizzy spells?"

Másání Mildred has a whole list of health issues; the most concerning is her heart. Years upon years of eating unhealthily has clogged her arteries and messed up her blood pressure. It's all that frybread. I've tried explaining to Másání Mildred that frybread is horrible, but she just laughs and goes on eating her golden crusty delicacy with extra salt. I mean, she's lived a long life and deserves to eat how she wants now. But it's hard to keep quiet when her health issues get worse because of her eating habits.

"Usually in the mornings," Másání Mildred answers. "When it happens, it's right when I wake up."

"Do you feel a little confused?" Dr. Platero asks.

"Yes," Másání Mildred firmly states.

Dr. Platero nods. "Do you use an oxygen machine when you sleep?"

"No, she doesn't," Grandma Rosie answers when Másání Mildred takes a little too long to respond.

"Let's start there. I'll put in an order request for you. For the time being, I want to keep you on your current regime of medications."

Másání Mildred scrunches her face, creating folds and valleys. "They give me headaches. And I want to eat breakfast."

"I know, shimá." Dr. Platero tries to soothe her. "But you

must follow the directions and wait two hours after taking your medicines to eat. If you don't take them, you may experience sundowning-like symptoms. You mentioned you get confused in the mornings?"

"'Aoo', in the mornings," Másání Mildred answers.

"Then you'll have no choice but to move in with me," Grandma Rosie chimes in. She folds her arms across her chest. We've all been wanting Másání Mildred to move in with Grandma Rosie.

"Fine," Másání Mildred relents. "I'll take the medicines."

"I want to do another round of tests to check on your current blood oxygen levels. Your previous tests are a little outdated. Once we have more information, then we can assess our options—some that might even allow us to reduce your medications." Dr. Platero smiles widely.

"What do you mean?" Grandma Rosie perks up.

"There is a procedure called the TAVR procedure," Dr. Platero explains. "This is getting a little ahead of ourselves. But it's an option that I think shimá would benefit greatly from. Again, we'll need more information before we can even consider it. I'll have someone call you, shimá."

Grandma Rosie stands up. "Actually, shideezhí, can we update her records to have them call me? I should have power of attorney."

"That will have to be taken care of in our records department. Just pop in and they can update that information. We'll figure out our best course of action, shimá, so that you're not dizzy all the time."

“’Ahxéhee’, shich’é’é,” Másání Mildred says to Dr. Platero. She pulls her down to wheelchair level for a hug.

Then Dr. Platero turns to me and says, “Grandson, you’re going to have an amazing time at Sagefield. Soak up all the information and have as many experiences as you can. Graduates of those prep schools go on to do great things. Just remember, after you conquer the white world, help your community. You don’t have to live on the rez, but you still can give back in many ways.”

She squeezes my shoulder and leaves the room.

Both my heart and mind flutter with excitement. If Dr. Platero went to a college preparatory boarding school, does that mean I could be a doctor? I could even be the Navajo Nation president! My soul inflates with all the possibilities before me. I feel like I’m floating when I leave the hospital with my grandma and great-grandma.

Around six, I stand in front of Grandma Rosie’s kitchen counter, which is now filled with food for my going-away dinner. I hold a large rectangular Styrofoam plate for Másání Mildred. Grandma Rosie is to my left and my mom is to my right.

“Mama,” I say.

My mom looks up at me. Her long black hair is pulled into a tight ponytail. She has rolled up her sleeves to above her elbows. I can spot a few blots of motor oil around the bottom of one of her biceps. She clocked off her job as a bus maintenance mechanic for the Navajo Pine School District and rushed over from where we live in Navajo, New Mexico. When we were little, Chris and

Jayden used to be scared of her because she always looks mad. Even though she's five-three, I'm sure she'd have no trouble beating down a grown bear with only her fists.

I hold out the plate so my mom can scoop a whopping amount of potato salad that Grandpa Dominic had picked up from Bashas' in Window Rock. The weight of the salad bends the sturdy plate as she slams it on.

"Here," Grandma Rosie says, and she adds a big scoop of Jell-O with bits of canned fruit floating inside it.

"I think that's enough," I tell them.

"Is that for me?" Grandpa Dominic says behind me. He has pushed back his dusty tan cowboy hat on his head. His heeled boots clack on the linoleum floor.

"It's for Mom," Grandma Rosie answers him, in a serious voice that siblings use to pick on each other. "Make your own plate."

"How about you make one for me?" Grandpa Dominic chuckles. "Can't forget this." He places a large golden disc of frybread onto the plate, which is loaded with food. I'm not sure how great an idea it is for Másání Mildred to be eating frybread with her heart condition. A small bag of chips is one thing, but this is deep-fried dough.

Grandma Rosie bonks him on the head.

"Mom!" Grandpa Dominic calls to Másání Mildred. "She's hitting me."

Másání Mildred sits at the end of the kitchen table in her wheelchair. A thin blanket rests on her shoulders, and a flower-print scarf is wrapped around her head.

"Na'." I hand her the plate.

She grabs my hand and pats my knuckles. "'Ahxéhee', sha'awéé'."

Before I can leave to grab another plate, she motions with her hand to bring my ear to her mouth. "What's up, Másání?"

A little louder than a whisper, she says, "You don't have to go to that school, sha'awéé'. You can stay here and go to high school in Navajo." There's a hint of a plea in her words. I can't see her eyes, as her transition lenses shield them.

I smile. "I want to go."

She gasps and holds me in a firm hug.

She mustn't want me to go. As far as I know, I'm the only great-grandchild who goes to see her. When Demi, my older sister, enlisted in the air force, just my grandma, my mom, and I were left to take care of Másání Mildred. Grandpa Dominic and others pitch in every now and then, but we can't always rely on them to step up. I'm certain Másání Mildred will miss me as much as I will miss her. I kiss her forehead. Her skin feels a little cool to the touch. Hopefully with the help of my new doctor grandma, her circulation will improve and she won't be as cold all the time.

Just then, someone knocks on the front door. Másání Mildred releases me and looks up.

"Sorry we're late!" a distant family member shouts. I forgot the actual relationship, so I just call him Uncle Joshua. It's so rare to see him here. Uncle Joshua closes the door behind Másání Gertrude, my other great-grandma.

"Hi, Másání." I quickly hug Másání Gertrude and then

hurriedly grab a sturdy chair and place it next to Másání Mildred. Másání Gertrude hooks her walking cane onto the chair, and I help her sit down. I smile when I see both matriarchs hug each other.

Like Grandma Rosie, Másání Gertrude has permed hair, though hers is all white now. She still has good enough vision to not need glasses. Unlike her older sister, Másání Gertrude has a bit of a sharper nose and rounder cheeks. Even her brow seems to be a little less prominent. Only when they are this close together do I notice these small differences.

Once, when I was eight, I asked why they looked so different. Both of them immediately said, "Doo 'ajínída'." That means "Don't talk about that." It's more than a command. It's a philosophy. After most Diné ceremonies, you are considered holy and must act as such. That includes thinking only good thoughts. By thinking and saying good things, you are attracting positivity into your life. If you think or talk about bad things, then all the good the ceremony is supposed to do is nullified. "Doo 'ajínída'" is an extension of that thought process. If you talk about bad things like death, you are sort of inviting death into your life. So, with a lot of the traditional Diné Elders, they won't talk about bad things because they are afraid that they'll attract what they are talking about into their lives or the lives of those they love. I don't fully agree with this thinking, but I must respect it. It is my culture, after all. I hurry back to the counter. Grandma Rosie, my mom, and I quickly prepare a plate of food for Másání Gertrude.

And that's all the people who are going to arrive for my going-away party. I absorb this.

Someone left the Crock-Pot open, and the smell of mutton and roasted green chili fills the kitchen. Grandma Rosie chastises Grandpa Dominic. The two másánís are busy chatting away in Diné. My mom stands next to me. She holds her phone at arm's length, waiting for Demi to video chat with us from where she is stationed in Alaska. But it's anyone's guess if it'll go through. Grandma Rosie's internet is rez internet and therefore inconsistent on a good day.

An ache replaces the swelling of my heart. I'm not going to be here for almost three months. At least, not until Thanksgiving break. I'm going to miss family dinners. I'm going to miss the last Ndáá-s of the summer. I'm going to miss overnight meetings in the hogan in Sawmill. When my mom gives up on calling Demi, I hold up my phone and sneakily take a picture of everyone. I know that when I'm in Connecticut and feeling lonely I can look at this picture.

2

Nida'iiníísh, Bini' Anit'ą́ą́ Tsoh 6
Friday, September 6

The night before I fly out, Chris, Jayden, and I sit on the arch of the Window Rock. During these last days of summer, the sun doesn't fully set until eight. My phone says it's seven, so we have plenty of time to chill before we have to make our way back through the walking paths behind Window Rock.

Jayden inhales his vape pen and lets out a long exhale. I can make out the cannabis scent underneath the mint flavor as the white cloud disperses against the orange horizon. "Sure going to miss having you around, D-sauce." He offers his pen to me.

"I'm good," I say. I'm not a fan.

"Driving," Chris says when Jayden offers it to him.

"More for me." Jayden inhales again. He tucks his long hair behind his ears. The sunset glares off his glasses and into my eyes. I look away.

The three of us have been friends since second grade, when we were all in the same class. During recess, Chris and Jayden would fight each other on their portable video game system. Chris was the first one to let me play his. Mom was in trade school at the time and barely making enough money to keep our Navajo Housing Authority apartment. Otherwise known as NHA. Otherwise known as No Happiness Allowed.

We've grown up together. We are ride or die. Even though, now that we are in high school, we are all changing. And it's a little scary that we are.

As his Fishbone T-shirt confirms, Jayden is in the ska punk scene playing bass, probably because of his older cousin Starletta, who I might have a little crush on. And also more than likely because of Starletta, he's been really into getting high during the weekends. He's got so much talent. He basically taught himself bass, guitar, and piano. And he's so good at all three of them. Good enough that the music teacher at our high school has no idea how to mentor him, so he lets Jayden do what he wants during music class. Last I heard, Jayden was teaching himself something called the "Appassionata" on the piano.

Chris, meanwhile, is going down the jock path. If it has a ball at the end of it, he's on the team. Both he and I do football during the fall. But during winter, I wrestle while he plays basketball. Chris wants to sign with the Arizona Diamondbacks. He wears a faded and wind-torn baseball cap as a reminder that every day he can take a step toward that goal.

And here I am, tallest in my grade. I'm not the smartest in school. I'm not the most talented. I'm not the most athletically capable. But somehow, it was me who got the scholarship to Sagefield.

"Bet those white chicks won't be able to keep their hands off you," Chris teases me.

Jayden smirks. "And guys. Don't discriminate." Last year, when we were freshmen, Jayden told people he was bisexual. His parents didn't take it that well. Jayden had thought that his parents would be cool, what with all the positive stories in books and movies concerning our LGBTQIA2S+ relatives. But in small corners of the world like Navajo, the lesions of homophobia still exist. Jayden explained to me that our tribe didn't hate on our queer relatives until we were colonized and our Elders were forced into boarding schools to be indoctrinated. "For reals, though, enjoy it."

There's a tinge of jealousy in Jayden's words. All three of us applied. Last year, this amazing woman Ms. Thomas visited our school and pitched to all of us that there were college preparatory schools on the East Coast and that Sagefield was the best. If we had the drive, she would find the scholarships. That's what she said. And out of the three of us, I never thought I'd be the one. It was a struggle for my mom to even afford the hundred-dollar application fee, let alone the testing fees.

Jayden lies on his back and stares at the sky. "Don't worry about us."

"What makes you think I'm worrying about you two?" I joke.

"You get all quiet when you're thinking," Jayden says.

"Just thinking about all the white girls, n'aye," I say.

"You think our little switch-up would work with them?" Chris asks.

I lightly chuckle. We used to mess with our white third-grade teacher and pretend to be the other. To be fair, all non-Diné people say that Chris and I look the same.

Down in the parking lot, a van pulls up. A crowd of white missionary teenagers floods out of the sliding doors. From this distance, I spot that they are wearing the same shirt. Probably something about their Bible camp.

"Speaking of white girls," Chris says with a mischievous smile.

We watch them crowd around the statue of the Navajo Code Talker and loudly babble about how pretty the Window Rock is. After a bit, one of the older boys spots us and points.

Jayden sits up and looks at them. "Yo. Let's moon them."

"I'm down," I say, playing into it.

"Shyeah!" Chris laughs. "They're going to get all offended and call the cops on us."

Jayden stands up and is already unbuckling his jeans.

"Oh damn, you're for real!" I say, and stand next to him.

"Guys!" Chris says. "Seriously. Don't."

"C'mon!" Jayden encourages Chris.

Chris looks at me, pleading with his eyes.

"You don't have to if you don't want to," I say. "But then . . ."

Jayden chuckles. "You said *butt*."

I continue, "You should take a picture."

"Fine, then, gaw!" Chris gives in.

"Still need a picture," Jayden says. He pulls out his smartphone and opens the camera app. "On the count of three."

We are all holding up our jeans and wait.

"Three. Two. One!" Jayden yells at the top of his lungs while holding the phone at arm's length. "It's a full moon tonight! Guys, howl."

All three of us drop our pants and howl, then burst into laughter as we hear screams from down below. They might be more scared that we'll fall off the arch than they are of the public indecency.

"Hey! You three! Stop!" an adult yells. "Come down here right now!"

We are busy pulling up our jeans and tightening our belts.

"I'm calling the cops!" the adult says. He holds his phone against his ear.

"Oh snap!" Jayden says. "Go! Go!"

In a second, the three of us are running to the trails behind the Window Rock and hurrying toward Chris's truck, which is parked in front of the Navajo Nation Fish & Wildlife building. We nimbly rush through cedar trees and horsetail grass. The setting sun darkens the land.

Blood filled with bubbly laughter and warm adrenaline flows through my veins. I know that even though I'll be leaving these two, we'll forever be brothers and have each other's backs. Nothing will change between us.

3

Dimóo yázhí, Bini' Anit'ą́ą́ Tsoh 7
Saturday, September 7

The first thing I notice about Sagefield Preparatory Academy is the smell of freshly mowed lawns, like newly cut watermelon. Robust, dark green grass carpets the hills around campus. Grand deciduous trees are planted in perpendicular rows, with leaves twice as big as my hand. Also, I notice that the sun shines a few longitudinal degrees more south in the horizon than I'm used to. The morning heat has more moisture, too, unlike the droughty heat I'm used to back home on the Diné reservation that has turned Mother Earth brown and dry.

"We're here!" Ms. Thomas cheers. She looks at me through her red-rimmed glasses, which match her vivacious lipstick. Her short curly gray hair bounces with every turn of her neck. Her dark skin gleams in the midday sunlight. She's the director of Diversity and Inclusion, and one of the reasons I'm able to attend this college preparatory high school in the small town of Merewell (pronounced "Merry-well"), Connecticut. Earlier this morning, she picked up my mom and me from Bradley airport. She now drives us onto campus on pavement that's as smooth and dark as fresh black paint. I'm overwhelmed that this is where I'm going to spend my last three years of high school. This could be where I graduate from!

A dark metal plate with old English letters spelling out *Sagefield Preparatory Academy* hangs on a fancy redbrick arch. The buildings all have the same clean red bricks. No graffiti anywhere. To our immediate right are three dark bronze sculptures of bulls. Right in front of us is the main school building. It's a large two-story building with big broad windows. To the right of the main building is the three-story library. To the left is the school chapel.

All around the main building are the dormitories. To the east are the girls' dorms and to the west are the boys' dorms. Splitting them apart is the smooth pavement that we are driving on. According to the map in the brochure I hold in my hand, there is a gender-neutral dorm behind the main building. There are separate fields for football, soccer, field hockey, and baseball, and an eighteen-hole golf course. Like, a baseball field specifically for baseball and not a football field doing double duty. Northward, beyond campus, is Lake Lavender, where the rowing team practices.

I wish I could do rowing. However, I'm certain that football and wrestling for the Dire Foxes are two major reasons that I was accepted to Sagefield. Even though I am a decent defensive football player, I excel in wrestling. Not to brag, but I placed third in the Arizona state wrestling championship as a freshman last year. So, obviously, I have to participate in those two sports. Ms. Thomas didn't have to tell me, but I'm pretty sure my full-ride scholarship is conditional on my sports abilities.

Ms. Thomas veers left toward the boys' half of campus and then parks behind the boys' dorm named Tristan Galloway. "This dorm is for Preps and Lower-Mids," she explains. "Preps are freshmen, and Lower-Mids are sophomores."

Everything here has a weird, stuck-up name. The cafeteria is called the dining hall. The principal is called headmaster. The buildings and wings of classrooms are called learning centers. And not only that! They have to have some name attached to them. It's the Wilma Reynolds Athletic Center. It's the Rachel Eiselberg Dining Hall. And so on.

My mom steps out and inhales the humid late-summer air. She quietly surveys the dorm building and whispers in awe, "Damn." She folds her arms and squints. She has on her nice polo shirt that she wore at Demi's high school graduation two years ago.

I smile and stand next to her. "Yup."

"Oh!" Ms. Thomas says. She yanks out her large handbag from the car to grab her phone. "Photo! Someday, years from now, Derrick, you'll look at this picture and think, 'Wow! I was just a baby!' You too, Darlene!"

My mom turns from looking at the golf course nestled next to a thick northwestern Connecticut forest. She rests her head against my shoulder, and I hold her. We smile. Click. Ms. Thomas tosses her phone back into her bag and then says, "Let's flag down a proctor to help with your luggage."

"I don't need help," I say. I have just one large black suitcase with wheels. I don't really have that much. I have six sports coats, just as many khaki pants, several button-down shirts, and some ties that I was barely able to afford with the money I earned from Grandpa Dominic. That's the boys' dress code. Alongside those, I brought my wardrobe of comfortable shirts, pants, shorts, and athletic wear, including my very own lucky wrestling shoes.

"Eric!" Ms. Thomas yells to a group of seniors sitting at a white desk with a large banner reading *Check-In*. They all wear dark blue shirts with *Proctor* in silver letters; those are the school colors.

"Hi, Mama Sandy!" Eric waves. His fancy leather sandals smack against the bottom of his heels as he approaches us. His skin is a gentle bronze. Not the tan of someone who works outside all day but of someone who spends a few hours outside in a bathing suit to get some color. The first word to cross my mind is *preppy*.

"Can you help us with getting Derrick moved in?" Ms. Thomas commands.

Eric asks, "Derrick? You're on my floor. Wow, you're huge for a Lower-Mid!"

"Nice to meet you," I respond, lowering my voice. I squeeze his buttery-soft palm in a firm handshake. A surprised expression crosses his face.

"Strong grip," he yelps. We release, and he reaches over to shake my mom's hand. "Your son is going to be well taken care of, Mrs. Hoskie."

"Miss," my mom corrects him. "Thanks for saying that." I wonder where her fire has gone. She's timid, reserved, and quiet.

Grandpa Dominic told me that my mom used to get into a lot of fights when she was in high school. Now she stands there twirling her thumbs, the way Grandma Rosie does when she's nervous.

Eric turns to Ms. Thomas and says, "You're personally hand-delivering this one? He must be special."

Ms. Thomas grips his shoulders, and he winces subtly. I rub my shoulder and remember her tough grip when she picked up my mom and me earlier this morning. "I want you to keep an eye out for Derrick. He's fresh off the reservation and may need some extra guidance!"

"Reservation?" Eric asks.

"From the Navajo Indian reservation," Ms. Thomas says.

Eric mouths a "Whoa!"

Not that I want to hide my Diné-ness, but having someone else tell others that I'm Native doesn't feel cool. I didn't have to deal with it on the rez because, well, everyone is Diné. But in border towns, like Gallup or Farmington, non-Natives often treat you like dirt. How will people here treat me when they find out I'm Native? I want to leave this conversation before he has a chance to mention his distant Indian ancestor, which all white people say they have, or the ancestry test he recently took.

"My dad and I took a 23andMe test, and we're three percent Cherokee. So I'm Native, too!" Eric says. Yup. Called it.

"No, you're not," my mom shuts him down. She folds her arms and stares directly into his eyes. Almost daring him to say it again. Eric doesn't know how to respond to that and just stares back, dumbfounded.

I love my mom. Just like that, she's out of her shell and back to the warrior woman who once cooked for a one-hundred-person event with fifty bucks, four sheep, and only me for a helper.

"Let me show you your room," Eric says, handing me my dorm room key.

Eric takes us to my room on the fourth floor of the Tristan Galloway Dormitory using the elevator. I can't believe there's an actual elevator in my dorm!

"All dorms also have faculty members on their floors," Eric explains. "For underclassmen, there is an additional senior proctor who helps with anything you might need. If you have any questions, come to me and I can point you in the right direction." We step out of the elevator. The floor is quiet and empty. "You're the first on the fourth floor to arrive. It's going to get busy this afternoon when everyone else shows up."

"Just as well," Ms. Thomas chirps. "We could only bring Darlene for a few hours. But it's so important for parents to be here when they drop off their babies."

"You can say that again," my mom says. Her voice wobbles. I know she wanted to stay longer but couldn't get the time-off request approved.

"He's in football, so he'll need to go to the field tomorrow morning for practice," Ms. Thomas explains.

Eric rubs his chin, which has the beginnings of a five-o'clock shadow. "Football, huh? Reese Carter on the second floor is in varsity football. Galloway has a bunch of soccer players and water polo."

"Water polo? I'd sink right to the bottom," I joke. Though it's probably accurate. I'm a mean doggy paddler, but that's it.

"You should try out!" he says.

I can't believe he said that right in front of Ms. Thomas! If I were to try something other than football, would that negate my scholarship? Mom and I can't afford this place.

Ms. Thomas saves me. "Not this one, Eric! He's skipping JV and going right into varsity football."

"Varsity?" Eric says. His eyebrows rise almost to the brim of his hat.

"Coach Price saw Derrick and his football team play and knew that he belonged on varsity." Ms. Thomas sounds like she's bragging.

I half smile, excited that my ability to tackle hard helped get me here, as well as a little bitter that I can't do another sport like rowing. I turn my gaze downward so that he doesn't think I'm overly proud. "What sports do you do?"

"Cross country in the fall, private study in the winter, and golf in the spring." He holds his nose high. It's official. This guy sucks. "I take it you got it from here. Again, if you need any help," Eric says, "reach out."

Eric leaves as I fumble with the brass key. Then I open the door to my new room and lead my mom and Ms. Thomas inside. So this is the space I'll be living in for the school year. Opposite the door is a large rectangular window. Underneath it, in the sunlight, is a light brown wooden desk. Next to my desk is a large chest with five drawers. Pushed up against the wall to my right is a long twin bed frame with a mattress. To my left is a sliding door that has been left open, revealing my large closet.

"Come on, you can unpack later. I want to give both of you a tour of campus!" Ms. Thomas says. She claps and squeezes her hands together.

I leave my luggage in the middle of the room and follow Ms. Thomas to wherever she wants to take us.

Ms. Thomas leads us across campus as more students arrive in black Mercedes SUVs, Cadillacs, and Rolls-Royces. We enter the dining hall through the main building, which is the oldest of the buildings and connects the auditorium for all school meetings, the language wing, the English wing, the music hall, the student activity center, and the Grillery. The ceilings of the dining hall reach high and host three sparkling chandeliers. There is a large center area with round walnut tables.

"The dining hall is equipped to handle all your dietary needs." Ms. Thomas beams. Her low-heeled pumps tap against the light wooden floor, which is reflective from polish. "We work with several local farms and bring in their produce for the salad buffet. One of the farms near Buffalo supplies our school with fresh-ground bison from their herd! It's so fresh you'd think it came right off the animal!"

My mom and I share a smile. "When you come back, Sandra," my mom says to her, "we'll butcher a sheep fresh for you. Then you can have some off-the-animal meat." Mom is relaxing more, not twirling her thumbs. Her shoulders aren't scrunched. She's even crossed her arms. Diné tend to cross our arms. I'm not sure why. There's probably some cultural reason. Like how, in the hogan during a ceremony, you have to cross your legs whenever you receive food, water, or medicine. So I cross my arms. It feels respectful. It might also just be my family that does this.

Ms. Thomas rubs my mom's shoulder. "As long as I can cook you a big meal."

I love that my mom and Ms. Thomas are becoming friends.

Ms. Thomas leads us to the exit. There are three pairs of doors. She points to the ones in the middle: "Don't walk through the middle doors. Only seniors do. If you're not a senior and walk through them, you'll be cursed and end up expelled. It's a silly superstition, I know! But it's always fun to play along."

After avoiding the middle doors, Ms. Thomas leads us to the science building, or rather the Grant McClintock Learning Center for Science.

"This whole building is for just science?" my mom asks. She looks completely awestruck and mesmerized. She had told me long ago that she wanted so badly to go into robotics. That's probably why she now works as a mechanic, doing maintenance for Navajo school district buses.

Ms. Thomas is more than happy to explain. "Yes! Sagefield has physics, chemistry, biology, psychology, sociology, anthropology, earth sciences, and even astronomy! Look at the top; the telescope is set up for night viewing."

My mind takes a minute to absorb all this info. I really love the idea of taking physics for my science requirement. Then I look up to the top of the building and see this expensive telescope that's the size of a fifty-five-gallon barrel.

"During the last lunar eclipse, the astronomy teacher, Ms. Winters, invited the whole community to view it. You should go if that happens again!"

"I can't," I say.

"Why is that?" Ms. Thomas asks.

My mom answers, "We believe that eclipses, lunar and solar, are the deaths of those beings. Back in the old days, our ancestors would sit inside their hogans to pray while the eclipse happened. These days, we can't be outside, nor can we look at it in person, otherwise we'll get moon sickness." There's another explanation of eclipses, but we aren't allowed to share that version.

"That is so interesting!" Ms. Thomas says.

"That's our way of life," my mom says. "It's more than superstition."

We get to the massive glass doors of the Grant McClintock Learning Center for Science and enter a chilly dry atmosphere. Ms. Thomas points out the classrooms, or whatever stuffy name they have for classrooms. A number of classrooms have four electric microscopes that she explains cost a few thousand. Each. A wealthy family donated them. Toward the end of the building, we walk upstairs to the second floor.

Ms. Thomas points out of the windows of the staircase. "That's the Wilma Reynolds Athletic Center, Derrick. You'll be going there for football tomorrow morning."

I stare out and see a large modern building. Unlike the redbrick main building and learning centers, this one is made of smooth concrete and panes of glass. Oh man, I can't wait to work out at the gym here. Leading to the front entrance is a large curving black path that Ms. Thomas describes as being made from recycled sneakers.

Ms. Thomas continues, "And just south are the administrator houses, where I live." Beyond the parking lot and across the glistening, smooth paved road are two rows of pristine wooden houses with white picket fences. "When you come back for Parents' Weekend, Darlene, I'll be hosting you. I have this coffee that is to die for!"

"I'm already saving up money to come back," my mom says.

"Darlene," Ms. Thomas says. She pushes her fists into her sides and raises an eyebrow like my mom just said the most ludicrous thing in the world. "Do you understand what world we are in yet? There is money set aside for everything. We had a student from Thailand whose parents couldn't afford international tickets for his graduation. When I heard about this, I got on the phone, called up the headmaster himself, and I said to him that if we are going to commit to diverse students, we are going to commit. None of this half-behind stuff is going to fly. We were able to secure funds to get all his family members to graduation. All of them. Mom, Dad, grandmami, grandpapi, two brothers, two sisters. Darlene, you tell me what you need, and I'll make it happen. You better be ready to come back here for Parents' Weekend in October."

There are tears in my mom's eyes. She has been scared of letting me, her youngest child, go. I'm sure hearing what Ms. Thomas just said reassures her that Sagefield is going to be a place for me to grow and be enriched. "All I ask is that you check in with Derrick."

Ms. Thomas says, "I'm going to be keeping both eyes on this one. If he so much as sneezes and doesn't say 'excuse me,' I'm going to hunt him down and wring him out myself! With my own two hands!"

They both laugh. I appreciate what she says, hunting me down if I step out of line. Growing up on the rez, there are tons of family members everywhere that get on your case if you act up. I don't mind being chewed out because it usually comes from a place of love. Ms. Thomas is like a long-lost auntie, and I hope she will correct me if I mess up. Because I don't want to screw up my opportunity to be here.

"Look at the time!" Ms. Thomas says.

I look at my phone, and it says 2:30, which means it's almost time for my mom to leave for the airport. Ms. Thomas guides us outside, and I emotionally prepare myself to say goodbye.

When we get back to my dorm, a few students have arrived. I see mostly white faces. It hits me that I'm a minority here. Ms. Thomas said I was going to be the only Native on campus this year. But I didn't understand what that meant until now.

"Mama Sandy!" shouts Eric, waving her to come to him.

"I'll meet you both in your room," Ms. Thomas tells me.

My mom and I navigate back to the fourth floor. As the elevator door opens, there stands a woman who looks like she belongs on television. The sunlight that pours in from the skylight above makes her tanned skin and voluminous wavy blond hair glow. I try to be polite and not stare at her body underneath the fancy polo and golf skirt she wears. Behind her is a mountain of a man. For some reason I get this urge to fight him, if just to prove that I can take down someone six feet and four inches tall. They both smile at us and move to let us out of the elevator. Their teeth are straight and bleached, and they could be in a toothpaste commercial. There are actually people like this in the world!

"Hi!" Her voice is deeper than I expected, with a touch of sultriness, like a jazz singer's. She shakes my mom's hand. I catch my mom checking out the dad. "I'm Sharon Ecclestone, and this is my husband, Terrance!" She shakes my hand, too.

"I'm Derrick," I say, still dazzled by her smile. My mom and I awkwardly slide out of the way to let them into the elevator. But they continue to hang around and talk.

"Pleasure to meet you, Derrick," Mr. Ecclestone's voice booms. "Caleb! Come out and say hi!"

Behind them, Caleb shyly walks out of the room directly across from mine. He has thin dark brown hair like his father and his mom's green eyes. He's taller than I am but lanky. I'm more muscled than him. There are pimples covering his cheeks. He doesn't look happy to be here.

"Hey," he says, then looks at the floor.

Mr. Ecclestone walks over to me and shakes my hand and pats my shoulder. "Wow, that's a man's handshake."

"Thank you, sir." I like these people. My arms fold behind my back. I point my toes forward and stiffen my neck.

"Military?" Mrs. Ecclestone asks, looking at my mom.

"His grandpa, uncle, and older sister," my mom responds.

"Sharon served twice after high school," Mr. Ecclestone explains.

No way! How does she just keep getting cooler every minute?

"So did Terrance," Mrs. Ecclestone says, and leans her head on his shoulder.

"Are you planning on enlisting?" Mr. Ecclestone asks.

"I'm considering it," I admit.

"As long as you're not unemployed living under my roof," my mom snarks.

"Maybe you and Caleb can enlist together," Mrs. Ecclestone says. She motions him over to shake my hand.

Caleb tries his best to hide his frustration. We shake hands. He avoids looking at me. Is he mad at me or something? Whatever, I don't need him to be my friend. I'm sure I'm going to have tons of friends on the football team.

I ask, "Do you guys need help?" Even though it would take up what little time I have left with her, my mom would chew my ear off for not offering.

"No, we already got all of Caleb's stuff in," Mr. Ecclestone says, thankfully.

"How thoughtful," Mrs. Ecclestone gushes. To which I almost blush. "Are you available for a late lunch? We're just about done."

"No," my mom says. "I actually have a flight to catch this afternoon."

"Next time . . ." Mrs. Ecclestone trails off.

"Darlene Hoskie," my mom finishes. "Yes, next time."

The Ecclestones head into the elevator while I unlock my door.

* * *

We stand back in my dorm room. My mom bites her lower lip with enough force that her jaw pops out slightly.

I know she loves me. But I've seen her struggle to buy me decent clothes, regularly feed me, and keep me away from the gangs in my neighborhood. I'll finally be on my own. She'll no longer have to scrounge around or work overtime to be able to support me. I'll have breakfast, lunch, and dinner consistently here. She should feel a huge load has been lifted off her shoulders. I hope she's proud of me.

It takes the length of an exhale for her to cry. She pulls me into a hug and rests her head on my chest.

"They always say the youngest one leaving hurts the most," she tells me. "It does."

Everything I felt before evaporates. I hate seeing her cry. I hate that it's me who is making her cry. "I'm sorry."

"Don't apologize." She releases me and pulls a napkin out of her purse. "This is just something mothers go through."

"Are you going to be okay?"

"Don't worry about me," she says.

"I *am* going to worry about you."

"No, you're not. You are going to graduate from here. You're getting into an Ivy League school with a full-ride scholarship because you have that drive."

"I get that from you," I say to soften her sadness.

But it does the opposite and sends her into another crying session. I hold her. This time, her entire body heaves.

"Doesn't matter when you leave, I'd still cry like this," she says. "Does this place make you happy?"

It makes parts of me happy, but I'm not fully in love with the place. Not yet. I tell her, "Very."

"That's all I need," she says as she pushes out of my hug.

Just then, Ms. Thomas knocks on the door and enters. "Oh, Darlene," she says. "I cried for twelve whole days when my youngest left the nest. Twelve! I would hover outside her room and just stare at her bed."

"I thought empty-nest syndrome was made up." My mom chuckles through her sobs.

"You feel those feelings. You call me when it becomes too much to breathe, because it will get to that point. Trust me, your son is safe. He's going to get a world-class education from the very best teachers in the nation. So many opportunities will be available to him, like study abroad programs and school trips to Broadway shows in Manhattan. I promise you that I will be on his behind the moment he steps out of line! And remember: you're coming back for Parents' Weekend in October."

My mom nods. One more hug. "My heart, I'm going to miss you."

Her hair brushes against my cheek. I want to scratch it but don't for her sake.

She inhales, and then we are no longer hugging. She wears her neutral face. Her lips are scrunched together. Her eyes glint. She breathes evenly, intentionally. Everyone else would assume she's angry, but I know she's suppressing her sadness.

"I'll call on Sundays," I tell her.

"Damn right you will. Don't forget Grandma Rosie and Másání Mildred." She leaves with Ms. Thomas, and they walk down the stairs to the parking lot in back. My door closes.

For the first time I feel the weight of everything I did to get here. Raising most of my grades to As. Becoming the best guard in football. Placing third in Arizona state wrestling. I even had to cancel hanging out with Chris and Jayden several times.

I look at my luggage and am thankful for the distraction. I will take my time moving in, because once that is done, there is nothing left to do but miss my mom, my friends, and my home back on the rez.

4

Dimóo, Bini' Anit'ą́ą́ Tsoh 8
Sunday, September 8

Walking on the recycled-sneaker path to the athletic center feels like stepping on condensed marshmallows. Today, I have a lot going on. First is football practice in the morning. Then I have a Lower-Mid meeting and finally an all-school meeting. I look at my phone, and I'm thirty minutes early to practice. Good. Coach Atcitty, my football and wrestling coach at Navajo Pine, drilled his athletes to be fifteen minutes early. Any later earned you sprints, which I absolutely hate. A powerful gust of air conditioning blasts my bare neck when I enter through the sliding glass doors.

My footsteps echo in the lonely three-story-high grand hall. A bronze statue of a dire fox, the school mascot, stands at the center. It has the stature of a large silver wolf as well as the triangular face, bushy tail, and large ears of a fox. It bares its fangs and swats a massive right claw. There is a smooth, slightly golden patch on the tip of its nose.

This whole place is just awesome. I wish Chris and Jayden were here with me. Even though it's two hours earlier back home, I start a video chat with both. After a few rings, Chris answers first. He's still lying in his bed.

"Sup, duders?" he says through a yawn.

"Check this out, man," I answer. I flip the camera around and show him the dire fox statue.

"Yiiyah, yeenaldlooshi!" he says.

I chuckle. Then I hear Jayden enter the conversation.

"It's five thirty-five, jerk," Jayden says. He rubs his eyes, then squints at his screen. "Whoa, what's that place?"

"This is the athletic building. Check this out." I show them the two Olympic-sized swimming pools to my left. I turn, holding my phone close to my chest, to show the four basketball courts. I tilt the phone up to show them the indoor running track above. Farther down the hall, I stand in between two more halls. I spot the sign that reads *Boys' Locker Room*.

"Damn," Chris says.

"Four indoor basketball courts?" Jayden says. "Which one do they use for games?"

"Those are just their practice courts," I brag. "The stadium basketball court is somewhere else."

"Nice, D-sauce," Jayden says. "I'm going back to sleep. Send me pics."

"The only nudes I do are noodles," I joke.

Jayden lazily smirks, then says, "You know you want to send me your angles. Hit me up later. Happy for you, D-sauce." He hangs up.

As I walk to the locker room, I say, "This place is nuts, man. They practically have a building for each school subject."

"That's cool, brother-man," Chris says. "But I'm going to follow

Jayden's lead and get more sleep. Post some more pics when you get a chance."

"All right," I concede, feeling a little disappointed.

"Later," Chris says.

I end the video chat. I really wanted to share my first tour of the athletic center with my two best friends. Chris would have really enjoyed the athletic building. I'm certain Jayden would get a kick out of the music hall. I take some pictures and load them onto my PicsPress account. I notice that Jayden has already uploaded the photo of us on the Window Rock arch.

My mom doesn't allow me to have more than PicsPress at the moment. I've thought about signing up for other social media sites, but if my mom ever found out I did something without her permission, she would confiscate my phone. And she has, like, hardcore mom knowledge. She just knows things about me. She also has access to all my passwords on my phone.

The moment I enter the locker room, I am overwhelmed by the smell of artificial pine. The aggressive scent coats the inside of my nostrils. Real forests do not smell this strongly. Dark cherry wood doors line the walls all the way down the enormous space. First initials and fully spelled-out last names hover above the lockers in golden letters. I notice IIIs in several of the last names. Whoa, buddy, there's a V!

At the other end, I see shower stalls with neatly labeled bottles filled with shampoo, conditioner, and body wash. I bet the water is always hot and never in danger of being turned off because of late payments. There are actual curtains here that have the texture of fabric. I squirt the body wash and sniff its subtle masculine smell.

Beyond the shower and toward the back are metal lockers. None of them are rusted, torn open with pliers, or graffitied. Mine has my first initial and last name spelled out for everyone to see: D. Hoskie. The lonely Diné last name. Inside are royal-blue cotton athletic shorts, a pair of socks that are too long for my comfort, a jockstrap that I'm never going to use, white compression shorts, and a white T-shirt with our mascot printed on the chest. I best get ready. I want to be the first on the field to earn my spot to belong here.

The football field sits behind a dense row of pine trees. The home bleacher has *Dire Foxes* painted in royal blue on the metal edges so the visiting team can clearly see it. That's right. I'm no longer a Navajo Pine Warrior. I'm a Sagefield Dire Fox. My school colors are now silver gray and royal blue.

It's ten minutes to eight, and still no one has arrived. My heart pumps and my legs ache for activity. Then, finally, a senior, probably, with long curly brown hair leads two other guys who are my height. Their exposed shins and forearms don't have any bruises or nicks.

"Hey there," Curly Hair says.

"Good morning, name's Derrick," I say, and reach out to shake. It feels weird that I don't introduce myself with my clans to the guys. Curly Hair smiles, ignores my hand, and says, "We go by last names here. Name's Finnegan—I'm team captain and quarterback. So you're the sophomore. Damn, you're huge!"

"Thanks," I say. The other two say their last names: Mancini and Harris.

"My dad took us to Aspen," Finnegan complains, continuing a conversation he was having. "There's nothing to do in the mountains outside of ski season! Vacationing in America is so lame."

First off, it's weird as hell hearing him use *vacation* as a verb. Second, I am not a fan of how he uses the word *lame*. I'll keep my mouth shut for the time being. These guys are going to be my new friends, and I don't want to start anything with them this early in the school year.

"My family and I went to Bulgaria," says Mancini, who is pretty stocky and has a cleft chin. Harris, by his side, remains quiet about his summer plans.

"Traveling transatlantic sucks!" say Finnegan.

"The flight's so boring and long," says Mancini. "None of the girls were pretty, either. Such a waste."

"Hoskie, what'd you do this summer?" Finnegan asks me.

"Oh, uh, me?" I stammer, not wanting to admit that I spent most of my summer cutting down dead trees in the Chuska Mountains to sell for some spending money this year. "Just hung around." There are more guys coming down the path to the football field.

"Wish I could have relaxed," Harris mumbles. "I ended up doing an internship in Montreal."

A few minutes later, Coach Price finally shows up, with the rest of the team trailing behind him. He stands between two burly men, who make him appear normal sized. All three wear khaki shorts as well as shiny polo shirts with *Sagefield* in curved lettering on their chests.

I stand tall, as Grandma Dominic taught me. Toes pointed forward. Knees locked. Shoulders broad. This should impress them.

"All right, gentlemen," Coach Price says, his deep voice shushing the entire team. He smiles, showing his broad, straight white teeth. Specks of gray hair peek out from behind his ears. "If any of the gear isn't the right size, Defensive Coach Donnell or Offensive Coach Owens can get you the right ones." He points to the two men at his sides. Donnell is a mountain of a man with enviable facial hair. I haven't shaved in months, and I only have a scraggly chin hair to show for it. Owens, on the other hand, looks like he belongs on the cover of a fitness magazine and not on a football team. He's tall and looks like he can outsprint a sports car. "Without further ado!" Coach Price blows the whistle and lets it drop onto his chest. "Coach Owens, warm up these Dire Foxes!"

"My pleasure," Owens says. If I was told that he arm wrestled an elephant and won, I would have no trouble believing it. "Line up!"

All of us organize into roughly six rows standing on the white lines on the green grass. Now that the sun is rising, I can feel the air heating up and becoming moist. The guy next to me, I believe he is called Goldman, smells like sunblock. I can only imagine how uncomfortable it will be for him once we start doing afternoon practices in the full heat of late summer. Sucks for him. I quickly do ten push-ups as per Owens's warm-up instructions. My heart pumps, and I feel a rush of excitement building in my limbs.

* * *

After our warm-up with Coach Owens, Coach Price leads us to a wide-open area behind the row of pine trees on the other side of the stands. A thick cloud of buzzing insects flies in our faces as we walk down a well-worn path.

"Man, screw these gnats!" says a guy whose skin color is close to mine. He could be Latino. I also assume he said *screw* because we are in earshot of the coaches. I notice a colorful tattoo of a Día de los Muertos skull on his left calf. So he's at least eighteen and probably a senior.

The hell are gnats? In seconds, the gnats introduce themselves to my face and exposed neck area. These are like peppercorn-sized mosquitoes! I angrily wave a hand in front of my face and smack the ones that have landed on my skin with my other hand. A few fly into my mouth, and I spit them out. They leave a weird flash of taste like condensed fart and burnt rubber.

Tattoo Calf guy next to me chuckles.

Before I can warn him to close his mouth, he also gags and spits.

"They flew into your mouth, too, huh?" I ask him, and spit the remaining taste out of my mouth.

"¿Saben como nalgas, no?" says Tattoo Calf. Yup, he's Latino. "Soy Ramirez. ¿Cómo te llamas?"

"I don't speak Spanish," I respond with agitation. It pisses me off that he just assumes I speak Spanish. That happens a lot in Albuquerque and Phoenix. People see dark brown skin and assume I'm Latino.

A look of confusion crosses his face. I bounce before he can get mad at me for "not knowing how to speak my own language."

I catch up with Finnegan, who walks with his head tilted

slightly upward. A gaggle of six guys hover near, each trying to suck up to him. I'm embarrassed for them. I slow down enough so that I'm not a part of the group desperate for Finnegan's attention.

Finally, we reach the training field. Workers are placing bright orange cones on the unpainted grassy field. Agility drills. Not quite sprints, but still not my cup of tea.

"Linemen!" Coach Donnell shouts, holding a thick fist in the air. "If you would so kindly follow me!" Despite his gentle request, his tone holds the threat of *you will listen to me or else.*

"Running backs, tight ends, wide receivers with me!" Coach Owens commands.

The team splits roughly in half. I walk behind Ramirez toward Coach Donnell. Then I get this huge urge to scratch my forearms. Small pink bite marks dot my exposed skin. Those damn gnats! First chance I get, I'm going to grab the strongest insect repellent I can.

I stop with the rest of the team and scratch at the bites. They may call them gnats here, but they look like mosquitoes and itch like mosquitoes. Screw it, I'm calling them ts'í'ii-s.

Bam, someone charges into my back, nearly knocking me to the grass.

"Yo!" I growl, turning to face the idiot who wasn't paying attention.

"Sorry," Ramirez says, raising his palms. "Didn't mean to run into you."

Okay, so he's speaking English to me. My defenses soften. I nod. "It's cool."

He searches my face. I can practically hear his thoughts as he tries to figure out what ethnicity I am.

I should give him a break. I'm not going to make many friends being defensive. "I'm Diné. Native American."

His dark eyes widen. Yup, that's what I was expecting.

"Indígena, that's cool," Ramirez says.

"Sure." I smirk. I've never known how to respond when someone tells me being Native is cool. But don't get me wrong—it totally is.

"Hey, I'm sorry for assuming you were Latino," he says. "There aren't too many of us brown folks here."

Before I can respond to Ramirez, Coach Donnell yells, "Dire Foxes!"

I immediately place my attention on him while all us linemen form a semicircle around him.

"We will start with reviewing our stances. It's the foundation of any great football team."

It completely shocks me to hear other players lightly chatting while Coach Donnell speaks. And I'm 90 percent certain that Coach Donnell hears them talking. Coach Atcitty would be up in their faces yelling and tearing their hides a new one for talking while he was. I shake my head when I realize that Coach Donnell isn't going to do anything about the chattering players. There's just so much to adjust to here.

After practice, I have to rush over to Cornelius Longhorn Student Activity Facility, where we Lower-Mids are having our class meeting. The SAF—I'm not calling it by its full name—is a long lounge room, by my estimates fifty yards long and about twenty-five yards wide, filled with rows of extremely comfortable black leather couches. There are detailed Persian carpets that cover light brown wooden floors. Of course, there's a chandelier. Yeah, Sagefield doesn't do anything low-key.

It's apparent who the new students are. We are the ones who are not excitedly talking with our cliques. We kind of just hover around and smile. Everyone else is busy catching up with their friends and bragging about their summers. It's not much different than when the football team was talking about their extravagant vacations. There's a healthy amount of southern European cruises, some humanitarian excursions to developing countries, and some summer internships at places I'd never even think of like Google, Apple, and even in DC. As in Washington!

I spot Caleb being friendly with some other guys. He looks at me and immediately averts his gaze. Weird. Whatever.

Suddenly, I see the prettiest girl in the world, and everything quiets. She has black hair, a slight tan, and designer glasses. Unlike everyone in this room, she seems to be listening instead of trying to impress her friends.

I look away and spot a tall, imposing man with curly pale hair holding his fists up. His sports coat is the same royal blue of the school colors. A few students notice him and quiet. Gradually the entire room pays attention to him.

"Who's that?" someone to my right asks. He has a strong German accent.

"No clue," I admit to him.

"Welcome back." The large man's voice isn't exactly booming or as commanding as his frame. It's surprisingly soft, but each syllable is distinct. As a result, we have to work to pay attention to what he's saying. "I have missed you all very much. And I hope that summer was restful and productive. For all the new incoming students, we welcome you to our family and our home."

All the returning students shout, "Welcome to Sagefield, hoo-rah-rah!"

The imposing, soft-spoken man continues, "Hoo-rah-rah, indeed! My name is Mr. Fairchild, and I am your class dean. Now, you are all entering this exciting school year as Lower-Mids, and that means several things. Firstly, you will be assigned Human Development class."

A bunch of students stifle laughter and hide blushing cheeks. I have no idea what that's about.

"Remember that when you are in Human Development, you not only represent yourself but your entire graduating class. As we have a big day ahead of us, I want to give our incoming classmates the opportunity to introduce themselves. Now, if you would, please stand in a line right here."

Mr. Fairchild points to the side of the room opposite the wide windows. I stand near the middle of the line.

The entire class stares at the twenty of us who are new. I'm the tallest. I'm estimating ninety students total, including us newer ones. There's a mixture of white, Black, and Asian students, as well as some who look Latine.

I nearly gasp as I catch my crush checking me out. She quickly looks away. Then she tucks her straight hair behind her ear. I smirk to hide my bubbling excitement.

“Now, tell us your name, where you are from, and one thing you want people to know about you,” Mr. Fairchild explains.

The first kid adjusts his thick glasses and smooths out his pink polo shirt. “My name is Anton Wagner,” he says with a very thick German accent. He even pronounces his *w* as a *v*. “I’m from Rothenburg ob der Tauber, Deutschland—er, I mean Germany.” This straight-from-Germany kid is in my class!

Down the line the rest of us talk. One is from Manhattan. Another is from Bolivia. One is from Los Angeles. It dawns on me that, yeah, I’m special, but so is everyone else. I find myself relaxing and letting down my guard a bit. This is exciting! I might somewhat fit in.

My turn. “Hi, everyone. Um.” I think about it for a second and decide to go for it. “My great-grandma Mildred taught me to always introduce myself in my language. So, yá’át’ééh. Derrick Hoskie yiníshyé. Ts’ah Yiskidnii nishłį. K’aa’ Dine’é báshishchíín. T’ó tsohnii dashicheii. Kinyaa’áanii dashinálí. Those are my clans. I’m Diné from the Navajo Nation in Arizona.” That’s more than enough.

Everyone stares at me like I’m this weird creature made of Western fantasies and cowboy fever dreams. This type of attention makes me uncomfortable. My forehead warms and my palms sweat.

“That was something truly special,” Mr. Fairchild says after a few quiet seconds. “What did you say?”

I explain, “I just told you my four clans. I’m Sage Brush Hill clan. Born for Arrow People clan. My maternal grandpa’s clan is Big Water clan. And my paternal grandpa’s clan is Towering House clan.”

"That's so wonderful," Mr. Fairchild says. "Thank you for that. And you are . . ."

The girl to my left is awestruck and staring at me. It takes her a few seconds to snap to and introduce herself.

It may have been a mistake to go full-on Diné on them this early. But I'm not going to regret introducing myself in Diné. I'm proud of my clans. Still, with everyone looking at me, I'm uncomfortable.

After the last of us, a girl from Nigeria named Ife Achebe introduces herself, Mr. Fairchild softly says, "We have a few minutes before we must make our way to Gertrude Claasen Auditorium for the school assembly address by our headmaster. So please mingle and make new friendships." He claps twice, and everyone stands up and returns to their original cliques.

Suddenly, three female students approach me. They gawk and stare at me.

"Wow, so you're Indian, right?"

"You have such beautiful cheekbones."

"You should grow out your hair."

"I bet you would be hot with long hair."

"You don't look Indigenous."

I only have enough energy to respond to the last one. "Neither do you." Even though the girl who said it didn't mention anything about having Native heritage.

"Really? But my mom says that we are Indigenous because we have really high cheekbones!" Her tone becomes defensive like I'm the one in the wrong. "And my uncle took an ancestry test and it said he was part Indigenous."

I'm pissed. Demi used to talk about how weird white guys would have this absolutely horrible Pocahontas fantasy. That's what it feels like with these three. I'm their racial fantasy.

There is chattering all around me. My ears prick up when I catch the words *Indian*, *Navajo*, and *cheekbones* from the surrounding conversations.

Grandma Rosie taught me to be proud of my clans and to always introduce myself to new people in Diné. My ancestors, my language, and my culture survived colonization and Bible-based religions. I'm not about to be ashamed. But still, everyone is looking at me as this exotic thing instead of as a person.

"Hey," says the guy now standing in front of me. "If you're Indian, why don't you have long hair?"

I sigh loudly. Everyone stares at me, waiting for my response.

"Chicks dig long hair," I reply. "You don't want me to steal all your women, do you?"

Someone chuckles, and hopefully that shuts him up.

I see Caleb and my chance to leave these students. "There's my friend. He and I were going to . . ." I don't even bother finishing the statement and walk away. Before I can reach him, he has turned his back to me. I try not to take that personally and walk into the hallway to breathe. Sagefield is a hell of a weird place. I wonder if I'll ever feel like I belong here.

5

Dimóo biiskání, Bini' Anit'ą́ą́ Tsoh 9

Monday, September 9

I arrive five minutes before the start of Lower-Mid history; my first class on Mondays is at 8:30. My schedule isn't the same every day, as it was at Navajo Pine. It's like college, with some open blocks throughout the day. Today, I have history, then Human Development, geometry, and Latin.

I find a seat four chairs away from Mr. Henderson, who sits at the large oval table. His fingers furiously tap on his laptop keyboard. He's in his mid-fifties, I want to say, with a big bald spot on the back of his head and scrawny shoulders. He wears a tie and a button-down shirt with a brown plaid sweater vest. I stare beyond him out the wide windows at a dense pocket of pine and oak trees. Farther beyond the tree line is Lake Lavender. I chomp on a banana that I grabbed from the dining area as the other students sit down.

The bell rings.

"Before we begin, a reminder." Mr. Henderson's speaks with a gruff and raspy voice. He closes his laptop. He sorts through papers from his briefcase as he dryly talks to us. "At the end of the semester in December, you will be required to write a twenty-page essay using only primary sources. It's been my experience that some of you will put it off. I'll give three more reminders throughout the semester. When December comes along, extensions will not be permitted. I highly, highly recommend that you choose a topic by the end of this week to maximize your time for research."

It's the first class and this dude is already talking about starting a twenty-page essay! He must have seen me and two other students react. "Relax. It's not required that you choose your topic this week, only highly recommended. It's your responsibility, not mine, to ensure that you meet the required deadlines."

"Excuse me, Mr. Henderson," says Ife Achebe. I hadn't noticed when she entered.

Mr. Henderson looks at her with a hard-to-read expression. "Yes, Ms. . . ." He trails off and rubs his temples. "No, wait, I'll remember your name. Ms. Achebe. Did I pronounce that right?"

"It's Aa-chay-bee. How did you know my name?"

"We teachers get a list of your names with your photos. Helps with attendance. Give me time; I will pronounce your name correctly, Ms. Achebe." He slowly pronounces her name with care. "Now, did you have a question?"

"What's a primary source?" she asks. I'm glad she does.

"Ah yes," Mr. Henderson starts. He pauses and pulls a stylish pair of glasses from his briefcase. "Primary sources are firsthand accounts of events. They can be diaries. They can be photos. Interviews, even. But they must come directly from the person who experienced the event themselves."

Ife smiles and nods.

"With that out of the way . . ." He looks at me. I wish I could become invisible because I know he's going to call on me. "Mr. Hoskie." To his credit, he pronounces my name decently enough. "Summarize our readings."

It's just my luck to be called on the first day of the first class of my first semester here. It was so rude of Sagefield to have required summer reading for both English and history.

"But it's just the first day of class," a student across from me says. Thank god someone said it.

"Be that as it may, Mr. Choi," Mr. Henderson dryly responds. There's no note of annoyance in his tone but his face expresses otherwise. "An email was sent to each of you detailing my expectations of your work ethic as well as the assigned reading for today's class."

Mr. Henderson smiles. "Who here has looked at the syllabus and completed the readings?"

Eight out of twelve of us raise our hands, including me.

"Very well, you four, try your best to contribute to our discussion," Mr. Henderson says to the four who didn't raise their hands. "Mr. Hoskie, please summarize for the class," he directs me.

My mind works in overtime to recall all the details of the assignment. "We read about the initial thirteen colonies that were established after the landing at Plymouth."

"Who were the ones that landed?" Mr. Henderson asks.

"The Pilgrims and the Puritans," I say.

"What is the difference between the two?" he asks the class. I want to say that both Pilgrims and Puritans displaced the Native people that inhabited the area. They both spread their diseases everywhere.

A white student speaks up to discuss their differences. It's funny how white students can separate Puritans and Pilgrims but have trouble distinguishing between Cherokee and Diné. This is also why I really don't care about history class. It's always about dead white guys who screwed over Native people again and again. The white student finishes talking.

Mr. Henderson asks the class, "Who were the main players?"

I want to say the Wampanoag and the surrounding eastern tribal Nations. This is basic Google-level research information. But I prevent my thoughts from forming into words. It's history, and I have to regurgitate the information from the textbook. I spend the rest of the class not motivated to participate in the class discussion.

After history, I rush to the English wing for my next class, Human Development. When I walk into the classroom, there are already three other students sitting at the large elongated oval table. As I sit down, they stare at me like I've got something on my face.

"What's up?" I say, holding down my urge to stare them down.

"Is it true?" a white male student asks.

"Is what true?" I steel myself and prepare for the inevitable stupid question to follow.

"That you live in a tepee?" he asks.

Geez. The other two students gawk at me, awaiting my answer.

"No," I say. My annoyance brims. I'd roll my eyes, but my mom raised me better than that.

"Oh, I am so sorry," he says. Hopefully, he realized what he asked was layered in prejudice.

"A wigwam?"

"No." I glare at them, and they back down. In border towns by my rez, if a white person called any of us out for being Native, Chris, Jayden, and I would be kicking their ass. Because usually there's legit racism behind those comments. But here, I can't figure it out. This question isn't exactly overt racism, like being called a tepee n-word, which happened once. But it also ain't cool to be put in the spotlight for my ethnicity like this.

Suddenly, all the fire in my chest is extinguished when that really pretty girl at the Lower-Mid meeting walks into the classroom. She smiles when she notices me, and in order to hide my own goofy smile, I quickly open my backpack and pull out the laptop I have borrowed from the library for the school year. She sits a few seats to my left.

A few more minutes pass, and two other students sit down before the teacher walks in. She has short gray hair and some wildly pink glasses that hang at the edge of her nose. She counts us, then closes the door behind us. I thought there'd be more students. That's something else I have to get used to here. Classes are so much smaller than at Navajo Pine! Back on the rez, my largest class had thirty-five students. And there were only twenty-five desks. So if I arrived late, I'd have to sit on the floor. True story.

"Good morning!" the teacher sings, sitting down. The rest of the students pull out their brand-new laptops. "Oh, pishposh! There's no need for laptops. We won't be taking notes in Human Development."

We all awkwardly put our laptops into our bags. I'm low-key glad, because my loaned laptop looks like a chunky lunch box compared to their slim and, dare I say, sexy ones.

"A reminder, there is no grading in this class. It's pass/fail. Participation is highly encouraged. Let's start with introductions! Name and something you are a big fan of. Could be your sport. Could be your instrument. Could be your pet! Now, I'll start. I'm Mrs. Fairchild." I nearly gasp. Compared to our class dean, who must be her husband, she's a prismatic rainbow of refracted light. Her voice fills the room, and her entire body moves with warm energy. "And I used to be a big fan of Harry Potter, but nowadays, I'm a huge fan of reading diverse authors. All righty, let's start!" She points at the pretty girl, who confidently smiles.

"Hi, I'm Wendy Bernadotte," she says. "And I'm a fan of Late Romantic period piano pieces."

"Oh. I absolutely adore Mendelssohn's 'Songs without Words,'" Mrs. Fairchild says.

When it's my turn I say, "Good morning, everyone. Name's Derrick. And I'm a big fan of SPAM and potatoes." True story. No one has any idea what I'm talking about, and they just stare blankly at me.

After we all finish our introductions, Mrs. Fairchild rubs her hands. "Is everyone fine if I say a quick enchantment to this space?"

She looks at all of us. None of us respond. We're all confused.

"It's perfectly fine to say no. Not everyone is a fan of enchantments. But if there are no objections, I will begin in three, two, one!" She reaches to the ceiling, like she's praising the sun. "May this space we enter be one of safety, respect, understanding, and growth!" She claps with joy. "If it's okay, I would love to start our classes with an enchantment. If at any point down the road, you discover 'Hey, I'm not entirely comfortable with that,' I encourage you to voice your concern. It's perfectly fine to change your mind later if you aren't liking how things are going."

Her energy and vivacity are infectious. I feel like I could tell her anything and she would hype it up. Mrs. Fairchild squeals. "Now we can begin in earnest." She walks around the table. "Today we will get to know each other and develop foundations—safety being the biggest one! You can never have too much safety."

It may be a bit early to say, but I think this may be my favorite class. Mrs. Fairchild seems to be the coolest teacher ever, and of course, Wendy's here. Not to forget, no homework.

A little after noon, I stand in the food line in the dining hall behind Finnegan, Harris, Mancini, and other footballers. Some girls say hi as they walk past us. They are wildly cute. Since I'm off the rez, I don't have to ask for their clans. That's definitely a positive of coming here. I'm not clan-related to anyone!

I overhear a girl say, "That's the Native guy."

I brush off the comment and try to enter the chat with the guys.

"So what does your dad do?" Finnegan asks one of the running backs. I try to be as invisible as possible in case they think of asking me about my dad. I'm still not fully over how he raised his hands at my mom the last time I saw him. Their voices blend together as I wait to get my food.

"He's a lawyer."

"Nice. What kind?"

"Entertainment. What about yours?"

"Anchor for ESPN; what does your dad do?"

"State senator for Massachusetts."

That's when I realize they are asking all of us new guys this question. They are essentially figuring out whose dad makes the most money and who has the most power. It's a pecking-order thing. Like, because of what their parents do, they are also on that same level of accomplishment. I stand next to Carter, another defensive lineman, who is asking the cafeteria man for another grass-fed burger.

"Thank you, sir," Carter says.

"Good to see you, Reese!" the cafeteria man says, then smiles at me. "You want two patties, as well?"

"Very much so," I say to him. I read a small name tag. *Art.* "Thank you, Art."

"No problem." Art smiles.

"While you're at it, make mine a double," Finnegan says. The rest of the team demands the same. They don't even say thank you.

Art cheerfully says, "On it!"

After I get my burger, I make my way to the football table. I recognize Goldman with his fancy glasses and sit next to him.

"No, man, Chelsea has really filled in," says Goldman.

Harris says, "Chelsea got crater face."

"Just put a paper bag on her head," Goldman says. There's laughter around the table.

I've done my fair share of appreciating the opposite gender. But the way these guys are doing it makes me uncomfortable. A no-BS single mother will smack the disrespect of women right out of you. Finnegan, Harris, and Mancini sit down at the table.

"Yo, Finnegan. You seen Lynne, right?" asks Mancini. "She's lost so much weight!"

"Bulimia looks good on her," says Finnegan. Several of the guys whoop in agreement.

I nearly spit out my burger. My mom would expect me to take a stand and call these jerks out. But instead, I swallow my annoyance. They are the only source of friends I have right now, and it's too early for me to make enemies. Do enemies exist in boarding schools? Like, do fights even happen here? If I were to get into a fight, would I be expelled?

Finnegan asks me, "Yo, Hoskie, any girl catch your attention?" He horribly mispronounces my last name. It's not that difficult to say.

"It's *Hoss-key*," I respond. "Not yet. Just got here."

"Newbie!" Mancini says with a mouthful of burger. "Wait until the swimming team arrives."

I let them talk for a little bit.

Then, someone from another team, I assume soccer from his uniform, comes over to our table and sits next to Mancini. Everyone else still talks about which of the female students they'd want to bang.

"I just Venmo'd you," says the soccer player.

There's an attempt to be sneaky. But they are super obvious when Mancini hands over something. They do a bro handshake of bumping, slapping, and finger snapping, and the soccer dude takes off.

I'm just going to ignore what happened. It's not my problem. I eat more of my organic, grain-free, grass-fed, non-GMO burger and get this huge craving for a greasy green chili cheeseburger combo from That's-A-Burger.

After another football practice and dinner, I navigate my way to the English wing again from my dorm room. Ms. Thomas enrolled me in something called Mandatory Study Hall. Basically, all Preps and Lower-Mids have study hall from seven to nine, which they do in their own dorm rooms. Students who are having a hard time, need a little extra help, or are brand-new to this boarding school world, like me, are in Mandatory Study Hall. So I'm heading for a classroom that has a tutor. I open the door and see other students there. A friendly-looking woman smiles at me.

"You must be Derrick. Hi, I'm Ms. Laramie." She shakes my hand, then writes a check next to her list of students. There's a genuine warmth coming from her. She has brown hair that is short and gelled. She wears a crisp baby-blue polo shirt with cargo pants.

"Pleasure to meet you." I smile.

"Please sit at the table and we will begin studying in"—she looks at her watch—"two minutes. In the meantime, please turn off your phones and the Wi-Fi setting on your laptops. We're still waiting for one more student."

With the others, I sit down at the oval table and take out my boxy plastic laptop. The guy sitting across from me uses a shiny stylus on his sleek Samsung laptop. The girl sitting to my right has this drool-worthy dark MacBook. Someday, I'll be able to afford one of those. I hope.

Sitting to my left is a small Asian guy with parted hair wearing bourgeois clothes. Being as friendly as possible, I say to him, "Hey."

"Me?" the stylish guy asks. He looks a little surprised. Then he replies, "Salutations." He searches my face, then says, "What Asian are you?"

I'm taken aback. "What?"

"What Asian are you?" The question is like a wildfire burning through my patience and kindness.

"I'm not Asian," I respond. My chest warms with anger.

"Oh. But you look Asian," he states. "You sure? Maybe a half mix of Mongolian."

Just then, the door swings open and in walks Caleb himself. He hesitantly grins at all of us and avoids looking at me. Seriously, did I do something to get on his nerves?

"Cutting it close, Caleb," Ms. Laramie says. "Please find a seat. It is now seven p.m., students. I like to start study hall sessions with a five-minute meditation to exercise our focus muscles. The more we practice letting go of distractions, the easier it'll be to focus. For now, pay attention to the sensation of breathing, and anytime you feel yourself slip away, just give yourself a little nudge to get back on track."

"Will do," I say. It makes sense that the more you practice focusing, the easier it becomes.

We all close our eyes. My mind wanders around the word *Mongolian*. As I focus on my breath, the fire inside my mind cools. The five minutes are up quickly. I open my eyes, a little calmer.

"We'll have a quick five-minute break in one hour," Ms. Laramie states. "Raise your hand if you need help. And we begin now." She starts a timer on her phone.

I reach into my backpack and pull out my history textbook. A brief flash of Mr. Henderson's face pops into my consciousness. Bleh. I can do this later. I was having some trouble with Latin words, and it's my only class that meets daily. So I pull out my college-ruled notebook and begin to write down all the words we are studying.

Before I can finish the week's set of words, Ms. Laramie approaches me with a welcoming smile. She whispers, "Good evening, Derrick. May I ask what you are doing?"

"I'm, uh, memorizing my word set," I answer. If it had been any of the teachers at my old school, I would have been on high alert and ready to argue. "I was going to write the word and its translation over and over again until I got it."

"For each word?" Ms. Laramie says in a surprised voice.

"Yeah," I shakily respond. It's not like there's another way—at least, that I know of.

"Let's try a different approach. Here." Ms. Laramie quickly

tiptoes to her bag and pulls out a thick stack of index cards. "Use these to make flash cards for yourself. Latin on one side, the English translation on the other."

"Okay," I say.

She must sense my uncertainty. She explains, "One of the benefits of using flash cards is that you can mix them! Once you're done doing one round, shuffle them and do it again. Another benefit is that the more certain you are of a word, you can take it out of the deck and focus on the ones that are giving you the most trouble."

"Sure," I say. It takes me a moment to absorb what she said.

"I'll check back with you in twenty minutes," she says. The student across from me has raised his hand. Ms. Laramie approaches him.

While it's all well and good to have her helping me, I hate how it makes me feel like a kid. Back home, when Mom was working two jobs, Demi and I were responsible for ourselves. Cooking. Cleaning. Homework. We even had food ready for the family when Mom came home. I liked that I could do my own thing on my own time. Here, everything has a strict structure and schedule. It really feels like I gave up my independence to be here.

6

Dimóo, Bini' Anit'ą́ą́ Tsoh 15

Sunday, September 15

After dinner on Sunday, I hole up in my dorm room. A few of the guys are going to hang in Mancini's room later to watch movies. And I said I'd go.

But first things first. I hold my phone to my ear and wait for Másání Mildred to answer. I've been looking forward to talking with my family. I still feel homesick, but it's getting easier to deal with, and these phone calls back home will definitely help.

"Yes, hello?" she answers.

"Másání! Yá'át'ééh!" A smile spreads across my face.

"Oh! Yá'át'ééh, sha'awéé'! I miss you!" I press my phone against my ear because she speaks a little too softly. My volume is already maxed out.

"I miss you, too, Másání. How are you?" I ask.

I can hear some scuffling in the background. Her voice is energetic. "Are you at that school?"

"Yes. I just finished my first week. And it's a lot tougher than Navajo Pine."

“You don’t have to stay there, you know. You can come back.”

“I know.”

“They’re just going to teach you the same math. Might as well stay here.”

My reflex reaction is to smile, even though I’m alone in my room. She doesn’t get it. An opportunity like this, my being here at Sagefield, is huge. This could set me up for life! A lot of the students here go on to attend Ivy League schools. As a freshman, I barely even dreamed of going to college because my mom and I couldn’t afford it. But now that Sagefield has provided a scholarship, I feel like there’s a chance I could go to an Ivy League! Me, a rez kid! When Másání Mildred says stuff like that, it hurts a little.

I explain, “It’s different here, Másání. I don’t have to worry about the gangs.”

“Oh, okay, then.”

That’s usually how this conversation ends. When I bring up the gangs in my hometown, she understands. But lately, we’ve been having the same chat. It could be her age. Sometimes, she forgets stuff and is confused.

I ask, “Have you heard back from Dr. Platero?”

“No, huh-uh,” she answers. “I’m supposed to go for blood tests sometime in October, jiní.”

“I’ll be sure to call then,” I say. “Are you taking your medicines?”

“Yes,” she says a little grumpily. “When are you coming back?”

I ignore that she changed the subject. “I should be back for Thanksgiving.”

"Oh, that's too long, sha'awéé'. Who's going to chop wood for me?" she teases me.

There is a shard of truth in what she asks that bothers me. Mom, Grandma, and I were the only ones going up to help her prepare for winter. All my uncles and aunties that live nearby don't bother to check in on her or even drop off food supplies. With me and Demi gone, it's going to be my mom doing the wood chopping. Was it selfish of me to want to come here and not be around to help Másání Mildred?

I force my voice to be steady. "I'll chop more chizh for you when I'm back. I'll even bring some Church's chicken."

"Hágoshį́į́," Másání Mildred says.

I check out the time because I need to call my mom and Grandma before I head to Mancini's. "Well, I just wanted to check in on you. I'm going to hang out with some new friends I've made over here."

"No one's hitting you?" Másání Mildred says.

"No one's hitting me, Másání," I assure her.

"You can tell me the truth, sha'awéé'." There's desperation in her voice.

"It's the truth," I say. My chest churns with homesickness and something else. It feels a little like fear.

I've been told that Másání Mildred was in a boarding school as a young girl. Her generation barely speaks of that era. Grandma Rosie tells me not to ask her about that time or else it'll upset her. She'd tell me "Doo 'ajínída'" and "It's best not to talk about that time" because of her age and heart. All I know is that when

Másání Mildred was a girl, she was possibly kidnapped by the US government and forced into a boarding school.

"Hágoshį́į́. Thanks for calling me, sha'awéé'. It makes me feel special," she says.

"No problem. I miss you and I'll call you again next week," I say to assure her, but also myself.

"'Ahxéhee', sha'awéé'," she says. Then she hangs up.

I'm left alone in my dorm room. I take a moment to conquer this homesickness welling up in my throat. My mind races through all the scenarios of her not having enough firewood for winter because I'm not there. She's suffering because I wanted to come to school here. Instead of sadness and longing, I feel guilt. I hope Sagefield is worth what I'm putting Másání Mildred through.

7

Dimóo biiskání, Bini' Anit'ą́ą́ Tsoh 16

Monday, September 16

"What is the colonial era?" Mr. Henderson asks the entire class.

I hold my tongue, hoping that he doesn't notice me. To my right, Ife raises her hand.

"I don't understand the question," Ife says. "Are you asking for a definition or something else?"

"First the dates, then the definition," Mr. Henderson suggests. "Mr. Hoskie. You've been quiet throughout the entire class."

Crap. I guess it's hard to not be noticed when there are only twelve students and one teacher. I state, "The dates are 1600 to 1775. Give or take a year."

"Didn't even look at your notes," Mr. Henderson says. There is a hint of a compliment there. "That is correct. What are the thirteen colonies? Let's start with the three groups."

I spit out, "There's the New England colonies: New Hampshire, Rhode Island, Massachusetts, and even little ole Connecticut." I remember seeing this highlighted in my used textbook last night. "Then there's—"

"That's enough," Mr. Henderson interrupts me. "Don't steal the fun from the entire class." He doesn't even smile at his own weak joke. His eyes squint as he scans the other students.

I want to respond to his comment about *stealing the fun*, "Like how the colonies stole land from the eastern tribal Nations." But I keep quiet and lean into my wooden chair. Maybe that'll be enough for him to leave me alone for the rest of class.

"Mr. Choi, what are the other colonies?" Mr. Henderson says to James.

James riffles through his notes frantically. "Um. It's right here. Somewhere."

Meanwhile, Mr. Henderson polishes the lenses of his glasses with his tie. "Ms. Achebe, venture a guess while James finds his answer?"

"Yes! I can do the middle colonies. New York, New Jersey, Pennsylvania, and Delaware." As she talks, she looks back and forth from her notes to Mr. Henderson, and her gold string earrings sway. I bet they are actually made of gold.

"Yes," Mr. Henderson says. He slowly turns to James. "Are we ready, Mr. Choi?"

"Yes!" James says with some fear. "Southern colonies. And they are Maryland, Virginia, North Carolina, South Carolina, and Georgia."

I try to hide a yawn by squeezing my lips together. But a small sound vibrates from my throat.

"Mr. Hoskie," Mr. Henderson says. "Why is this considered the colonial era, and what major event occurred to end it?"

Mancini was correct. Mr. Henderson's class is simple fact

regurgitation. "Probably because they were colonies still under the thumb of the British Empire. As for the major event, well, 1775 isn't too far from 1776, which is when the colonies unified and formed the United States." I don't add that this is when the colonists grew from thousands to millions and displaced the same number of Native peoples from their homelands. I don't mention that the treaties they brokered with those same eastern Native Nations were fundamental in proving to the British Empire and the world at large that the colonies were self-sufficient. Our treaties were the spine that built this country.

That's enough to keep Mr. Henderson off my back for a little bit. He continues to pester the other students into spewing out more dates, names, and events until the end of class.

I'm so grateful when the bell rings and allows me to leave this class. When I've stuffed my loan laptop into my backpack, Mr. Henderson says, "Mr. Hoskie. Mr. Choi. Ms. Achebe. A moment before you leave."

"Uh, I have to hurry to the science building, Mr. Henderson," James says.

"You three have yet to submit your topic for the semester essay," Mr. Henderson says. He latches his briefcase and stands. "This is your second reminder. That is all." He walks out of the room, leaving the three of us stunned.

"Mr. Henderson!" Ife says, chasing after him. "I could use some help."

"Sure," Mr. Henderson says in the hall. His voice gets lost in the murmurs of the busy hallway. "Let's schedule a meeting . . ."

I shake off my annoyance. Mr. Henderson grates on my

nerves. It could be how he picks on everyone with his questions. Whatever. My next class should be a little better. At least Human Development is pass/fail and I'm not expected to write a twenty-page essay.

Later, I sit in the middle of Human Development, and Mrs. Fairchild has a projection screen showing her desktop. She has several social media tabs open. Today, we are examining various influencers who are incredibly fit. The male influencers talk about some pre-workout that boosts testosterone and muscle growth. They apparently have an allergy to shirts. The female influencers talk about supplements that tone the midsection and promote smooth skin and are obsessed with leggings that highlight their curves.

"Notice how they exhibit their bodies," Mrs. Fairchild states.

Wendy raises her hand. "The lighting that they are using is soft. It creates a smooth-looking tone for their skin and creates deep shadows that highlight their physiques." When I heard that Wendy was dating someone on the JV football team, my levels of crushing on her dropped. I ain't going to pine after someone in a relationship.

"Good observation. Anyone else?" Mrs. Fairchild asks the class.

"They are all white," I blurt out.

There is a moment of silence. It seems like no one in my class knows how to process what I just said. I mean, it's true. All the ones that Mrs. Fairchild showed were young, fit white people.

Mrs. Fairchild smiles and then says, "Yes. We cannot ignore

this fact. While preparing for this presentation, I did my best to incorporate BIPOC influencers. But the dummy account that I used for research exclusively began to show white influencers. That's not to say there aren't any BIPOC influencers; there are. But the algorithms that social media employs either know I'm white or . . ." She trails off.

Anton finishes her statement when no one else speaks up. "The algorithm prefers to push white influencers over BIPOC influencers."

"Exactly! And what does that do?" Mrs. Fairchild asks us.

Wendy says, "It implicitly tells the audience that there is one standard of beauty: white, young, cis-gendered, and physically fit."

I decide to add, "Even if social media's exclusion of BIPOC influencers isn't racially motivated, the effect is still the same as if it were."

Mrs. Fairchild claps, startling some of the students. "Precisely! Intentionally racist administrators or computer-generated formulas, it doesn't matter. Because you, the content consumer, are still being informed that you all should be white, young, and hot!" She emphasizes the last word with a funny voice that makes us chuckle.

I add, "But what if you manipulate the algorithm to focus on things other than hot, young white people? Like, say, dogs?"

"Aw, I love dogs!" Wendy says. Out of my control, I smile.

Mrs. Fairchild squeals, "Yes! You have the power to change what you are exposed to! But no one tells you that you can. No one, not even the apps themselves, tells you how to manipulate what you are exposed to. You must intentionally search out the content that you want. That's work that frankly not everyone will want to do or knows how to do. Back in my day, before the internet and apps, we got our content from magazines and commercials. Back then, we had no control over what was directed at us. And it was all hot, young white people. Now, how do you think that affects what you think of yourself when what you see doesn't represent you?"

"Body shaming," a girl named Jessica contributes.

"Yes. Body shaming is a very big result of targeted ads."

Wendy says, "Underrepresentation has been shown to contribute to higher rates of mood disorders in marginalized communities."

In my mind, this speaks beyond targeted ads. For so long, Natives hadn't been meaningfully represented in any medium. I can only imagine the types of ads that my mom, that Grandma Rosie, that Másání Mildred were exposed to and how that made them feel. How did it affect them?

"What other areas of life can we relate this exercise to?" Mrs. Fairchild asks us.

"Stereotyping," I say without raising my hand. Immediately, everyone looks at me. "When the information you receive about people comes from one incorrect source, you treat those people as stereotypes and not as human beings."

"Yes. Stereotypes—that's going to be a topic that we will visit in a future class, so we will discuss that then. Thank you, Derrick, for giving me the opportunity to foreshadow!"

Just then the bell rings.

"Okay, class! I'll email the next batch of readings tonight. Great conversation, and I will see you all next week!"

Before I realize what I'm doing, I ask Wendy, "What's your favorite dog?"

"All of them," Wendy says. "But I have a Shiba and a corgi at home." She hides her smile by looking away from me, like she's a little embarrassed. "Their names are Mary Puppins and Indiana Bones."

"That's funny!" I say, laughing. "Those are some good names."

"Do you have any dogs?" she asks. We're both done packing and begin to walk out the door.

"I got two at my grandma's house," I say. "Their names aren't as cool as your dogs', though."

"What are they?"

"Pubby and Yáadilá," I say.

"Wow, Yáadilá is such a pretty name," she says.

I laugh. "It's a Diné expression. On the lighter joking side, it can mean 'Good grief,' but on the angry mom side of things it can also mean, like, 'You should know better!'"

"Oh!" She laughs. "I stand by my assessment. Still pretty. Well, I go this way."

"Later," I say.

"Later." She walks in the opposite direction from me.

You know, she's actually kind of cool. I wouldn't mind just being friends with her.

After Human Development, I make my way over to the administration wing of the main building. Of course, there's a name. It's the Dagny Aagaard Administration Wing. I enter and go to the front desk, where the receptionist has a tag hanging on a lanyard that reads *D'Angelo*.

"Good afternoon," D'Angelo says to me. "What can I do for you?"

"I have a meeting with Ms. Thomas," I say, ready to pull up the email that I received yesterday.

D'Angelo responds, "Did you read the directions in her email, or will you need help finding her office?"

"I read her email," I say.

D'Angelo smiles. "She's very descriptive."

"That's an understatement," I add. For real, reading her email and the directions to her office was like reading a ten-page essay complete with thesis and antithesis. She even described D'Angelo's lanyard!

"Let me know if you still need help," D'Angelo says.

I walk down the hallway. Through tall windows, I see tons of adults in business suits and skirts sitting in front of large computer screens. According to her email, Ms. Thomas's office is the last one on the right.

When I stand outside her office, I see Ms. Thomas tilting her head up to read the computer screen through her bifocals. Her lips move as she reads whatever is in front of her. I knock, and she looks startled. She gives a wide smile and motions me in.

I walk through the door and am impressed with her office. It's neat, clean, and full of plants. To her side is yet another expansive window that stretches from floor to ceiling. Outside is a beautiful view of Lake Lavender underneath the dark clouds. The wind creates small waves that bend and roll across the water's surface.

"Derrick!" Ms. Thomas shouts at me with joy in her voice. She gets up and hugs me before we both sit back down.

"You wanted to see me?" I say, still not entirely sure what her "check-in" means.

"I do," Ms. Thomas says. She grabs a folder from the desk behind her. "I've emailed your teachers to tell me how you are performing."

A chill spreads from my spine to my fingers and toes. It's only been a week since school started! They wouldn't have already submitted grades. Or would they have? I'm doing all right in my classes. Maybe I could improve in history. But I've turned in all my assignments, and my homework is being returned to me with B-pluses.

Ms. Thomas continues, "You *are* doing a good job. Your teachers have positive things to say about your work so far. Keep it up."

I relax. It's such a relief to hear that I'm doing well in my classes. The work is definitely more than I'm used to, and more in depth than what was expected at Navajo Pine. But yeah. I can tell Grandma and Másání I'm doing well when I call them this Sunday. They'll be proud.

I'm also relieved that Ms. Thomas is checking in on me. It feels a little like when my mom would make me show her my completed homework or when she'd grill me for getting a C-minus on an assignment. Because beneath the strictness is concern and care for me. Or maybe I'm just missing having a tough mom figure nearby. "Thanks for telling me, Ms. Thomas."

"You will keep your grades up," Ms. Thomas instructs me. She looks directly into my eyes. "Your mama specifically told me to tell you that. I told her no need to say that. I was going to anyway."

My emotions are alight. My homesickness has been hurting less and less, but I still miss my mom and Grandma and Másání. Any interaction with my mom, even through Ms. Thomas, is enough to rekindle my longing to be back home and in my own bed.

"There's another reason why I wanted to talk to you in person," Ms. Thomas says. She takes off her glasses and leans forward. Her elbows rest on her desk. "I've been thinking about reaching out to our Native alumni to see if they're interested in talking to you about their experiences at Sagefield."

This surprises me. There were other Natives here on campus before me? I mean, it checks out. Why wouldn't there be Native Sagefield alumni? But it also gets me thinking. Maybe I could talk to them about how to deal with these stupid questions and attitudes. I still get asked why I don't have long hair. Rather, now people are asking if I'm growing it long enough to have braids. My hair is not even two inches long and they are asking me that! I dread letting my hair grow even longer. "For real?"

"Is this something you'd want me to do?" Ms. Thomas asks.

"Yes, please."

Ms. Thomas takes a Post-it and scribbles down something. Then she adheres it to her desktop screen. There are at least fifteen other Post-its on the perimeter.

"I can't promise that any of them will respond. But if one does, we will do a chaperoned video call with me joining you."

That sounds like a glorified babysitter. It sucks being treated like a kid, man. Whatever, as long as I can talk with another Native person who has gone through what I'm going through. "Thanks, Ms. Thomas."

"Now, keep on keeping on."

"Will do." I stand up and walk to her side of the desk for a hug.

"You're such a sweet boy!" She squeezes me hard.

"See you, Ms. Thomas," I say, and hurry out of her office. She's already back in her chair reading something on her computer screen.

I leave the administration wing feeling renewed, hoping that one alumnus responds.

8

Dimóo dóó dį́'íjį́, Bini' Anit'ą́ą́ Tsoh 19
Thursday, September 19

Even though Mandatory Study Hall is two hours long, it feels like twenty minutes. I finish my Latin homework and start my reading for history. I open the PDF files that Mr. Henderson sent via email. I have to push with determination on my loan laptop's touch pad because it won't register my click otherwise. Caleb, sitting across from me, vigorously taps his fancy stylus against his large touch screen tablet. All the other students work on their expensive tech, their large pro headphones that cover half their head and their four-thousand-dollar pro laptop systems. Someday, I want to be able to afford these things.

As I read the PDF that accompanies this week's textbook section, I remember that I need to figure out what I'm going to write about for my twenty-page essay for history, using only primary sources. I don't even know where to begin. Ms. Laramie walks behind me. I suppress my urge to ask for help. If I can't do this on my own, do I even belong here?

I literally feel my brain twitch. I massage my temples and roll my neck around. The stress builds up in my chest and swells my brain. This amount of homework is cruel and unusual.

Then Ms. Laramie announces, "All righty, scholars, it's time to finish what you're working on. I'll see you all tomorrow. Same time. Same place."

I immediately take my phone off silent mode and see a string of texts from the group chat with the football team. I've also missed a video chat from Chris and Jayden. I'll respond to my rez friends when I get back to my dorm room.

You better be coming to study break Hoskie! is the first message I read from the group chat. There's a bunch of thumbs-up icons next to it.

I groan. I had been avoiding this as long as possible. But I don't have other friends at the moment and I need to make an appearance. I wave goodbye to Ms. Laramie as I make my way to the Grillery near the student activity center.

Right off the bat, Study Break is something that I don't think I'll be a big fan of. It's like all the Preps and Lower-Mids have convened in the student activity center. There are loud conversations, and I notice that a few couples are sneaking away toward the music wing.

"Hoskie!" Mancini yells.

I see both Mancini and Harris smiling at me from one of the black leather couches. They wear skimpy sleeveless shirts to show off their scrawny arms that they believe to be muscly.

"What's up, guys?" I say, sitting down next to them.

"Is this the first time you came to Study Break, or are you avoiding us?" Harris asks, wearing aviator sunglasses inside. He has the douchiest smile.

I explain, "First time." A big reason I didn't want to come is because the Grillery is where students can buy overpriced burgers, ice cream, and other delicious stuff. My budget doesn't allow me to buy anything. And I don't want people to realize that and make it weird.

Then I notice that Caleb has entered the student activity center and is walking with the bourgeois Asian kid. His name is Xavier, if I remember. Xavier spots me looking at them. I'm not going to be cheap and avoid them. I nod and wave at them. Xavier excitedly waves back at me as they get closer.

"Why are those losers waving at you?" Mancini asks.

"We're in Mandatory Study Hall together," I respond.

"You don't have to be nice to them," Harris says.

"I know," I automatically shoot back.

Just then, Xavier walks up to us. Caleb stays at a distance, looking worried and anxious.

"Look, he is actually approaching us." Mancini smirks.

"Good evening, gentlemen," Xavier says. He extends his hand.

Harris takes one look at Xavier and the rainbow bracelet on his wrist. He doesn't even make an effort to say hi. Mancini looks at me and whispers, "This is awkward."

I reach out and shake his hand. "You don't have to be so formal."

"Caleb and I are heading to the Grillery and wanted to know if any of you wanted to join?" Xavier asks all of us. He stares directly into my eyes, like he was saying it specifically to me.

I take the hint. "Yeah, sure. I could get something to eat. You guys coming?" I know they won't.

"No thanks, dog," Harris says.

"All right," I say so that I can cut them loose.

Caleb, Xavier, and I move toward the Grillery. But then Mancini says, "Hold up one minute, Hoskie."

There's a seriousness to his voice that I haven't heard before. I can't ignore him. I say to Caleb and Xavier, "I'll catch up."

The two of them make their way to the back of the line.

"Hey, not to pry, but do you have any Parents' Weekend plans?" Mancini says.

"I haven't thought that far ahead," I admit. Parents' Weekend is when parents come to campus in mid-October for the weekend. Yeah, pretty self-explanatory. Saturday classes are canceled. Most of the students are already planning weekend trips to Manhattan or some beach resort. Several of the seniors are planning a huge rager somewhere that I as a Lower-Mid am not privy to know. My mom and Grandma Rosie, however, are coming, so I can't wait. And I wouldn't miss that for any rager.

"You can crash at my place if you've got nowhere else to go," Mancini offers. "Harris is coming over and the more the merrier."

That's actually pretty nice of him. "I appreciate that. I'll let you know."

"It gets a little expensive when you go home for every break," Harris says. "So if you ever need a place during any of the breaks, hit us up."

There's also a hint of understanding in Harris's words. "Will do." I fist-bump them.

"See you at practice," Mancini says, then pats my shoulder.

I navigate to the Grillery and find Caleb and Xavier standing at the end of the line. I join them.

"You have some quality friends," Xavier says.

"Thanks for the save," I say.

"You couldn't have looked more desperate to get away from them," Caleb contributes.

Damn, I was that obvious? Xavier and Caleb begin to talk about what they are going to get.

Suddenly, I feel a tap on my shoulder. I turn and see this gorgeous Black girl smiling at me. She has some nice glasses that highlight her eyes and smile. Her hair is short and curly. I smile back.

"Hi, I'm Andrea."

"Hi. Derrick."

"You're that Native guy, right?" Andrea asks.

Here we go. I sigh. "Yes, I'm Diné."

"Wow. I've never met a Native before," Andrea says. Before I can respond to that, she says, "You have such pretty hair."

"Thanks?" I reply.

"Can I touch it?" Andrea asks. Her hand immediately reaches for my head.

"Dude, don't," I automatically spit out.

"Oh, I'm so sorry," she apologizes. She looks genuinely embarrassed. Before she can say anything else, she quickly leaves.

"What do they got here?" I ask, shaking off the interaction.

"Fries. Burgers. Pizza. Ice cream. Candy bars. Soda. Coffee," Caleb lists.

I open my wallet and see that I have only three bucks left for this week. Mom sends me a twenty here and there, but I can't rely on that. She has her own expenses. I have to make the money I made with Grandpa Dominic last, otherwise I'm going to be broke sooner rather than later.

Caleb must sense my worry. He says, "I gotcha covered."

"I'm not that hungry," I say to avoid the embarrassment of having him pay for me. But, right on cue, my stomach growls as I sniff the aroma of a cheeseburger.

"Not hungry, huh?" Xavier asks.

"I'll be good," I explain. "I got some snacks back in my room."

"It'll be our pleasure," Caleb says. "Plus, I'm going to eat all the things before wrestling season starts and I need to make weight."

"Oh, for real?" I ask, genuinely excited. "What's your weight class?"

"One sixty," Caleb answers.

"Nice. I was one seventy-two last year, but it's looking more like one eighty-nine this year," I tell him. "What about you, Xavier?"

"Me? Wrestle?" He laughs. "Not in a million years. But I do like those singlets."

I catch his little smile. I don't miss that this could possibly mean that Xavier is queer. There's some surprise in Caleb's expression. Caleb looks like he wants to disappear.

"They aren't the most comfortable," I say to dispel the awkwardness. "But if you ever want to try out, I'm sure Caleb and I could help ya."

"No thanks. I'm committed to squash," Xavier says. "I noticed you didn't care about my comment about the singlets."

"Xavier!" Caleb tries to shush him.

"Yeah? So?" I respond.

"I just want to make perfectly clear whom I'm attracted to," Xavier says.

"Dudes," I supply.

"Yes, dudes," Xavier says.

Caleb looks so nervous that I wouldn't be surprised if he just sprinted away from the two of us.

"Cool," I say.

"That's it?" Xavier asks.

"Do you want me to say anything else?" I respond. "As long as you're not a jerk, we're cool."

"Well said," Xavier says.

Caleb seems to calm down some. Then Xavier asks, "Are you?" Caleb tenses up.

When Jayden had asked about my sexuality, it had upset me a little, because it had felt like an attack on my own identity. Now I don't care. People are just trying to get to know me. And, honestly, I'm more pissed off that people still ask me if I grew up in a tepee, which happened again yesterday. It's probably why I haven't gone to Study Break. I'm trying to avoid meeting new students and a whole new set of those questions.

I relax a little. "No."

"Okay," Xavier says.

Caleb fully relaxes his shoulders. I begin to suspect that Caleb might be queer, as well, and that his awkwardness around me might stem from that. It's not for me to speculate. If he is and feels comfortable telling me, cool. If not, also cool. It's his decision and his life.

"Okay. Feel free to order what you want. My mom would kill me if she found out I let you go starving," Caleb adds.

"She would," Xavier says. "She's always trying to feed me. She once even ordered me an entire pizza for my birthday."

"Well, I can't let your mom think that," I say, relenting. "Fine. I would appreciate a slice of pizza."

"There, that wasn't so hard now, was it?" Caleb says.

But it was. If my mom found out I was accepting charity, it wouldn't be pretty. Even without my mom here, I'm disappointed in myself. For the rest of Study Break, I do my best to enjoy myself. And I'm glad that whatever weirdness was between Caleb and me is lessening. I'm reminded a bit of when Jayden came out, but I force myself not to equate them. They are two separate individuals.

Back in my dorm room, I take out my textbooks and organize them on my desk by what I need to finish first. I roll my neck and pull out a bottled coffee drink that I bought when Caleb and Xavier weren't looking.

I sprawl on my bed and just stare at my ceiling for a few seconds. I don't miss home as much now that things have truly gotten going here. With that, I open my phone and call Chris and Jayden.

Jayden is the first to answer. His hair covers one of his eyes. "D-sauce! I was just thinking about you."

"How sweet of you," I respond.

"Nothing good," Jayden jokes. Man, I miss hanging with him.

"What's going down?" I ask over the continued ringtone on Chris's end.

"Check this out," Jayden says as he sticks out his tongue. A kernel-sized stud sparkles in his bedroom light.

"What the . . . ? Dude, that's awesome!" I say. "Where'd you get it?" Jayden is a few months younger than I am, and we're both not old enough to get piercings without parental supervision. His parents would also never allow it.

Just then, Chris answers. "Gents!"

"Chris!" I say.

"You show him yet?" Chris asks Jayden.

"Yuppers," Jayden says. He sticks out his tongue again.

I'm a little hurt. Had I been there, I would have gotten something pierced, too. Like maybe my left ear or something.

"Starletta is dating this tattoo artist who also does piercings," Jayden explains. "Thinking about getting a tattoo. Chris is a little too much of a wimp to join me."

"My dad would kill me," Chris says.

"You want in?" Jayden asks me. "I can wait till you get back."

"It'd have to be somewhere my mom can't see," I explain. I'm also in a parent-will-kill-me-if-I-get-a-tattoo-before-I'm-eighteen scenario.

"You could get an *I love Mom* tattoo on one of your cheeks," Jayden teases.

Both Chris and I chuckle.

"What would your tattoo be?" I ask.

"Horned toad on my chest," he says. And I'm instantly jealous. That's a real cool tattoo idea. Horned toads are signs of protection. If you ever catch one, you're supposed to place it on your chest and it will bless you, jiní.

"Just real tradish," Chris says.

"Damn, can you wait till we're eighteen? We can be tattoo twins," I offer Jayden.

"No dice," Jayden says. "I'm not sure how long this guy is going to date my cousin. Got to get when the getting's good."

"Snag discounts are the best," I say.

"Besides, we can still be tattoo twins. Or triplets," Jayden says.

"Oh, guess what, man?" Chris says.

"You're going to tell him now?" Jayden asks.

I know they are both hanging out without me. Even though I know it's not because they don't want me with them, I still feel left out. And with these two, this feels something like betrayal. I shove it down because I'm not some child who gets all butt hurt when he doesn't get what he wants. "What's up?"

"I got a job!" Chris says.

"What? Everything all right?" I respond. Chris and his family, like mine, haven't had it the easiest when it comes to money. He has had to step up in more ways than one to help his parents. But then I realize this also means he has had to quit football. And he loves football.

"Everything's good," Chris explains. "I convinced my parents that I need to start saving now if I want to go to college."

That sends me into a thought spiral. Do I need to get a job, too? I mean, I want to go to college, too. But then I refocus. I shouldn't bring up football right now because he might be sore about it.

"I'm going to be dishwashing at Quality Inn," Chris says.

"Nice, man," I say. I try to sound as encouraging as possible.

I notice that Jayden is looking away. He doesn't want to go to college. He thinks that everyone who goes gets into massive financial debt to work jobs they hate just to pay off their student loans. He doesn't want to be paying students loans until he dies.

"How about scholarships?" I offer.

"They don't always cover everything," Chris says.

That is so very true. While I do have a full-ride scholarship to Sagefield, my mom still had to pay up front for books and other stuff. If I want a nice laptop, I'll have to work for it during the summer. At least I'll be sixteen by then. And hey! Maybe I could wash dishes by Chris's side! Chris could be my reference!

We talk about nothing for a few more minutes. But when it gets to 10:35, I tell them I need to finish some homework. Jayden boos me, and Chris salutes me.

After we hang up, I feel the rush of joy that I had talking to my best friends subside, and all I'm left with is silence. The bare white walls of my room reflect the bright light, and the sounds of my breathing echo against them.

I chug the bottled coffee in a few loud gulps. I pull off the top textbook, Latin, and begin to do some translations. This is going to be a long night.

An hour later, I quickly check my email for the history reading. That's when I notice a new email from Ms. Thomas.

Derrick,

I am writing to tell you that an alumnus has responded to my email and is open to virtual chatting with you. He is currently a senior at Yale University. He says he has some time available this coming Wednesday, September 25, if that works for you.

I quickly respond to her email, saying that I would love to chat with this alumnus.

After that, I get back to studying. My mind lingers on Jayden's new tongue piercing and Chris's new job. They are both changing and growing. And I'm here at Sagefield, where I'm doing homework every single day. If Chris had gotten accepted here instead of me, would he still feel the need to get a job? If Jayden did, would he have gotten that piercing? I feel a little guilty that I want to be back home with them and not stuck here.

9

Dimóo dóó tágíį́į, Bini' Anit'ą́ą́ Tsoh 25
Wednesday, September 25

After my first class, I rush back to my dorm room. As I set up my boxy laptop, I quickly scarf down the rest of the bagel that I grabbed from the breakfast bar at the dining hall. I gulp down mouthfuls of coffee from my sixty-four-ounce Nalgene bottle and toss my dirty laundry into a corner of my room that won't show on my camera.

So this Sagefield alumnus is named Bryan. And he's studying political science at Yale University. Is it weird that we're both in the same state? And why am I so nervous?

I open the link that Ms. Thomas sent. After a few seconds, my computer screen fills with a live view of Ms. Thomas. She's in her office.

"Good morning, Ms. Thomas," I brightly say to her.

She nearly jumps out of her chair. "Oh, you scared me!" After she composes herself and looks into the camera, she says, "Good morning to you, too. Are you ready to talk with Bryan?"

"Yes, ma'am," I say. I turn my loan laptop to the side so that the bare white walls behind me don't blow out my camera with overexposure. If I had one of those newer laptops with the latest software and camera system, I wouldn't have to do this.

Then a third person appears on-screen. It's him! And he looks like he's also in a dorm room. He smiles widely at Ms. Thomas. "Mama T!"

"Bryan!" Ms. Thomas beams with a grand smile. "Thank you so much for agreeing to talk with Derrick. He's from the Navajo reservation."

"Oh, Diné," Bryan says. His eyes shift slightly to his left. I guess that's where my face is on his screen. He has a long thick braid of black hair. His dark eyebrows highlight the whites of his eyes. His face isn't fully square, but he has a wide jaw. I even see some turquoise earrings dangling off his ears. "Yá'át'ééh," he says with a broken, choppy pronunciation. "I butchered it, didn't I?"

"Good enough," I say to him.

"All right, before we get started," Ms. Thomas says, "school policy requires that a chaperone be present in all extracurricular interactions with our students, Bryan. I will turn off my camera, but I will still be on the line."

I'm beyond excited to talk to him no matter the conditions. "Thank you for setting this up, Ms. Thomas. And thanks to you, too, Bryan, for agreeing to talk to me."

Bryan grins. "Listen, whenever Mama T asks you to do something, you do it. She has changed so many lives for the better, mine included."

"I'm just doing my job," Ms. Thomas says. "Okay, talk away."

Her video screen darkens and displays her professional headshot, and it's me and Bryan.

"So Sagefield is weird," Bryan says.

I nearly laugh. "Yes!"

"Are they asking if you live in tepees?"

Now I do burst out laughing. "Yeah."

"Happens all the time. New sport. New people asking it. Then, new year, and it's the same process all over again."

"That doesn't sound like a good time."

"Just wait until they read the two paragraphs about the Trail of Tears in history. Everyone will wrongfully assume that your family was relocated along with the five tribes. Something to look forward to."

"Thanks for the heads-up."

"Yeah, so any questions for me? I was at Sagefield for my last two years, Upper-Mid and Senior. That was, like, four years ago?"

"I mean, I have a few. I don't know where to begin." I lean into my chair and cup the back of my head with both hands. My mind swims in a sea of questions, unable to pinpoint one.

"I can start. There are a few things I wanted to hear when I was there."

"Yes, please."

"This has to deal with all those people who keep asking you those questions. It comes from a place of ignorance. The reality of most of your peers is so much different than ninety-nine percent of the population's. You are literally going to school with the children of the wealthiest people in the world."

“Did those questions also piss you off?” I ask Bryan.

“They did and do. Those ‘Do you still live in a tepee?’ questions stem from a lack of knowledge and not always from a sinister set of beliefs,” he explains. “I had to figure that out myself. But that doesn’t mean you shouldn’t have reactions to it. Far from it.”

“I get so annoyed. Because it’s the same questions over and over.”

“And it feels like you can’t be pissed off because they aren’t the kind of racist questions that come from a sinister mindset.”

“Yeah! And it just makes it more frustrating.”

“Derrick, you *can* be pissed off. I mean, don’t take it out on them. But you have every right to be annoyed. You’re only human.”

“But I’m the only Native on campus.”

“Ah, gotcha. It feels like you have to be on your best behavior because they’re going to think every Native person acts like you.”

It feels so gratifying to hear someone else say this out loud. I’m glad that Ms. Thomas can hear this conversation.

Bryan continues, “Listen. Mind if I call you little brother?”

“I’d love that,” I say, and focus on what he’s saying next.

“I’m sorry to say, it’s not just Sagefield where you’re going to experience this. I’m still dealing with it at Yale. And my boss at my online internship, oh, she works in the White House! No biggie. Anyway, she says that she also still deals with these things at that level.”

“That sucks,” I say.

“I’m here to tell you you don’t have to deal with it!” He opens his arms out. “You are not obligated to engage with it.”

"What? Do you just ignore them?"

"If you want. If you feel like you want to invest your energy and time into teaching them and correcting their fallacies about Natives, by all means. But not all people will want to be corrected. They'll prefer their stereotypes over the reality of Native peoples. Because they don't have to deal with the fact that the land they stand on is stolen. They don't have to recognize that the founding fathers stole ideas from my people, the Seneca, and the Nations of the Haudenosaunee Confederacy, when they wrote the Constitution of the United States."

"Wait. What's that last part?" I ask. I immediately open my notes application and write down his response.

"The Haudenosaunee Confederacy has the Great Law of Peace, which predates colonial arrival. If you look at it and compare the Great Law of Peace with the Constitution, you'll be surprised at the similarities. Some even say that the founding fathers plagiarized a great deal of the Great Law of Peace but intentionally neglected to incorporate women into positions of power."

That's actually really cool. Not the plagiarizing nor the disempowerment of women, but the part about the Great Law of Peace predating the Constitution. Hey, I could write about this for my twenty-page history essay!

"Back to what I was saying," Bryan says. "You're at Sagefield to learn. That's your priority. You can teach and share yourself with the community when you want, and if you want. Some days you'll be able to be patient and teach people. Other days, it's not your problem. Take it day by day, and person by person. A good tactic I use is to ask them why they are asking me something. That usually forces them to think about what they're saying. The ones you want to invest your energy teaching will recognize that they aren't informed."

"Thanks," I say to Bryan. It feels like a weight has been lifted off my shoulders.

"Hey, September thirtieth is coming up. You gonna wear an orange shirt?"

"No, huh-uh," I respond, a little bit of my rez slipping out. "Why?"

"Orange Shirt Day, little brother! The National Day for Truth and Reconciliation," Bryan says, searching my expression. "It started up north in Canada. But the idea is you wear an orange shirt to raise awareness about the residential school systems in Canada, and the boarding school systems in the United States. It sheds light on that dark history. We, Native people, are all descendants of boarding school survivors."

His last sentence echoes against my bare walls and creates ripples of pain throughout my spirit. Másání Mildred.

"I didn't know about Orange Shirt Day," I manage to say. "Yeah, I'd like to do that here. But the only orange shirt I have is this." I run to my closet and pull out one of my tank top workout shirts.

"You should ask Mama T if you can wear that next week," Bryan says.

"Yes?" Ms. Thomas's video reappears in our feed. She looks at the both of us and narrows in on my orange shirt.

I ask her, "Can I wear this on Monday for Orange Shirt Day?"

"It's not approved for the school dress code," she says. "But seeing as it's for the National Day for Truth and Reconciliation, email your teachers explaining the situation and cc me. Next year, be sure to have an orange button-down shirt."

I barely register that she's giving me permission to go against the dress code. The words *next year* grow to fill every crevice in my mind. Because it means I'll be back here. It might mean I'll graduate from here. "Yes, ma'am."

"I need to head out for my next class. But one last thing I think you should hear. Sagefield is hard. It's one of the most difficult things I have ever done in my life."

"Even more so than Yale?" I joke.

"Yes," he says seriously. "You can do it. Because you come from a long line of warriors. Remember that. You inherited your ancestors' strength, wisdom, and tenacity. When you graduate from Sagefield, so many opportunities will be available to you."

Excitement pumps through my veins. When I graduate. Not if.

"Thanks for your time, Bryan," I tell him.

"No worries. I could just dump a bunch of advice. Let's keep in touch. If you ever need to talk about anything, email me or set up another one of these chats with Mama T."

"I really appreciate that!"

"Later, little brother. Bye, Mama T!" Bryan says. Quickly, he signs off.

The yellow light of the sun washes my blank walls in color and warms the air.

Ms. Thomas's phone rings, and she picks it up. "Yes, Mr. Wordsworth."

She continues the conversation. She probably forgot that she's still in the meeting, so I sign off to give her privacy.

Wow. Bryan is proof that Natives can succeed at Sagefield and at Yale. Just knowing that there are Native alumni from these elite schools makes graduating from here seem like it's doable. Could I be one of those big shots with a high-paying job? Maybe, if I am, I could buy my mom an actual house and we can move out of that NHA housing unit.

While hope percolates in my heart, I quickly request an add to Bryan on PicsPress and then get ready for my next two classes.

10

Dimóo yázhí, Bini' Anit'ą́ą́ Tsoh 28

Saturday, September 28

I shouldn't be surprised that the football team chartered a luxurious bus for an away game with Chadley Rosenfeld, one of our rival schools. The seats on this bus are stitched black leather. There's enough space for each guy to have two seats to himself. I even have my own air-conditioner vent above me! It's nuts. The late-afternoon September sun shines brightly outside on the field of grass.

Most of the guys watch movies on their large OLED tablets with their super-expensive Bluetooth headphones. Meanwhile, I'm reading the first chapters of *The Great Gatsby*. I've had to read a full book every week for English. At the end of each week, I have to write eight-page papers. I'm in the early chapters, and it's about New York City in the 1920s or something. My eyes ache from all these long hours of reading.

After a quick neck massage, I rub my eyes. Inside the darkness of my closed eyelids, red fireworks pop and spread where my fingers press. I yawn, wishing I had brought some coffee with me. I can't afford to keep buying three-dollar bottles. I have to find a more affordable option for my growing coffee habit. One more hour until kickoff. I open the book and force myself to read.

How am I supposed to care about a city I've never been to? In 1923, the Navajo Nation government was established, and the Diné of that period would have been voting for our first Navajo Nation Chairman, which was what we had before our current presidents. That has more inherent value and affects my life far more than some rich white douchebag named Gatsby. I look out the window. I run my fingers through my hair, which is longer than I'd prefer. The tips of my hair tickle my forehead. I need to get a haircut.

"Dude, hook me up," I hear one of my teammates behind me whisper, bringing me out of my own thoughts.

"How much?" asks a voice I recognize as Mancini's.

I close my book, unable to focus on the assigned reading. Mancini and the second guy aren't making any effort to hide whatever it is being slung.

"Ten milligrams."

"All I got is twenty."

"I can send you money."

"No problem. Just keep working your computer magic."

"Thanks, man. I'm just about done with the infiltration for the 'extra help.' Also, I got a paper due for Mr. Henderson on Monday."

"Mr. Henderson?" I blurt out.

I turn around and look at them. The other voice belongs to Goldman. He is the one asking for whatever Mancini is distributing.

"I have him for History 101," I explain. "Dude's an ass."

"He is!" Goldman says. "The way he expects you to memorize every detail is borderline psychotic."

"For serious!" I respond with my full rez accent. I continue my rant. "He wants us to know the names of all the Pilgrims, their birthdates, their astrological signs, and all that nonsense."

Goldman responds, "He only gets better in 301."

"You guys got nothing on me. I have 601 with him," Mancini says.

"Does history even go that high?" Goldman asks. "What do you even study at that level?"

"Dinosaurs?" I pitch in.

"World history, my brothers," Mancini answers.

"Why would you do that to yourself?" Goldman asks.

"It's rote memorization with a pinch of bullshitting. Easy stuff, if you ask me. All you got to do is spout out names and dates and say how you think people's actions affected historical events."

"So what exactly are you studying?" I ask.

"We're doing a survey of terrorism in America from 1865 onward," Mancini explains in a bragging tone. "We're starting with racial terrorism and lynching during the Reconstruction period in the South."

"That actually sounds really interesting," I say, and open my book to exit the conversation. I'd rather be learning about that than about the American Revolution. When Goldman returns to his seat, I look out the window, still struggling to focus on the reading. Rolling hills rise and fall like sine waves. Everywhere there is vibrant greenery. Grass. Trees. Bushes. Even the bodies of water that we pass have a greenish hue to their blue depths.

I grab my phone from my pocket and send a quick picture to my mom and Grandma Rosie. Then I send a picture to Chris and Jayden. Before any of them respond, I notice that Carter, who is sitting in front of me, is playing a first-person shooter game on his large laptop. Across, to my right, is Ramirez. Huh, he must have gotten his hair shaved. He's busy reading a massive book. I glimpse the title, *War and Peace* by Leo Tolstoy. I bet I have that behemoth to look forward to.

Ramirez must sense that I'm looking at him and closes the book. "These readings." He scratches his newly shaved head. His forearm muscles twitch with every movement. I suddenly remember the tattoo on his calf.

"Yo, Ramirez," I start. "What was it like getting a tattoo?"

He reaches upward to stretch. After a loud exhale, he says, "It stung the entire time, like a beesting. You thinking of getting one?"

"My friend at home says he knows someone who could do it."

"What? You're not eighteen, right?" he asks.

"I turn sixteen in March," I answer.

"I didn't know tattoos were allowed for sixteen-year-olds."

"No, my friend's cousin's boyfriend is a tattoo artist and can do it," I explain.

"Is he a professional?" Ramirez questions. He leans closer to me. "Because you don't want to be a guinea pig for some newbie tattoo artist. They last forever."

"Good point. I'm not sure," I respond. And yeah, that does

make a lot of sense. I wouldn't want to walk around with a subpar tattoo on my body. I'll just wait.

Ramirez continues, "I don't think he's a professional if he's doing tattoos on underage people. Besides, it's better to research tattoo artists."

Carter turns around and asks, "So what would your tattoo be?"

I don't want to copy Jayden's cheii tattoo idea. At least not without his permission. But I did have a thought. "I am thinking maybe the four sacred mountains around my arm."

"What are those?" Ramirez asks me.

"In each direction, we have a sacred mountain. Sis Naajiní in the east. Tsoodził in the south. Dook'o'oosłíίd in the west. And Dibé Nitsaa in the north."

"Do all Natives have sacred mountains?" Ramirez asks. Carter fully faces me. Both are eager for my answer.

My initial gut reaction is to recoil and not respond. But Ramirez and Carter are super cool. If I were to explain to them, they would listen. Unlike Mancini or Harris, who might not be as respectful. I remember what Bryan said to me. Pick and choose, if I feel like it. And I feel like it. "I can't speak for all Native Nations. For Diné, there are the four primary ones. But there are so many other sacred mountains."

Both their expressions are soft and attentive. After I explain, they nod.

"That's pretty cool," Carter says.

My hair has been tickling my forehead. I scratch and push it to the side.

"What's very cool?" asks Mancini from behind us.

"Hoskie was just talking about his culture," Ramirez explains.

"Oh, like how you're all supposed to have long hair?" He faces me. "Why is that? And why don't you?"

My gut churns and my brows furrow. I think this is what Bryan meant when he said some people only want to confirm their stereotypes of Natives. "Not all Native guys have long hair."

"But, like, you should, though, right?" Mancini asserts. "I'm not saying it's not cool. The opposite."

I take a deep breath. I feel annoyance bubbling in my veins and chest.

"That's what all the movies show," Mancini pushes.

I'll give him the benefit of the doubt. "Are all movies factually accurate?"

"I mean, documentaries are," Mancini says.

Yeah, I'm not going to get through to this guy. Like Bryan said, I don't have to teach him a thing.

"Sure," I say curtly. Changing the subject, I ask Carter, "Yo, what were you playing?"

Carter answers, "*Angelic Ring Infinity*. You game?"

"How is it?" Ramirez asks.

"It's all right," Carter says.

"The previous games were better. Especially when they were with the original developers," Mancini contributes.

And just like that, the conversation changes. Bryan's right. I don't have to give anyone a lesson about my tribe, especially if they don't want to learn. It's not my responsibility. I smile with that realization.

As I again brush my hair aside, I get this idea to shave my head. If I do it, then maybe no one will ask me about my hair again.

We get back to Sagefield campus from our game around eight that night. I got to play on the defensive line and even sacked a running back who was carrying the ball. There are some new bruises on my arms and calves. My legs ache as I walk the three flights of stairs to my dorm room. I wasn't in the mood to wait for the elevator.

As I enter my hallway, I catch Caleb exiting his room. I smile and say, "What's up, Caleb?"

Caleb says, "Whoa! What happened to you? You look like you just got into a fight with a diesel truck."

"Something like that. I was on the defensive line for a few plays, and Coach told me to just create chaos. So chaos I created." I make my way to my door and fish in the top pocket of my backpack for my keys. My hand brushes against my tádídíín, which I keep there. My stomach, as if on cue, grumbles.

"Hungry much?"

"All the time," I admit.

"Listen, I'm going to hang with some friends and we're going to order pizza and watch a movie. If you want, you can join us."

He just invited me to hang with him? I'm a little surprised. "That sounds great." Then I remember. "Crap. Sorry. I got to pass tonight. I already said I'd join Carter and Ramirez in a bit." I'm also planning on shaving my head tonight.

"Oh, okay," he says. His head droops a little bit.

"But I'm down for a chill sesh later. Outside of Mandatory Study Hall."

"You don't have to if you don't want to," he says.

"Let's hang out," I assert. "So that way you can send a picture to your mom and prove that you're being courteous."

Caleb laughs. "You saw right through me."

"I have a very involved mom, too."

"All right. Cool. Yeah. I'll catch you later."

"Sounds good," I say, and wave at him.

He leaves, and I enter my dark dorm room. After I turn on the light, I dump my heavy backpack on the floor and tumble into my bed. Outside my window, the unnatural white light of the streetlight contends with the yellowish tinge of my ceiling light.

Then I plug in my phone to the wall to charge, and after a few minutes, it vibrates and turns on. I need a new phone. It can't hold a charge for a can of beans. The crack on my screen slowly navigates across the entire front panel the same way a pothole creeps across an ignored street. Once the phone fully boots up, I get a string of texts and missed call notifications.

I send a quick text to Chris and Jayden. Shaving my head!

I stand outside Carter's door on the second floor of my dormitory. Should I shave my head? Why am I stalling? Of course I want to. Shaved heads are much easier to maintain. And I won't have to deal with people telling me that I should grow my hair long and put feathers in it. At least, I hope so.

I knock on Carter's door and find Carter standing behind a

chair where someone I haven't met yet is sitting. A loud buzzing sound tells me that the guy is having his head shaved. Ramirez sits on Carter's large comfy futon.

"Hoskie!" Ramirez shouts.

"Ramirez!" I excitedly say.

"We can use first names if you prefer. If you forgot, mine is Reese. We aren't in football now," Carter—I mean Reese—says.

I'm briefly reminded of hanging out with Chris and Jayden. A whole afternoon of the three of us just chilling, binge-watching an entire TV series. I miss them. A sense of newfound brotherhood wells up in my chest. There's enough camaraderie to share between these two groups. Rez friends. Sagefield friends.

Reese stops the clippers and turns to smile at me. "Welcome to the barbershop."

"You have a nice clandestine haircut operation," I say.

"Everything I do is clandestine!" Reese says, and then goes back to shaving the rest of this guy's scalp.

I realize I never got Ramirez's first name. So I ask, "What's your first name, Ramirez?"

"I was just about to ask you the same," Ramirez says. "Gabriel."

"Derrick," I reply.

Reese asks Gabriel, "How are things with Julia?"

"We cool," he says.

"Just cool?" the new guy getting his head shaved says, and laughs. "I saw you two sneaking out of the music hall!"

I gather that the music department must be where everyone goes to hook up.

“Things must be going cool with Yasmine, too,” the new guy says.

“Nah, I ain’t a player,” Gabriel says with a simple smile. “Yasmine’s nothing more than gossip. Right, Derrick?”

“What?” I ask.

“People are saying that you and Caleb are a thing,” Gabriel says.

I nearly laugh my head off. “Oh. I’m flattered to be his rumored boyfriend. Are we a happy couple?” Man, people here just spit gossip all the time. Nothing else to do, I guess.

“Mancini said he saw you hanging out at the Grillery and everyone was wondering if you’re into guys,” Gabriel explains from the couch.

I grow defensive. I remember Jayden and how scared he was of being himself. The words come out a little more aggressive than I intend. “Does it matter if I am?”

“Easy,” Gabriel says. “I told Mancini to shut his mouth. We’re not in the 2000s.”

“Thanks,” I say. There is a very impressive computer setup on Reese’s desk. A large, probably thirty-two-, maybe thirty-seven-inch screen 4K UHD display hovering above a neatly organized desk. A large glass tower box sits on the floor. There are neon blue lights highlighting a water-cooling system and some large computer graphic cards. Reese is a computer gamer! On the screen is the pause icon and a dark screen. “Damn, you got some impressive gear!”

Reese smiles. “I’m fortunate.”

“This is nothing compared to Goldman’s,” the new guy says.

"Then again, if you're doing high-level hacking, you'll need all the professional-level chips and cards."

I don't pay attention to the last comment because I'm still transfixed by Reese's computer screen. "What are we going to watch?"

"A classic," the new guy says. "After the buzzing concludes. Can't hear a thing otherwise."

"Gotcha." I have to ask, "So how do you know Reese?"

"I'm on the wrestling team."

"Seriously?" I nearly shout. "I'm in wrestling!"

"Well, sit down and have a beer!" The new guy motions to Reese's closet, where I assume Reese is hiding his stash from the floor faculty members.

I respond, "No thanks. Do you have anything else to drink? Nonalcoholic?"

"I got some Gatorade. Coffee," Reese offers. He hands the clippers to Gabriel, who continues shaving the new guy's head.

I'm not really in the mood for anything sweet. "Coffee sounds good. Thanks."

Reese opens a drawer and pulls out a big bag of powdered coffee. "Powdered okay?"

"Sure." I nod.

"Damn, that's a lot of coffee, Reese," the new guy says.

Reese scoops some dark, delicious-smelling granules into an empty RTIC bottle and then pours some Evian water into it. "Had to pull a few all-nighters recently."

"I feel that," Gabriel says, focusing on the areas by the new guy's ear.

"You want some?" Reese asks Gabriel, handing me the bottle.

"Mind if I take a picture so I can buy some for myself?" I ask Reese. He holds the bag of powdered coffee for me to snap a picture.

"I'll just give you some," Reese says. He opens another drawer and begins scooping a healthy amount of coffee into Ziploc bags.

Before I forget I say, "I didn't know you were in wrestling, Reese."

"He's not just in wrestling," New Guy starts. "He's the team captain."

Excitement starts in my chest and rushes outward to my limbs. I couldn't have asked for better news. This made my whole night, week, month!

"Yeah," Reese says. I can sense some nervousness. He hands me the bag of powdered coffee and takes the clippers from Gabriel to finish New Guy's hair. "There!" Reese says, and turns off the clippers. He raises his hand and slaps the back of New Guy's head.

"Damn!" New Guy shouts. He stands and looks at a mirror on Reese's closet door.

"Next!" Reese says, cleaning the teeth. Done, he points the clippers at me.

I nod and sit in the chair. The clippers buzz by my ears like a thousand angry bees. In a few seconds, I feel clumps of hair fall onto my shoulders and fresh air on the patches of my exposed head. I have never cared about the length of my hair and regularly get it cut so that it doesn't become a morning chore. With hair, you have to shower in the morning and all that stuff. I'd much rather just roll out of bed and head to breakfast.

When Reese has finished, he slaps my bare head. The sting from Reese's palm feels like energizing lightning. Yeah, this feels good. I take a quick selfie and upload it to PicsPress for my friends and family to see.

I can only imagine how people here at Sagefield are going to react to a Native guy with no hair. Not all Native men grow their hair long. Good on the ones who do and everything. But not me. And with Bryan's advice, I feel empowered. I feel like myself. I feel a small sense of belonging with these guys.

11

Dimóo, Bini' Anit'ą́ą́ Tsoh 29

Sunday, September 29

The next night in my dorm room, I pull up my contact for Másání Mildred and call before I get ready to do some more late-night studying. It rings a few times. I imagine her reaching for her cell phone and not being able to find it in her pockets.

"It's Derrick," Grandma Rosie answers. My lips curl into a surprised smile.

Softly in the back, I hear Másání Mildred yell, "Who?"

"Derrick!" Grandma Rosie yells back. Then to the phone, "Hi, yáázh. How are you?"

My heart swells. I wish this was a video call so I could see them and they could see my newly shaved head. "Grandma! What are you doing with Másání Mildred?"

"I'm dropping off your great-grandma. I took her out for dinner in Window Rock."

"I'm glad you're there. I was going to call you after her."

Grandma Rosie says, "Call me tomorrow, okay? I'm going to be heading back to Fort Defiance."

"Let me talk to him!" Másání Mildred yells.

"Na'," Grandma Rosie says.

"Yes, hello?" Másání Mildred says.

A wave of homesickness floods my being. I wish I was there, helping Grandma Rosie with Másání Mildred. I should be there. "Másání! How are you?"

"Just peachy, sha'awéé'. We just got back from Window Rock."

"Did you have fun?" I ask.

"Yes. It's good to get out of this house. It's so lonely here," Másání Mildred says.

I can't help but want to hold her hand. I want to tell her that I'll spend the night so that she won't feel that way. "How was your week?"

"It was fine, sha'awéé'. Just the same things, day by day. I met with the doctor again."

"Oh? What did Dr. Platero say?" I ask. "How's your heart?"

"It's still beating. She has me on new medicines. She tells me that it'll help with my dizzies in the morning."

"You're still getting dizzy in the morning?" I ask.

"Yes. It happens every now and then. Nothing to worry about. My doctor ché'é says this'll help."

"Have you thought about maybe moving in with Grandma Rosie?"

"No. I'm staying right here, sha'awéé'," she firmly states.

I push no more. It's a touchy subject, one that might upset her. And with the condition of her heart, I have to respect her wishes. "I just had my first away game yesterday. Football."

"Oh! Jooł yitalí."

"'Aoo'. Coach put me in the defense line for a few plays, and they really like me." I look at the bruises on my arms, oddly proud of them. "My coaches say I'm really good at tackling."

"Be careful, sha'awéé'. If you want to come back home, you don't have to be there."

Again, I'm gutted. I do want to be home. It always hurts when she plainly states it like that.

In the background, I hear Grandma Rosie say, "Yooweh! He wants to be there."

"Are they treating you well?" Then, softly, a whisper. "Are they hitting you?"

"No one's hitting me, Másání," I assure her.

"Oh. Good. But you can tell me, sha'awéé'," she says. I'm not entirely sure, but she sounds kind of desperate and scared.

I change the subject again. "Are you still trying to get that surgery?"

"What? Oh, yeah. I have to try these new medicines first. If they don't work, then we'll try the surgery, jiní."

"I'll pray on my end over here that these new medicines work well."

"Do you have tádídíín over there?"

"Yes," I say. To be truthful, I haven't been praying as much as I did back on the rez. When you pray, you're supposed to stand on Mother Earth and face eastward during the sunrise. But with all the late nights I've been doing just to keep up with the workload, I've been sleeping past dawn. And also, I don't need someone spotting me praying. I'd never hear the end of questions about Native people praying in the morning. For Másání Mildred, I'll make an exception.

I briefly think of telling her that I'm going to wear an orange shirt tomorrow for the National Day for Truth and Reconciliation. Before I can, I hear Grandma Rosie yelling in the background, "Mom! How long has this food been in your fridge?"

"What?" Másání Mildred yells. I hold my cell phone away from my ear.

"It's all rotten! You don't have anything to eat!"

"There's potatoes in the back!"

"Mom, everything is rotten. Just come home with me. Then tomorrow I'll cook for you."

"Yáa! I'm fine right here."

I squeak, "Másání Mildred, go back with Grandma Rosie. Please." But she doesn't hear me. Then they start to argue in Diné and I'm lost.

"Másání Mildred," I plead again. Louder. "Go to Fort with Grandma Rosie."

But this time, the phone call ends. Másání Mildred must have closed her flip phone.

"You'll be safer with Grandma Rosie," I say to the silence.

A mountain of fear accumulates in my heart. Másání Mildred is getting up there in age. And a small accident could very easily turn into something very serious. If that were to happen while I was here, I wouldn't be able to help. I might not be able to see her again.

I feel my heart beating louder and faster. My ceiling light bulb flickers. I think of all my sacrifices and wonder if they are worth it. I belong there with Másání Mildred, Grandma Rosie, and my mom. I should be there.

12

ORANGE SHIRT DAY

Dimóo biiskání, Bini’ Anit’ą́ą́ Tsoh 30
Monday, September 30

I stand in front of the bathroom mirror before I head to my first class. I’m nervous as hell. Underneath my sports coat I’m wearing my orange tank top for National Day for Truth and Reconciliation. There are going to be a bunch of people asking me questions today. My throat tightens a little.

Yesterday I had sent out the email explaining why I’m not in full dress code to my teachers. Most of them responded with a simple acknowledgment. Mrs. Fairchild asked if I wanted to take a moment to explain the day to my Human Development class, and I agreed. I’m not dreading standing out. I have to get used to that. I’m dreading all the questions that will pop up. I don’t think I’m ready to talk or, as Bryan would say, teach.

But I have to do this for all our ancestors who were kidnapped and forced into boarding schools. I have to do this for the ones who returned silenced by the violence they endured. I have to do this for the ones who never returned and are still buried near these boarding schools. I have to do this for Másání Mildred.

I can do this. I squeeze my tádídíín in my top pocket before I put on my backpack and make my way to my first class. History. As I make my way over, I smell the wisps of cedar smoke.

When I walk into the classroom, I see Mr. Henderson and Ife talking at the round table. I dig into my backpack and hand him the essay that's due in two days.

He nods and places my paper into his briefcase. He quickly looks at me and my orange tank top. "It takes a lot of bravery to do what you are doing."

"Thank you, sir," I say to him, mainly for allowing me to not adhere to the dress code and not for calling me brave. I take off the sports jacket and rest it on my chair.

Ife stares at my orange shirt. She sees that Mr. Henderson doesn't do anything and continues with their conversation. Other students begin to come in.

"What happened to your shirt?" James asks me. "Didn't do your laundry?"

I smirk and respond, "Something like that."

"And your head?" James presses.

"Just prefer short hair," I say.

I'm surprised that it doesn't get more of a reaction from the rest of the students. I'm also thankful. I'm not entirely ready to start talking about my decision to wear an orange tank top.

Once the bell rings, Mr. Henderson immediately starts the discussion.

"Mr. Choi, summarize our readings," he says.

"Uh, y-yeah, no problem, Mr. Henderson," stammers James.

He quickly pulls out a notebook and reads. "Our weekend assignment was to read about the Constitution itself and how it came to be."

"Expand," Mr. Henderson demands, leaning back in his chair.

"Uh, I, uh . . ."

"First start with the dates," Mr. Henderson instructs.

"Okay," James says, looking at his notes. "It was created on September 17, 1787, and ratified on June 21, 1788."

"Who were the big players?" Mr. Henderson asks, this time to the entire class.

A student named Brandon raises his hand, "Well, there were seven." He massages his temples. "George Washington, Thomas Jefferson, John Adams, Benjamin Franklin, Alexander Hamilton, and . . ." Brandon stops and then opens his notepad. "Oh! John Jay and James Madison!"

I really want to step in and mention the Haudenosaunee Confederacy and how the "founding fathers" stole ideas from the Great Law of Peace. The Haudenosaunee had a democracy long before these colonizers infected the east. It frustrates me that this isn't being included in our readings. It feels like Mr. Henderson is spreading lies and not actual history.

"Nice work," Mr. Henderson says. "These founding fathers are credited with drafting the Constitution. Notice how it was created in September 1787 and not ratified until June 21, 1788. What was the reason?"

"Federalists and Anti-Federalists, primarily," Ife says. Her accent emphasizes the hard consonant sounds and trails the last *s*.

"Excellent, Ms. Achebe," Mr. Henderson says.

I lean back in my chair and fold my arms. I will just wait until class is over. I'm not at all interested in participating in this perpetuation of lies.

Eventually Mr. Henderson looks at me and says, "Mr. Hoskie, what say you to the viewpoints of the Federalists?"

"They were the ones who wanted to adopt the Constitution. They wanted weaker state governments."

"What about the Anti-Federalists?"

It becomes too much for me to hold back. I have to share my opinion. "I think it's just a crap show."

I hear a gasp in the room. Mr. Henderson has a stern expression that I can't read. Then he asks, "What makes this a crap show?" He leans forward and rests his chin on his hand.

Despite my bare arms, I feel the heat of my body increasing. "I think that there is too much credit given to the founding fathers. They didn't just come up with democracy on their own. They stole important ideas from the surrounding Native Nations. Specifically, the Haudenosaunee."

Mr. Henderson's right eyebrow raises. Is he mad that I'm dismantling his view on history? He commands, "Expand."

"The six Nations of Mohawk, Oneida, Onondaga, Cayuga, Seneca, and Tuscarora had their own functioning democracy dating back as early as the 1200s. Separation of powers—that was in their constitution. Individual freedoms and liberties were in their constitution. So to say that the founding fathers imagined this great government through their brilliant minds is a lie."

"Can you back up that claim?" Mr. Henderson asks me. He quickly scribbles down something on his notepad.

"Huh?" I respond, still recovering from the flood of anger and adrenaline.

"Do you have supporting documents?" he clarifies.

"The Haudenosaunee kept records of their government in wampum belts," I respond. Just a little something I dug up after my talk with Bryan.

"I want to touch base on this with you individually, Mr. Hoskie," Mr. Henderson says. "But, for now, if you are able to, I would like to return to the question of your opinion on the viewpoints of the Anti-Federalists. You think they are a, ahem, crap show." There is some apprehensive giggling.

"That's my stance," I say. "Crap. Show."

Mr. Henderson moves to another student to answer the question. For the rest of class, I notice that he pays more attention to me than normal. There are some occasional side glances from the other students at my shirt but nothing more.

After the bell rings, Mr. Henderson says, "Mr. Hoskie, stay an extra minute."

"No problem." I pack my things and then make my way to the chair next to him. He's going to punish me for something. I know it. Maybe for not contributing meaningfully to the conversation.

"About that outburst earlier, Mr. Hoskie," he states. And before I can answer, he continues, "I want more of that in class."

"What?" I'm caught off guard.

"Derrick," he says. I'm even further surprised he's using my first name. "You presented an opinion and argued it. You even supplemented your stance with the information about the wampum! I want to see this more in class. The way history is often taught in high school disregards so many facets and contributors. That fire you had. Use it! If you don't speak up about the history of the Indigenous peoples of the Americas, no one else will. My own knowledge is extremely lackluster when it comes to that side of history. I don't know what I don't know. Neither do your classmates. Now, you haven't chosen a topic yet for your final essay. I'd suggest the Great Law of Peace and its influence on the Constitution. That's something I'd be very interested in reading."

"Okay," I say.

"Think about it. Then email me. Preferably by the end of the day, Derrick. This is your third and final reminder."

He picks up his briefcase and then leaves the room.

Whoa, Mr. Henderson actually wants me to speak up about Indigenous history. And even more so, I think I have my semester paper topic. But I don't have the same passion for it as I do for some other subjects. This orange tank top and what it represents today weigh heavy on my mind.

I make it to my next class trying to avoid as many stares as possible. I briefly think about changing my shirt. Again, I'm doing this for the Elders whose abuse has been ignored and silenced. The voices of my peers echo as they pass me down the English wing.

“Dude, where’s your shirt?”

“Oh, he’s going to be in so much trouble.”

“What happened to your hair?”

“Hey, can I wear tanks now?”

“Why is he doing that?”

“I thought you were growing your hair long like a real Native?”

I sit in my seat in Human Development class, thankful to get out of the hallway.

It’s not just my arms and shoulders that feel bare when I take off my sports coat. I can’t shake this feeling that everyone is staring at me.

The bell rings and the talking quiets. After our enchantment, Mrs. Fairchild looks at me. I nod, and she addresses the entire class.

“Now, Derrick here is going to talk about his decision to wear an orange shirt today, which is to raise awareness. I’ll let him explain.”

I stand up, and now everyone’s eyes are on me. My forehead warms and my palms sweat. I awkwardly spit out, “It’s Orange Shirt Day today; that’s why I’m wearing an orange shirt. Today.”

There are some giggles. Wendy, on the other hand, remains respectfully quiet and attentive.

“It’s for the National Day for Truth and Reconciliation. You see, from the 1820s to as recently as the 1970s, Native Americans were forced to go to US federal Indian boarding schools far away from their families.”

A silence as thick as an iceberg envelops the classroom.

"There was this policy called 'Kill the Indian, Save the Man.' It justified any means necessary to whitewash Native children. Sometimes, if Native children spoke their tribal languages, they would have to eat soap to wash their own language out of their mouth. There was rampant abuse—physical, sexual, and psychological—at these Indian boarding schools."

My heart breaks. Másání Mildred might have endured that. She more than likely did. I force a cough to cover a choke.

"And in Canada, theirs was the residential school system. There was also death, both here and in Canada.

"A lot of our Elders went to these schools all across the United States and never returned. Their bodies are still buried on campuses."

I wonder if I have any great-grandparents who were buried off Diné Bikéyah. How many bodies of Native children are still buried at these US government boarding schools? I close my eyes and give myself a moment to calm down. I am strong. I am Másání Mildred's 'awéé'. I am Grandma Rosie's yáázh. I am my mom's son.

"So Orange Shirt Day is to bring awareness to this issue and to hopefully someday pressure the United States government to begin efforts to return the bodies of our stolen children to their homelands."

"Wow," says Anton. "I had no idea."

"That's terrible," Wendy says.

Mrs. Fairchild stands next to me, and it's all I can do to not let a single tear out. I'm not crying in front of anyone. She pats my shoulder. "Thank you for sharing that. Are you okay?"

"I'm good." I sit back down and count my breaths the way Ms. Laramie taught me.

"Does anyone have any questions or comments?" Mrs. Fairchild asks the class.

Wendy immediately raises her hand.

I wonder what she's going to say.

Her tone is even and somber. She looks directly into my eyes. She speaks from a place of honesty. "I don't know anything about this history. 'Kill the Indian, Save the Man' really captures and communicates what happened. I'm sorry that happened, Derrick. Do you have any book recommendations or further sources of information for those of us who want to know more?"

"I, uh. I don't," I admit. I realize that I'm on the same level of knowledge as most of my classmates right now. I told them all I know about that era.

"I actually did the honor of compiling a list of resources after I received your email, Derrick," Mrs. Fairchild says. She pulls out some papers and hands them to all of us.

I look at the top paper, and the very first web page is www.orangeshirtday.org. There are further resources and bullet points. It's not until the letters on the page start to shake that I realize my hand is unsteady. Breathe, I remind myself.

"Okay," Mrs. Fairchild says with a soft, gentle clap. "If any of you want to circle back to this topic, I'd be happy to listen. But for now, let's continue."

The rest of her words blur into my consciousness. I know nothing about this period of history. I know very little about Másání Mildred when she was younger. A carpet of goose bumps covers my arms even though the air in the classroom is hot and humid.

It's 6:00 p.m., one hour before study hall. I'm in the library, trying to avoid everyone in the dining hall.

I sit in front of one of the computers and mindlessly scroll through search engines, checking out resources on the Haudenosaunee Confederacy. I try to focus on Mr. Henderson's suggestion of writing my final paper on the Great Law of Peace's influence on the United States Constitution.

I quickly check my school email. I see a message from Harris with the title EXAM HELP. I hover my mouse over the message. Then it happens. I smell cedar and think of Másání Mildred. I ignore it and open a new message and enter Mr. Henderson's email address. I guess I should make my final essay topic official.

The Great Law of Peace is an excellent topic to cover. There are going to be plenty of firsthand documents. I could even broaden Mr. Henderson's definition of firsthand documents by describing the value of wampum.

Másání Mildred's smile pops into my mind. I'm drawn into one of my earliest memories. Both of us hold on to a smooth cane that she used before her wheelchair. I'm a toddler looking up at her smile, learning to walk. She whispers, "Hazhóó'ógo, sha'awéé'."

I open up another tab and search *founding of Sagefield.* Fear forces my jaws to clench. I try to focus on the sound of air flowing into my nasal cavity. My fingers uncurl like flower petals facing the sunlight. My eyes scan the Wikipedia page for a brief overview. Sagefield was founded in the 1890s. Originally it was an all-boys school, but it became coed in the 1970s. No. Sagefield wasn't a boarding school for Native kids.

I hear the echoes of Másání Mildred saying, "Are they hitting you?" "You can come home." "You don't have to go."

I shake her voice out of my ears. Sagefield was built as a feeder school for Ivy League universities. In fact, there are seven other schools like Sagefield, including Van Doren, our main rival school. They were all established in the late 1800s as polishing schools to send students to Ivy League colleges.

I search *Native boarding schools*.

The first result that pops up is an article that details the recent discovery of dead buried Native children at residential schools in Canada. Pain stabs at my heart. The search results go on and on. There are so many accounts, books, and articles written about Native children at boarding schools, both in the United States and Canada.

My great-grandma lived through this. My heart drops in my chest. I have no idea what happened to Másání Mildred.

This is going to be my history essay topic.

I spot a book that contains transcribed interviews from Elders who survived that era. It's called *Boarding School Seasons* by Brenda J. Child. Those interviews are my firsthand documents. But our library doesn't have a copy of it. Before I leave the library, I'm going to ask the librarian to order a copy.

Another thought pops into my head. Másání Mildred. If I can record her experiences, I could reference her interview as one of my firsthand sources.

More and more article titles pop on-screen as I scroll down. Common words are *abuse*, *torture*, *sexual assault*, *whitewashing*, *forced assimilation*, and *death*. Death? It should be called murder, because the kids didn't happen to just die on their own. They were killed! All things Másání Mildred lived through. Suddenly, I truly understand why she was terrified of my coming to school here.

I quickly sign off the computer and find a quiet, empty corner. I need a moment alone. I'm not going to cry. My breathing becomes shallow. I'm not going to cry. My vision blurs. I'm not going to cry. I'm planning on asking Másání Mildred about her boarding school years. I stare out the window at the green grass. I'm not going to cry. The moisture of my tears chills my cheeks as they trickle down.

13

PARENTS' WEEKEND

Nida'iiníísh, Ghąąjį' 18

Friday, October 18

A few weeks later, I anxiously wait for my mom and Grandma Rosie at the main building entrance. They had flown in late last night for Parents' Weekend. My mom texted that we would meet this morning at the main building entrance around 7:30 a.m. and eat a big breakfast together at Ms. Thomas's faculty house. I stare out the broad, freshly cleaned windows, searching for Ms. Thomas's car to appear. My heart and my stomach are excited to eat with my family.

This is the first weekend that homework wasn't assigned, and I couldn't be more grateful. And even better, all Friday and Saturday classes are canceled. It has given me some much-needed space to decompress and finally get caught up on sleeping.

I look at my phone, and it says 7:32. My mom is never late. Waiting for her is near unbearable. A brief wave of worry swells my throat. Then I remember the time difference and how long it took me to get over the jet lag. I can wait a little while longer. If I knew which house was Ms. Thomas's, I would walk over myself.

Then I see my mom walking on the path that leads from the dining hall to the science building. I nearly cry out to her. I open the doors and rush to her and hurriedly wrap her in a hug.

"Shiyáázh," she whispers in my ear.

"Where's Grandma Rosie?" I ask.

"She is helping Sandra cook," she answers. Then she holds me at arm's length and examines me. "So, you do shave your head."

"Every Sunday," I tell her. Ever since I decided I wasn't going to have hair, most of the "Why don't you have long braids?" questions disappeared. I don't know if it's because over time they just stopped asking or because I shaved my head.

"Ms. Thomas called me. She was agitated." My mom chuckles. "She was yelling, 'Did you know that your son cuts off his beautiful hair?'" She mimics Ms. Thomas's energetic voice. "She sounded concerned."

"She did?" I nearly shout. I smile at the ridiculousness of it.

"I told her that you do your own thing."

"I can't believe she was worried."

"You're in a very conservative environment, son," she explains to me. "Appearances here carry a lot of weight. Anything you do will be scrutinized."

"That's dumb."

"It sure is."

I never thought of it that way. Or at least, I never cared what everyone thought about what I did or how I presented myself. I'm not presenting myself for them.

"Txį'," my mom says. She wraps her arm around mine and guides me across campus. "There's a big pan of potatoes, bacon, and eggs with your name on it."

My stomach grumbles. It's been so long since I had a big meal of greasy potatoes. Don't get me wrong: The organic field-grown food they serve in the dining hall is awesome. But it doesn't hit the spot as much as fried potatoes.

As we walk to Ms. Thomas's house, my mom rests her head on my shoulder. I think I've grown, because she's an inch lower on my shoulder than she was when she dropped me off. Or maybe I'm holding myself taller since the last time I saw her.

A few minutes later, I sit down next to Grandma Rosie at Ms. Thomas's large dining table. Grandma Rosie sips on a cup of black tea. She laughs with Ms. Thomas, who sits on her other side. There's enough seating for ten people. An elegant gold-plated candelabra is at the center. Ms. Thomas's dining room is about the size of my mom's living room. It's huge. There are four display cabinets that have pictures of Ms. Thomas and her own family as well as students she's nurtured. I spot an empty area where mine could go.

"You're getting skinny!" Grandma Rosie says as she hugs me. When my mom was really struggling with finances, Grandma Rosie and Grandpa Greg would come over with a bag of potatoes and cans of SPAM to feed all of us. She would make a tall stack of tortillas that would help us get through the week. I was already grateful when both my grandparents would arrive because they always sided with Demi and me and chided my mom. It was funny to see my mom get yelled at instead of her yelling at one of us.

"I missed you, Grandma," I say again to her. This is probably the fifth time I've said it.

"Me too, shiyáázh," Grandma Rosie says. She rubs my stubby scalp with an open palm. Grandparents are healing.

A small ripple of grief runs over my heart as I wish Grandpa Greg was with us. I'm sure he would have loved to see this state and all the greenery on campus.

"Before I forget, shiyáázh," Grandma Rosie says. "Your great-grandma wants to talk with you. Dominic is taking her to her appointment at the hospital, so we can video chat with her. She really wants to see you."

Másání Mildred is going to the hospital? I ask, "Is everything all right with her?"

Grandma Rosie presses her lips together in a grimace. She carefully explains, "Dr. Platero is still trying to figure out the proper dosage of her new medicine for her. Sometimes it's too much and it interferes with her intestines. Sometimes it's not strong enough and she has these episodes of confusion. But don't worry about her, shiyáázh. She'll be fine."

"Yeah, I'd love to talk with her," I say.

I get up from the table and help Ms. Thomas place plates in front of my mom and Grandma Rosie. After everyone else has their plate, I accept mine.

Ms. Thomas finally sits down and says, "Do you mind if I say grace?"

Grandma Rosie nods and bows her head. My mom and I know not to go against Grandma Rosie and follow in line.

"Dear Lord, please bless this food so that our bodies are nourished in the same way that you nourish our souls. Thank you for watching over your children Rosetta and Darlene as they travel all the way from the Navajo reservation to Sagefield. Amen."

We all repeat the last word and begin to eat. I scoop a forkful of potatoes, bacon, and eggs into my mouth, and I nearly shout with joy. It's one of the most delicious meals I've ever had. Then I grab a cup of coffee.

"You're drinking coffee now?" my mom asks.

"Yeah," I state. My mom shrugs and continues to eat her breakfast.

"So, what do you think of campus, Rosetta?" Ms. Thomas asks.

"I'm jealous of Derrick," Grandma Rosie says after swallowing her food. "I never knew schools like this existed."

Ms. Thomas says, "I tell you, I grew up in the projects in Brooklyn, and those were some trying times. Trying times! My mama raised seven of us! And oh Lord! I could barely manage four on my own without pulling out my hair. But somehow, my mama always made things work. She pushed us to get our education, and I'm thankful she did. Because now I work for one of the best high schools in the world! And I love that it's my job to recruit kids who otherwise wouldn't have the opportunity to attend!"

"It must be very fulfilling," my mom contributes.

"Very," Ms. Thomas says, then eats some of her food. "Is everything all right? I didn't burn the bacon, did I?"

“It’s perfect,” I say. And I do mean it. “Sagefield dining hall has nothing on this.”

“Oh, this boy!” Ms. Thomas says. “I could just eat him up.”

“How’s he been doing?” Grandma Rosie asks.

I hold my breath. I’ve been staying up extra late and drinking more and more coffee to keep on track with all the assignments.

“He’s doing great,” Ms. Thomas says. “His teachers have written good comments about his work ethic.”

“Comments?” I ask.

“All the teachers are required to write reports on students by Parents’ Weekend,” Ms. Thomas explains.

Then it all kind of makes sense. This isn’t just an opportunity for homesick students to hang with family; it’s also Sagefield’s version of a parent-teacher conference.

“His grades are averaging B, B-minus,” Ms. Thomas flatly says.

I’m shocked my mom isn’t at my throat asking me to explain to her why I don’t have an A average. But she does lean forward and her eyebrows scrunch.

“Think nothing of it, Darlene! At this school a B average is something he should be very proud of. Trust me, if there were something that needed addressing, you’d be the first person I’d call. Then I’d ask you if I could yell at him.” Ms. Thomas laughs. A chilly wave of relief runs down my spine.

“For future reference, you don’t need my permission to yell at him,” my mom says jokingly, though she means it.

“Call me so we can both yell at him,” Grandma Rosie says.

“Thank you, Ms. Thomas, for helping me get here,” I say,

hoping to steer the conversation into a different direction. Flattery always distracts adults.

"You're such a sweet boy!" Ms. Thomas says.

And just as I had expected, my mom and Grandma Rosie both thank Ms. Thomas for helping me get to Sagefield. I relax a little more as Ms. Thomas recommends a few restaurants in the next town that the three of us can eat at. She mentions also that she won't be able to hang out with us for the day as she has a staff meeting to attend. She's always working.

My heart jumps at the thought of leaving campus and going to the next town over, Bridgeville, New York, with my family and maybe even eating some pizza! I think this will also be the perfect opportunity to ask them about my history paper. Maybe they can help me talk with Másání Mildred about her time in a boarding school.

After we finish breakfast, I take them on a quick tour of campus. Most of the students have already left with their parents to either go home or on a quick weekend vacation, and the campus is quiet and empty, like when I first arrived.

"I never imagined this," Grandma Rosie says as she examines the chandeliers in the dining hall.

My mom pushes against a tender spot on my forearm. "Who you been fighting?" she teases me.

"Better not be over girls," Grandma Rosie chides. But I know she's not kidding.

That's when I notice that several bruises have appeared on my forearms. "This is from football. Coach keeps putting me in the defensive line."

"Good," Grandma Rosie says as we exit the dining hall and make our way through a hallway to the main building. "Never fight over women and vice versa. Don't make them fight over you. In fact, no girlfriends until you graduate from college!"

"Until you have your PhD," my mom says.

I know they are somewhat serious. Mom had Demi when she was nineteen, a few months out of high school. She had wanted to go to U of A for engineering, but my jerk father convinced her that she belonged at home. And when I came into the picture, it became harder for her to argue with my father about pursuing her own education.

"I'll have a shotgun wedding when I'm defending my dissertation," I join in on the joke.

"Damn right you're going to defend a dissertation," my mom says.

"Language, Darlene!" Grandma Rosie snaps at my mom.

"Sorry," my mom says, but she doesn't mean it. She tries her best to suppress a grin.

I guide them into the student activity center. Grandma Rosie stares at the chandelier and expensive-looking couches.

Grandma Rosie asks, "What is this place?"

"This is the student activity center. It's where a bunch of the kids meet when study hall ends and before check-in. It's like an hour of mayhem," I explain, remembering the Grillery and Study Break.

My mom looks at her watch and then scrunches her face.

"We're going to call your másání in two hours. Your grandpa Dominic is with her right now."

This is the perfect time to ask them about my history paper.

Before I can ask, Grandma Rosie says in a serious voice, "Shiyáázh." There's a deep sadness in Grandma Rosie's voice. We find a large black leather couch and sit down. "I didn't want to say this in front of Ms. Thomas, but your great-grandma's health isn't great."

The news creates knots in my throat.

Grandma Rosie continues, "Dr. Platero says that her tests show that her blood oxygen levels are declining more than we thought. Next year is more than likely going to be her last with us."

It feels like I'm falling backward. Only a year left with Másání Mildred. My mom rubs Grandma Rosie's back.

"This is life." Grandma Rosie powers through a sob and regains her composure. "She's living a long, wonderful life with tons of grandkids and great-grandkids. She always asks about you and wonders how you are doing way out here. You're the only great-grandkid that visits her regularly, so she's curious about your life. I know that you're making her proud. You're making all of us proud."

"I try," I say to Grandma Rosie.

"Don't worry about her, shiyáázh," Grandma Rosie says.

I choke on a lump in the back of my throat. They always tell me not to worry about Másání Mildred. But I do.

"She's getting the medical attention she needs," my mom contributes. "She's at the hospital right now to discuss the next steps for her surgery. If she gets the TAVR procedure done, we could have more time with her. You just focus on your education. That's what she'd want."

I nod. In addition to all my essays, the books I have to read, the Latin verbs I have to remember, the geometry sets that keep getting more complicated, I now carry the knowledge that Másání Mildred will be passing away sooner rather than later. A storm of stress clouds my thoughts.

I hate this. It's such a horrible thing to hear that someone you love has an estimated timeline. I'm going to wait with my body clenched, my breath held, my spirit interrupted, until the hour, the minute, the second, when Másání Mildred is no longer with us.

"Okay" is all I can say. I rest my head on my mom's shoulder and find comfort. I'm glad mostly everyone has left with their parents for the weekend. There is no one here to see this weak side of me, to see that I need support.

The three of us sit in a pizza parlor in the town of Bridgeville for lunch. I wanted them to try the calamari pizza and get them out of their routine. But in the end we went with a standard pepperoni pie.

"Do you come here often?" my mom asks. Grandma Rosie listens for my response. They both must really want to know what my day-to-day is like.

"Not a lot. I take the weekend school bus here to shop at the Walgreens every now and then," I explain. Rideshare cars are forbidden from entering campus, so we are required to take the school bus to Bridgeville.

Just then, my mom's phone rings. It's the notification for a video chat. She holds her phone at arm's length away from her face and swipes the screen.

"Hey, Uncle Dominic," my mom says.

"'Aoo' yá'át'ééh, shimáyázhí. Ha'át'íísh'baa naniná?" Grandpa Dominic says. He smiles his large, goofy grin. Even though he's inside, he still wears his fancier black cowboy hat. His glasses, with the shade-adapting lenses, aren't fully dark. I can see still his eyes.

I know several of my white teammates would say that I should call him great-uncle or something. But I call him *grandpa* because he's my grandma's brother. I swear, if you're a young Diné, just call everyone *grandma* or *grandpa* and you're good.

"We're waiting for pizza," my mom says. "Do you want to talk with my mom?"

"Not until she pays me back the money she stole from me." Grandpa Dominic chuckles.

"You calling me a thief?" Grandma Rosie responds. "I took back my candy money that you stole from me plus the interest after all those years."

Grandpa Dominic says, with his goofy smile, "Don't listen to your mom, Darlene, and make sure to watch your purse."

"Oh, shut up," Grandma Rosie says.

"Yáadilá, don't talk like that to each other!" I hear Másání Mildred say in the background.

Grandma Rosie just smiles and shakes her head.

Then Grandpa Dominic says, "Rosetta, when I picked her up

this morning, I noticed that she hadn't taken her medicine for the past three days."

"Yáa! I told her she needs to take her medicine," Grandma Rosie says.

"She's a little disoriented right now," Grandpa Dominic says. "But she should be good to talk."

"Who's that?" I hear Másání Mildred ask.

"Mom," Grandpa Dominic says, "Na', Derrick kǫ́ǫ́."

"Shiyáázh," Grandma Rosie says, handing me the phone. "Tell her to take her medicine."

Másání Mildred lies in a bright white hospital gown that glows under the fluorescent lights above her. Machines beep behind her. There is a plastic tube underneath her nose that pumps oxygen. It scares me so much seeing her this feeble. A shiver runs down my spine. "Derrick?"

"Yá'át'ééh, Másání!" I say, trying to sound extra happy for her.

Her eyes scan me, and immediately she looks shocked. "Your hair!"

I smile and run my palm over the short stubs. "Yeah, I shaved it off."

"What's that on your arms?" Másání Mildred asks.

I display my arm for her and am just about to tell her about football, but she starts to cry. "Másání?"

"Are they hitting you?" Másání Mildred blurts out. "Did they cut your hair off?"

"I, uh, no?" I'm a little scared. Másání Mildred is upset. She hasn't even called me sha'awéé'. I was hoping to cheer her up and try to convince her to eat healthier.

"Get him out of there!" she yells. "Rosie. Darlene. I told you to not let him go! Look, he has bruises! This is because of both of you! They shaved his head!"

"Másání, no one's hitting me," I say, forcing my voice to remain calm and steady.

Grandma Rosie grabs the phone from me and talks to her in Diné. From her soothing voice, I know that she's trying to calm down Másání Mildred.

"What's going on?" I ask my mom. I hear Másání Mildred yelling at Grandma Rosie through the phone.

I'm at a loss for words and for thoughts. For a few seconds, my heart beats loudly, pounding against my rib cage. My ears ring. Then a million thoughts rush into my mind. I can't process them all. But one rises above the rest. Másání Mildred survived the "Kill the Indian, Save the Man" boarding school era.

"Let me talk to her," I say, and reach for the phone.

Grandma Rosie looks at my empty hand, then in a stern voice speaks some commands to her mother.

"Másání?" I say when I grab the phone. Másání Mildred looks at me. Her eyes are red, and the machines are beeping loudly to her side. "No one cut my hair. I did it." I want to say that I am frustrated explaining to the entire school that not all male Natives grow their hair long. I want to say I'm not happy out here. I want to say that I want to go home. "I'm in football, and that's how I got these bruises. I'm safe here."

"Sha'awéé', don't lie," Másání Mildred says. She's calmed a bit. "Tell everyone about how they are hitting you."

My face flushes. I wasn't prepared for this. None of this. "No one's hitting me, Másání. They take really good care of me." I say that last sentence a little louder but try to sound calm.

It's scary seeing how terrified she is for me. Only when my mom grabs her phone from my hands do I realize that Grandpa Dominic wants to finish talking with Grandma Rosie.

My mom's hand rubs the back of my neck. Her rough, calloused hands scratch my skin. I wish I had more than this short time with them. But they are flying out tomorrow evening and I will be left on campus alone with a handful of international students whose parents weren't able to make the trip.

When the pizza arrives, I'm too upset to take a single bite. I didn't even think about asking Másání Mildred about her time at the boarding school. Now that I have seen how upset she got, how can I ask her?

14

Dimóo dóó naakijį́, Ghąąjį'22
Tuesday, October 22

I make my way to the football field. The trees' leaves are as vibrant and colorful as a setting sun. For the past week, we've been in a heat wave. Today, it's eighty-two degrees! But starting Friday, there's supposed to be a big rainstorm that should bring the temperatures down, though not enough for snow.

I'm one of the handful of teammates who is early. Honestly, I'm just about done with football. Our whole season we've been mediocre. Nothing exciting to report.

"Man, I am loving this weather," I hear from a group of my teammates walking onto the practice field. Another says, "Global warming rocks!"

"Hoskie!" Finnegan says to me, and we fist-bump. "Shame you can't come to the homecoming dance with us."

Oh yes, homecoming is next weekend. Then, in three weeks, Thanksgiving break. It's still pretty far away, but I'm excited nonetheless to head back to the rez to be with family, including Másání Mildred. "Still got the next two years," I say.

I spot Harris, Mancini, Goldman, and a few others. It's too late for me to pretend like I forgot something in my locker. I'd never make it back in time for warm-ups.

"Dude, you going with Heather?" Harris says to Mancini. "She's so easy!"

"Hey," Mancini says in a serious tone. "Don't talk about her like that."

I do some arm swings and hamstring stretches to hide my surprise. Is Mancini standing up for someone other than himself?

"Just because you two are going out, you change your whole personality. Damn, you're whipped, dude."

"Better than not having a lady," Mancini says.

Harris pulls up his shirt to show off his muscular abdomen. "These make panties slide right off. Landing a lady is e to the z."

Goldman takes this moment to finish an energy drink, and he tosses the can to the side of a trash can. It's really the most obnoxious and lazy thing a person can do with trash. Meanwhile, I fight the urge to yell at them to grow the hell up.

"Oye, Hoskie." Harris reaches his fist to me.

"Sup," I say, not bothering to bump with him.

"What are the women like on your rez? I bet they're a bunch of smoking hot Pocahontases," Harris says.

"Dude," I say, making no effort to hide my disgust.

"What? I'm curious," Harris says.

I think of my mom and how she would handle this. She would punch them, easily. I, however, can't do that. So I say, "Diné women will kick your ass if you call them Pocahontas."

Harris looks like he has no idea how to respond. Then he smiles and laughs. “I could be into that.”

I walk to the middle of the football field and wait for my coaches to arrive. Meanwhile, I do some hip stretches and toe touches.

“Don’t let them get to you,” I hear Reese say to me.

I stand up and see his friendly face. “Was I that obvious?”

Reese joins me in some toe touches. “If Harris, or Mancini, for that matter, had one iota of a brain cell, they might have known they crossed a line.”

“They’re such assholes,” I say.

“Massive reeking assholes,” Reese says.

“If they don’t have one iota of a brain cell, how did they even get into Sagefield?” I ask. Now that I say it out loud, I am genuinely curious. “For serious.”

“Well, Mancini’s family has been coming to Sagefield since the early 1900s.”

“Legacy kid,” I say as I shake my head. I hate that I had to bust my ass to get here. Mancini only had to be born to get to attend Sagefield. I can think of twenty different students back on my rez who would be more deserving of coming here. Like Chris or Jayden.

In my dorm room later that night, I mix myself a cup of caffeine with the last of the powdered coffee that Reese gave me. In a few seconds I chug the whole thing and place an order for a three-pound bag. Buying three pounds of coffee at twenty dollars sure beats those overly sweet bottles at three dollars. I'm not planning on going to sleep early tonight. I have to study and get some translations done.

It usually takes at least thirty minutes for the caffeine to kick in. So prime study time will be around 10:30 or 10:45. I have to work on reading *Boarding School Seasons* first. Then physics. Another ten-minute break around 12:30-ish. Coffee time. I'll work on my geometry sets and then do some Latin memorizations in the next hour. Because if you do memorization before you fall asleep, your brain is more likely to remember it. I'll call it a night at 2:00. This schedule looks like it's going to be the norm for the next few days.

There's a knock on my door.

I stand up, slightly annoyed. But when I open the door, I'm excited to see Caleb.

"Yo," Caleb says. "You busy?"

"Oh man, sorry. Completely spaced on hanging with you!" I say. I feel the blood rush out of my face.

"Hey," Caleb says. He looks a little nervous. His head hangs, and his right hand holds his left elbow. Is he scared?

"Everything all right?" I ask.

"No. I mean yes, everything is all right." He stops speaking.

I offer, "I was planning on doing more studying. Would you want to do our own Mandatory Study Hall thing?"

His head lifts and his eyes light up. "Actually, yeah, I have work I have to do."

"Come on in," I say. Then I realize that I don't have any place for him to sit down. All I have is the bed, the chair, and the desk that came with the room. I'm a little embarrassed.

Caleb sees the bareness of my room. I don't even know what to say.

"Do you want to come to my room?" he asks.

Thankful for the olive branch, I answer, "I'll be over in a little. Just got to hit the bathroom."

"Okay. Cool," Caleb says, and he rushes to his room.

I make my way to the bathroom. Someone is in the showers. The smell of his musky soap fills the entire bathroom.

I remember that Grandma Rosie told me not to shower when it rains. Doing so would be an insult to the rain deities, because it tells the rain gods that their showers aren't good enough for you. Same goes for having a bath. So I'll need to shower real good before the storm arrives.

"Who's that?" Eric the floor proctor demands. His voice is so recognizable.

"What's up, Eric?" I respond as I stand in front of the urinal.

"Derrick! What's going on?" I hear joy in his voice. I haven't interacted with him much since I met him when I arrived on campus. I haven't had a good reason. He's a little bit of a tool.

"It's going." I can't help but feel awkward. How does he not feel weird talking to me when I'm doing some business?

The shower stops, and his hand grabs his expensive-looking cotton bathrobe. Eric asks, "Are you getting enough sleep?"

"When I can. Coffee when I can't," I say, finishing and flushing. I head toward the sinks that are in two rows opposite each other. I wash my hands, and I see the reflection of the back of my head.

"Caffeine doesn't replace sleep," Eric says, emerging from the shower wearing his robe. He looks me in the eye. "I used to do what you were doing and drink stronger and stronger caffeinated beverages. Last year during spring finals, I was drinking nothing but Red Bull. Horrible. I don't recommend doing that just to finish finals. There's more to life than good grades."

While I appreciate his concern, Eric has no clue what I'm going through. He can afford to not graduate. Both literally and figuratively. I'm sure that if he doesn't graduate or go to college, his parents will be able to hook him up with a job. Most of these rich spoiled brats here have that backup. I don't have that luxury. My mom made it very clear that when I'm an adult, I will be moving out and paying my own bills like my sister, Demi, did. However good his intentions may be, it's a little bit of an insult to hear from him that grades don't matter.

"I'll keep that in mind," I say. "Well, I'm going to get some studying done."

Before I can make my way to the door, Eric asks "Hey, can I ask a favor of you?"

I stop and consider my options. I can't come up with a reason to say no to him. At least not without a little more information. "What you need?"

"There's a group of students selling and buying ADHD medication. So if you hear or see some of that going on, please tell me."

Harris and Mancini pop into my mind. Is that what they are

slinging? "I'll keep an eye out," I say. I can't point Eric to Harris and Mancini. Not with the little information I have.

"You're a good man, Derrick," Eric says. "I don't have to worry about you one bit."

"See ya." Eh, whatever. I don't need to get involved with Eric. Just leave it alone. It'll play out how it needs to.

I hoist my backpack higher onto my shoulder and knock on Caleb's door.

"It's open!" he yells from the other side.

I push the door open and am immediately jealous. Caleb has extra lamps in the corners of the room that look like they are dimmable. He has a huge computer monitor, on which are Excel spreadsheets. He sits in his enormous papasan wicker chair. On the floor is a large bag of trail mix. In one corner is a large pile of clothes and trash. He probably did a rush job of cleaning his room.

"Nice space," I say.

He stands up and moves to his black leather computer chair, which just screams executive. "Thanks."

On his desk, just to the side of his computer monitor, is a picture of him and his parents.

"What are you planning on studying?" he asks me.

"Was planning on some reading for history, then physics, then geometry." I'm halfway done reading *Boarding School Seasons.* I had decided to hold off on talking with my mom about asking Másání Mildred about her past. But I'm not ready to explain what

I'm writing about to Caleb. He's a cool guy, but I'm not close with him like that. At least, not yet. I sit down in his wicker chair.

"I got snacks," he says.

"Thanks," I say. Wow, there is still some awkwardness between us. I don't think it's coming from me.

"I, uh," Caleb begins. "I actually took Physics 301 last year. If you need help with any of that, I can help."

"Whoa, I'm only in 101."

Just then, he gets a text, and he hyperfocuses on responding.

I pull out my physics textbook. Shoot. If he offered to help, I might as well take him up on it. Then something pops into my head.

"Yo, if you're in a high-level physics class, why are you in Mandatory Study Hall?" I ask.

He finishes texting and looks at me with a blank face. After a second of thinking he answers, "Oh. Got into a little trouble with not turning in assignments last year."

"What do you mean a little trouble?"

"I had an academic warning. So yeah."

I sense that he doesn't really want to talk about it. With a little smirk, I ask, "You want to start with a five-minute breath-counting thing?"

"Those are so boring!"

"Yeah, they can be." I chuckle. I don't want to admit that I find them helpful.

"If you want to," he says.

"I'm down to just start if you are," I say. I can feel the coffee beginning to work. My attention is becoming sharper. My chest feels lighter, and I have this urge to smile. It feels good. I get a little more comfortable and open my textbook.

His phone buzzes again. I look, and his face has lost its color. He squeezes his eyes shut and places his phone on his desk.

"You all right there?" I ask.

He looks like he's in excruciating pain. He breathes heavily and hard.

I stand up and approach him. I place a hand on his shoulder. "What's up?"

Another text arrives. My eyes notice that it's from Xavier. I respect his privacy and try my best to ignore it.

"I. Uh. I'm so sorry," Caleb sputters.

My brow involuntarily scrunches. I'm getting flashbacks of Jayden. I give Caleb time and space. It feels like he needs to make this next step on his own, so I don't rush him.

"Promise you won't get mad at me," Caleb squeaks out.

"You got it," I respond as calmly as I can.

"I'm—I'm gay," Caleb finally pushes out. The room is silent and growing increasingly warm from Caleb's nervousness.

I pat his shoulder. "Thanks for telling me that." I recall Jayden telling Chris and me about himself. How it took us both a moment to process. How Jayden had thought we were going to abandon him. How Jayden later explained it was the hardest thing he had ever done, even more than telling his own mom.

He looks at me, confused. "What?"

"It mustn't have been easy," I say.

His forehead is flushed. Then his body relaxes. He exhales loudly and leans back in his leather chair.

"You're the second person I've told," he confides in me.

"Honored," I simply say. Then some things connect in my head. "Is that why you were so awkward with me at the beginning of the year?" I lightly chuckle to help him feel more at ease.

"Yeah," he says. "I didn't know you would be so mature."

That's a word I don't get called often. It means a lot. But I had no other choice than to grow up. That's what living on the rez with a single mother does.

Caleb continues, "I thought you were going to be this homophobic jock that was going to pick on me. And it didn't help that my mom and dad instantly fell in love with you."

Whoa, hold up a minute. They fell in love with me?

"They just kept going on and on about how I should reach out to you and invite you back to our place for Thanksgiving. It sounds like you were the son they wanted."

"Easy," I say. "You're their son. They love you."

"It feels like it's a chore for them."

"How so?" Mr. and Mrs. Ecclestone didn't give me the impression that they didn't love Caleb. The opposite, actually. I'm not sure it's my place yet to call out his thoughts as insecurity. We're still fairly early into our friendship.

"My dad wanted me to do football. And of course that's why he's obsessed with you. You offered to help us move in, which no one else did. My mom's always going on about how polite you are."

Do I seem like this perfect son to them? I say, "They don't even know me."

"That's just it. They want to."

I feel a wave of awkwardness swell in my chest. I already have a parent. And she's awesome. "I don't know what to say."

"It's not your fault. It's my way of saying sorry for acting strange around you."

It feels like the air has cleared between us. "Dude, I honestly thought you were some sort of closet racist."

He just starts to laugh. "I don't know how to process that."

I hold my arms out. "Let's hug it out, man."

"What?"

"Come on." I encourage him and grab his hand and pull him into a hug.

"Thanks, Derrick," he says.

It's hard not to compare this moment with the time Jayden came out to me. I remind myself they are two different people. I'm ashamed to say that there was a month where I didn't touch Jayden: no hugs, no shoulder pats, no handshakes after he told me. Not this time.

We do the bro shoulder pat and sit back down.

For the first time, I see Caleb finally breathe easy around me. He's just existing, and that's so awesome for him.

15

Dimóo, Ghąąjį' 27
Sunday, October 27

Five days later, I immediately look outside my window after I wake up. Fat blobs of rain splatter against the window. It's been like this since Friday. Finally, the weather feels like fall. All the trees and their colors glisten under the dark blanket of clouds. It's glorious! Cold rain always feels magical when you can be inside sipping on something hot.

After a long yawn, I open my laptop and check my school email. Thankfully, there's nothing pressing. I can finish some of the schoolwork that I'm in danger of falling behind on. I am two-thirds done with *Boarding School Seasons*. I even found several PDFs to beef up my references. But I still want to know what happened to Másání Mildred. I have to fly this by Mom first. She'll know how best to go about it. My stomach grumbles, motivating me to get the day started.

I make my way to the bathroom with my shower pack. I splash some water onto my face at the sink. I'll fully shower later this evening when the weather report says it should stop raining.

Caleb slumps inside and goes to a urinal. He's wearing his Sagefield sweatshirt and sweatpants from the bookstore. "When will it stop raining?"

I was taught to be grateful for rain. That checks out, because my rez is mainly desert. So little questions like that or comments saying that rain sucks are a big no-no. "You down for grabbing breakfast in thirty minutes?"

Caleb finishes at the urinal. He takes a moment to open his eyes. "I'm going back to sleep."

"But you'll miss all the breakfast foods."

"Eh, I'll order something from Bridgeville," Caleb says as he washes his hands.

"Still down for studying this afternoon?" I ask.

"Yeah," Caleb says through a yawn. He dries his hands. "Going back to sleep. Good night."

"See ya," I tell him.

Later, after I toss on some sweats and a sweater, I emerge from my dormitory. A strong gale causes me to momentarily lose my balance. I force my umbrella open and point it into the direction of the wind. "Ah!" I smile like a child, holding the umbrella against the wind like a shield.

There is a huge puddle on the grass to the side of the paved walkway. When I get to the pavement, there's a stream of clean, clear water flowing down to the lake. Oh man, I wish I could go to the lake and see it! I avoid entering the main building and walk on the outside paths so I can enjoy the rain as much as possible.

I enter the student activity center area dripping wet. There is a collection of umbrellas leaning against the wall by the doors. I close my umbrella and place it on top of all of them. Before I go to the dining hall, I turn around and look outside. More sheets of rain continue to pour down. I understand why there is so much vegetation here. The leaves are now in their colors of autumn fire. Yellow leaves that have been stripped off by the strong winds lie on the ground. They look like pieces of leather. I can barely see the ground underneath!

I wish the rez could have this rain. There are so many people who live traditionally and rely upon the rain to grow their food and to refill the water wells. My stomach growls and brings me back to my goal of finding food.

I grab some food and immediately spot Reese and Gabriel sitting next to the windows with their girlfriends, Esme and Julia. They look like they are mid-meal. Great. I was hoping to have a quick meal so I can get started on drafting an outline of my boarding school essay.

"Derrick," Gabriel says.

"Good elevenses," Reese says.

"Is that a *Hobbit* reference, my good sir?" I ask him.

Reese nods as he shoves a huge mass of scrambled eggs into his mouth. Both Julia and Esme smile at me. Julia's bleached blond hair rests on her Sagefield field hockey hoodie. She looks like she just woke up. Esme, on the other hand, wears dark clothing to match her short ink-black hair that contrasts against her pale skin.

"What do you guys have planned for today?" I ask them.

Gabriel says, "Julia and I are heading to Bridgeville to watch a movie." He headbutts Julia, which causes her to drop her spoonful of oatmeal.

"Is it the new A24 horror movie *Allie Gory*?" Esme asks.

"No." Julia sighs. "Gabey prefers manly action explosion movies with booby helpless women. He doesn't like being scared. Don't you?"

Gabriel playfully huffs. "I don't see the point. Real life is scary enough."

"Hope you guys have a fun time," I say. "Reese?"

"Esme and I are going to study later," Reese answers.

"Julia, next weekend, would you want to watch *Allie Gory* with me?" Esme asks.

"Oh my god, yes!" Julia responds, dropping her spoon again. "I hear it's a conversation on gender stereotypes and expectations in horror movies!"

I notice Wendy entering the dining hall. She has on a bright purple raincoat and the largest smile I've seen. A friend of hers, about her height, walks next to her wearing a large yellow poncho. Wendy squeezes her friend's shoulder. Then her friend takes the poncho off and he's a guy. That must be her boyfriend. The guy is wearing Gucci sweatpants and a hoodie. They hold hands. Good for them. I ain't about to get jealous.

I bring my attention back to the conversation. Reese says, "I can't wait for the snow."

"Are you serious?" Gabriel says.

"Campus is stunning with a fresh blanket of clean snow. Plus, the Polar Bear Club officially starts," he says.

"What is that?" I ask.

Reese explains, "When the lake freezes over, a group of us cut a hole in the ice and jump into the lake. Then have hot chocolate after."

I don't need any more convincing. "I'm in. Just tell me when and where." I'm also really looking forward to doing a snow bath after the first snowstorm.

"Right on," Reese says.

"You jump into the lake in the middle of winter? No thanks. I like not having hypothermia," Gabriel says.

"When's the next time you'll get to do something like this?" I ask Gabriel.

"Solid point. Reach out to me before you go, and I might join," he says.

We chat a little more about football finally coming to an end in a few weeks. And before I leave, I head to the salad bar to stock up on fruit, and then to the coffee station to fill up my sixty-four-ounce Nalgene bottle.

Just then, I hear Wendy's voice and a deeper male voice near the coffee station.

As my bottle fills, she says, "Good morning, Derrick."

"What's up, Wendy?" I turn and face both of them. Her boyfriend has dark, smooth skin with full eyebrows and some facial hair at the baseline of his jaw. "Hi, I'm Derrick."

"Markus," he says with a booming voice.

"Derrick and I are in Human Development together," Wendy says.

"You're a Lower-Mid?" He sounds shocked.

I nod at Markus and tighten the lid on my bottle. I almost say that my sister stretched me twice at her kinaaldá, but neither of them would get that reference.

"That's a lot of coffee," Markus comments.

"Long day ahead of me."

"Word to the wise," Markus says. "During Thanksgiving break, don't drink a single drop of caffeine. That way, your caffeine tolerance will reset."

"Oh yeah? That works?"

"Like a dream," Markus answers. He's so friendly and chill.

"Thanks, man. I'll totes give it a shot. What do you guys have planned for this beautiful day?"

"Oh my gosh, I was just telling Markus how beautiful it is outside!"

"If you're into rain, then yeah," Markus says. "We were planning on getting some studying done."

"You should join us! We have this group study in one of the language classrooms," Wendy says.

"The more the merrier," Markus adds.

"Man, I'd love to. But I already have plans to study with some friends." I had already said I'd meet up with Caleb and Xavier later.

"Oh. Well, how about next time?" Wendy says.

"It would be good to have another guy in our group," Markus pleads.

"Poor Markus here is the only guy among my gal friends and I," Wendy explains.

"That's the story of my life." I laugh. "Surrounded by women.

Yeah, hit me up next time and I'll show up."

"See ya," Wendy says as I turn to leave.

Around four that afternoon, Xavier, Caleb, and I have claimed an empty classroom in the science building to do some homework together. My physics sets went a lot quicker with Caleb's help. Xavier also seemed to need some help with physics, though he's doing a higher level than I am.

"Do you two want to order some Thai food for dinner?" Xavier asks out of nowhere.

My gut twists. I'm in no position to be spending money that I don't have. I quickly come up with an excuse. "I'm eating with some football teammates at the dining hall. You guys go for it."

"That's a shame," Xavier says.

I finish off the last of my coffee that I got during breakfast. I think I'm going to need more.

"You sure do drink a lot of coffee," Caleb says to me, catching me off guard.

I mean, I'm not hiding it. "Got to get all this work done."

It's been a real struggle to keep up with the schoolwork. I've been handing things in on time, but just barely.

"I agree," Xavier says. "Though I'm not fond of coffee. Green tea is better!"

Someone's phone rings. All three of us reach for our phones. Caleb raises his hand and answers. "Hi, Mom."

"Oh, I bet she's going to ask to be on speaker when she finds out you're here," Xavier says to me.

"I'm studying with Xavier and Derrick. Really, Mom? But, Mom!" His voice raises in anger. "Can't you just be cool?" He's shouting into the phone. "Because you're making it weird. You always do." Wow, I'd never speak to my mom like that. "Fine!"

He taps his phone, and then Mrs. Ecclestone says over the speaker, "Hi, Xavier and Derrick!"

Xavier and I say hello to her.

"Xavier, how are you?" Mrs. Ecclestone asks.

"I'm well. Thanks for asking, Mrs. Ecclestone," Xavier responds.

"Please, just Sharon!"

Xavier and I share a look that friends have when their other friend's mom wants us to call her by her first name. A mixture of *Hell no* and *I guess I have to*.

"Derrick, what about you?" she asks.

"I'm fine, thanks for asking," I say, avoiding using her first name.

"Are you going to Caleb's birthday party?" she blurts out.

"Mom!" Caleb says.

"I wasn't aware of it," I say as politely as possible.

"Caleb said he was going to invite you."

"I was going to, Mom," Caleb says. With his free hand, he massages his temple. "Derrick, do you want to come to my birthday party in Bridgeville?"

"Just say yes," Xavier whispers. "She won't stop until you agree."

"I'd love to."

"Great! Please send pictures; I want to feel like I'm there!" Mrs. Ecclestone says.

"Can I take you off speaker now?" Caleb asks.

"One more question. Derrick, do you have plans for Thanksgiving? We have an extra guest room available."

All her niceties are overwhelming. "I'm actually going back home for Thanksgiving, but thank you."

"Is that Derrick?" I hear Mr. Ecclestone say in the background. "How's the football season going?"

"Dad!" Caleb groans.

"I'm just asking a question," Mr. Ecclestone says.

"It's an okay season," I tell Mr. Ecclestone. "I'm more excited for wrestling."

"Attaboy!" Mr. Ecclestone booms.

"Mom! Dad! We're studying!" Caleb grumbles.

"Okay, we'll leave you alone," Mrs. Ecclestone says.

Before they can say any more, Caleb just ends the phone call. I'm shocked. Had I done that, my mom would have immediately called back and torn me a new one.

"I was going to ask you tonight about coming to my birthday dinner," Caleb says. "And about Thanksgiving."

"No worries," I tell him.

"It might be a good idea to spend a weekend there," Xavier says. "Otherwise, she'll never leave Caleb alone. She spent two weeks texting Caleb about when I was going to visit."

"Oh, uh," I say.

"Don't feel weird; it's who she is," Caleb says. "She invites everyone. To her credit, she did invite our cleaning lady and her family to our New Year's Eve party, and we had a blast with them. My family sucks!"

Holy cow, he has a cleaning lady? I realize how little I know about Caleb. "Where do you live?"

"Upper East Side," Caleb answers. Those words don't mean anything to me.

"Is that like northeast Connecticut?" I ask.

"Manhattan," Xavier informs me. "We both do, except I'm in Greenwich Village. Hey, it wouldn't be a bad idea to host Derrick."

"My dad will make us tour some colleges," Caleb says. "Probably Columbia."

"That sounds amazing," I earnestly say. I'm probably never going to get another chance to visit universities in Manhattan. Also, I've always wanted to go to New York City. Maybe next year I could spend Thanksgiving break here. It would save some money on airplane tickets. "All right, guys. I'm going to get back to this essay."

"Good call," Caleb says. "Stupid mom. Just wasted our Study Break."

I bite my tongue. It's not cool that he calls his mom stupid. The room is silent again, save the tapping of Xavier's and my fingers on our laptops. Caleb is scribbling notes on his large tablet.

I get back to reading *Boarding School Seasons*. So far, I've learned that boarding school systems in the United States weren't really schools. They were more like job placement services in addition to offering religious indoctrination. Boys were expected to learn carpentry and other hands-on jobs. Girls were taught to sew and cater to white families. In Arizona, female Diné students were often sent to Phoenix to be maids for wealthy white families. Some of the young girls would get pregnant from the white men. I can't keep reading. Anxiety builds throughout my body, like carbon dioxide in a shaken soda. I can almost taste something metallic in the back of my mouth. I put the book down. It's a lot to grasp. There's a personal level to these stories that really corrodes my emotions.

I'm not ready to continue my paper. But I have to work on something. I decide to clean up my emails. Ms. Laramie did say that having an organized life can help with prioritizing tasks.

I click on old useless email messages and delete them. Then I come across an old email I had forgotten about. EXAM HELP. It's from Harris.

I click it open and see that there's a link to a Google Drive. I open the drive. There are rows of folders, each with a class subject written underneath them, like Lower-Mid geometry. Curiosity gets the better of me. When I open it, I see files that I probably shouldn't be looking at. These are the previous finals, and I see at the very top a file that says *Geometry Final*. I click on it. It's the actual final for this year!

I quickly close that file and am brought back to all the subject folders. These are all the finals that are coming up.

I shouldn't even consider using these files to study. I'm not. I'm determined not to click on the file that reads *Henderson's History 101*. But I do.

The questions he's going to ask are super specific and make no sense to me.

Farther down the folders, I see *Mrs. Laurenzi's Latin 101*. I want to know how much of the subjunctive case we will be tested on. I'll just take a quick peek so I'll know how to study. I have to maximize my studying efforts, after all. I see that subjunctive case is a huge portion. The ugly thing called pluperfect that we just learned in the last week of classes is making a big appearance on the exam. I close the entire Google Drive.

This is cheating. But I need to keep my grades up and I'm struggling as is to maintain the grades I have. School comes first. I have to be strategic in my studying. Using the cheat sheets is a strong way to be strategic.

I hate that I'm downloading the drive onto my hard drive. I don't have to open the files. They can just sit on my desktop. It makes me feel better knowing that they are there and, if I need them, I can find them. I'll feel far worse if my grades take a nose-dive and I'm kicked out of Sagefield.

A thought surfaces in my mind: Who am I turning into?

Later that evening, I video chat with my mom. She asks, "Are you excited for wrestling to start?"

"You have no idea!" I seriously can't wait. I won't have to be around the football jocks. From what I have overheard, all the jerks play hockey. Then, during spring, they'll be in lacrosse. So just a few more practices and I'll be free of them. "Hey, Mom. Question." I have to ask her about Másání Mildred.

"Shoot," she says.

"I'm required to write a twenty-page history paper. I want to write about the boarding school era when they would kidnap Native students and whitewash them."

"Okay."

I can see that she already knows where this is going. She rests her phone on the kitchen table and folds her arms. This is her I'm-listening-but-not-liking-what-I'm-hearing pose.

"I have to use firsthand documents. And I already got a bunch of resources through Sagefield's library with interviews from boarding school survivors. But I was thinking about talking with Másání about her childhood."

My mom massages her head. She doesn't like this idea. "Son. She's not going to talk. She hasn't talked to anyone about that time. Every time anyone asks, she says, 'Doo 'ajínída'.'"

"Okay," I say. Even though I want to say more, I can't because of the philosophy of silence.

"There's also the consideration of her heart, shiyáázh. She's getting up there in age. Any little source of stress could elevate her heart rate, and with the medicines she's on, it could be a very bad idea."

My heart drops. I didn't even consider her health. Talking about her abuse would without a doubt elevate her heart rate.

"How's her health?" I ask.

"As good as can be. The doctor got all the tests she needed done. It'll be about three weeks before we get the results."

"Three weeks?" I ask. "That's during my Thanksgiving break. Can I join whoever is taking her to the doctor?"

"About that. I just got your plane tickets and won't be able to send you any money. What you have is going to have to last," she says.

"That's fine. Thanks for letting me know," I tell her.

I want to ask her why she didn't reach out to Ms. Thomas for help with the airplane tickets. But I know she would never ask. Being indebted to another person is the last thing my mom wants, and we already owe so much to Ms. Thomas.

"Are you mad at me?" she asks.

"No," I immediately answer. "You're the best mom I've ever had." Other kids may want parents like the ones here, with tons of money. But my mom always fights for me. And that's something money can't buy.

I just wish there was a way that I could get a job. But I have to wait until after my birthday in March. Then I realize that's not an option for me here at Sagefield. There are no jobs here, and I wouldn't have time to work. So the earliest I could work would be in the summer.

"I love you, shiyáázh."

"Love you, too, Mom."

We say our goodbyes and hang up. I breathe with intention, to let my emotions ease. I concentrate on what I need to do. I remember my study schedule, which has me falling asleep around two in the morning. I open my Latin textbook and begin my translations. I don't even notice that I am taking extra sips of the coffee I made for my midnight study session.

16

Dimóo biiskání, Nìłch'ih Ts'ósí 11
Monday, November 11

I walk to the dining hall with Reese and a few more of my wrestling teammates for lunch because today is the first day of wrestling practice! I snap out of my happiness when I see Harris and Mancini sitting next to some other footballers.

"I'll catch up with you guys in a bit," I say to Reese and step out of the line.

I haven't looked at the cheat sheets since I downloaded them from the Google Drive, so I shouldn't feel bad. But it feels like I'm sitting at the edge of a cliff, looking into the wide expanse, the ground a mile below me. If I use the files to cheat, I'll be a different person. That's a line that when I cross, I can never uncross.

I approach Harris, who of course isn't too far from Mancini. We greet and fist-bump, and then I ask, "What are you planning to do for Thanksgiving break?" I need to find an opening to talk about the cheat files.

"I don't know," Mancini answers. "My dad wants to go on this stupid family trip to some stupid town in Greece."

"How about you, Harris?"

"I work a part-time job," Harris says. There is a note of shame in his answer.

"Dude!" I say. "Tell me about it. I'm still stretching the budget I got from some work I did with my grandpa this past summer."

"My dad took me on part-time for the summer at the company he works at," Harris says.

"I work, too," Mancini says. I bet he feels left out of the conversation.

"Working your mouth doesn't count," Harris says.

"Your mom works her mouth," Mancini says. They begin to gently punch each other.

"That's a pretty solid 'your mama,'" I say to keep them focused on me.

"Dude, grab a plate and sit down with us," Mancini offers.

"I'm going to eat with my wrestling team. We organized via email," I say. Thankfully it's true. And that's my opening! "I wanted to ask about the email that I was a part of back in September." This is about as subtle as I can be.

Harris catches on quickly, while Mancini is completely oblivious. "Oh, you mean the extra help?" Harris winks at me.

"Yeah, that," I say, winking back.

"Super helpful," Mancini says, finally catching on. "I wouldn't have passed my Spanish final last year without them."

"Yeah," Harris says to Mancini. "Not too loud there, Sherlock. What's up? You having trouble opening them?"

"No. I was wondering how you guys got them?" I ask.

"Goldman," Harris says. "He's a computer genius. He hacks things when he's bored. He was able to get into the teachers' systems to download all the exams. Teachers have to submit their exams weeks before assessments and upload them to the servers."

"Is there any way they know about it?"

"As long as we all keep cool about it, no one will know. No one's going to get hurt. You're not going to tell anyone, are you?" Mancini asks.

"Hell no," I say to them. "I ain't narcing. I just want to make sure that I don't get caught."

"This is your first time utilizing extra help, isn't it?" Harris says. He smiles. "Take a deep breath and relax. It's a victimless crime."

"How did I get the email?" I ask.

"I 'nominated' you," Harris says. "I knew you'd be cool and could use the extra help."

That explains it. "I appreciate it. So none of this can be traced to me. No one is going to rat us out?"

"Unless you talk," Harris says. "Which you said you won't."

"Got it," I say. "Won't say a thing."

"Attaboy!" Mancini says.

"Told you he was cool for it," Harris says.

"Hey, if you feel you need extra *extra* help, there's our other service," Mancini offers.

"Dude, not during lunch." Harris punches Mancini.

Mancini massages his arm and says, "Just connect with either of us if you need some pep in your step."

"Will do," I say to them. "Thanks, guys."

"No problem," Harris says. "Us scholarship kids got to look out for each other."

I head back to the line for food. Never in a million years did I ever think I would be chumming it up with Harris and Mancini. Much less did I think I'd be thanking them. I wonder how surprised the me from two months ago would be.

Back in my dorm room after classes, I get ready to head to the Wilma Reynolds Athletic Center for my first wrestling practice! My excitement swells, and all the negativity I was feeling earlier drains away from me. I can really show everyone why I'm here. I don't mean to brag, but I did place third in the Arizona state wrestling championship as a freshman last year. Wrestling is my sport, and winter is my season!

I do some light stretching while waiting for Caleb. I'm wearing my old sweatpants and a thick sweatshirt.

Caleb knocks and walks in. He's smiling. "Wrestling?"

"Yeah, boy!" I respond.

My phone vibrates. It's a text from Chris. Damn! I need to video chat with him and Jayden tonight. I keep forgetting. I'll do it later tonight after Mandatory. I leave him on read.

Ten minutes later, we walk through the glass doors of the Wilma Reynolds Athletic Center. The moment we enter, a loud heater blasts warm air onto us. The lights are all on, and below us on the acrylic floor are scuffs and gravel that has been tracked in from outside.

Caleb and I walk toward the locker rooms, through the hallway that reeks of chlorine. Down by the two Olympic-sized pools are the swimming and diving teams. Both guys and girls are stretching and warming up.

Caleb says, "So are you still down for coming to my birthday dinner?"

"Down like a clown," I say. It's still not until this upcoming Sunday. For a gift, all I could afford was a sentimental birthday card. "I got it in my calendar and everything."

"On that note," Caleb says, "when is your birthday?"

"Mine?" We enter the hallway to the boys' locker room. "March sixteenth."

"Any birthday party plans?" he asks.

"Honestly, I'm just trying to get through this first semester. I haven't even thought that far ahead."

We enter the locker rooms, and he heads to his locker, while mine is a little farther back.

At my locker, I use my phone to unlock the Bluetooth lock. I toss my sweatshirt and sweatpants into it and close it.

Caleb and I navigate through the massive athletic center, walking through three halls and up two flights of stairs, and finally come to the doors of the wrestling room. I can smell the mats. It has a smelly sock stench with melted plastic. It's so glorious.

Reese stands in the center of the room next to Coach Wright. Like everything here, the wrestling room is huge, easily twice the size of the one back on the rez. There is a wide opening in the center of the room with enough space for three full-sized wrestling mats lined up next to each other. The ceiling is high, and the room is well lit.

"Derrick." Reese smiles at me. "Caleb!" They hug.

"What's up, Reese?" Caleb says.

"Your team captain was just describing how tough you are, Derrick," Coach Wright says. He's a little older than most of the adults on campus. His hair is curly with patches of white.

"I hope I am," I say, and he shakes my hand.

"We can always use toughness," Coach Wright says. His voice is friendly yet stern. "And, Caleb," Coach Wright says, shaking Caleb's hand. "How's your father?"

"Oh, uh, he's doing fine," Caleb answers. "He got a promotion at his job."

Coach Wright smiles, then says, "Bully for him! He was a hard worker, something you've inherited from him."

"Thanks, Coach Wright." Caleb grins.

"Glad to have you back this year." Coach Wright pats Caleb's shoulder.

Just then, a few more wrestlers walk into the room. They are just as excited as we are. I wonder if I should have taken another scoop of coffee to power through practice. No, I reason, I can get through practice without it. But afterward, I will need some more so that I can stay up and finish my history reading.

Later that night, I sit at my desk and quickly call Chris and Jayden. A few rings pass, then Chris answers.

"Broski," Chris says. "How's it hanging?"

"My man," I say with a wide smile. Jayden doesn't pick up, and it's just Chris and me.

"Ah man, I was hoping Jayden would join," I admit.

"What's that? I'm not cool enough for you?" Chris jokes.

"I was going to tell him to get the tattoo without me."

"He already got it," Chris says. There's a weird tone to his voice. Like he's hiding something from me.

"What? How'd it turn out?"

"It's looks like a piece of turd, if I'm being honest," Chris says. "Yeah, his parents are pissed. He's cribbing at Starletta's right now until they cool off."

"They kick him out again?" I ask.

Chris answers, "He won't say. He got all quiet when I asked about it."

"Damn," I say. "I'll keep reaching out to him."

"Do that," Chris says. "Otherwise, how are things in the fields of sage?"

"All right. Yo, I just finished my last football game this past Saturday!"

"Nice," Chris says. He trails his *c* a little too long. There's a flash of sadness on his face.

"It was so nuts, man! I was on this crazy chartered bus. It was like sitting in a long limo!"

"That's cool," Chris says dimly.

"It was such a long drive! Like it was as long as going from Navajo all the way to Crownpoint."

"Dang, that's far," Chris says.

"And when we got there, man, they barely tackled. Like Coach Atcitty would call them something politically incorrect."

"Hey, man," Chris cuts me off. "I'm actually on my break right now and have to get back to work."

"What? Oh." My excitement deflates. I was hoping to hear what was going on with him. "All right."

"Just check in with Jayden when you get a chance."

"I will," I say. "Don't work too hard."

He softly chuckles. "I'll try. Damn, that's my boss."

He hangs up abruptly. After a second, I realize that he was in his bedroom. Maybe? Doubt creeps into my thoughts. Did he just shake me off? Whatever. He can be that way if he wants.

I scoop some powdered coffee into my bottle and shake it. I chug a third of it and open my laptop. I briefly look at the Google Drive on my desktop. I still haven't deleted it. My mouse hovers over the folders. Then I click open the Word document for my history essay instead.

A few minutes go by. I thought by diving into my schoolwork I could shake off Chris's cold shoulder. Are we growing apart? Eh, I'll see him when I go back for Thanksgiving in a little less than two weeks. We can clear the air when we hang out. Everything will be the way it was when I left.

17

Dimóo, Níłch'ih Ts'ósí 17

Sunday, November 17

Six days later, I follow Caleb down the stairs of our dorm. Even though it's five in the evening, it is dark as night. Which I guess it technically is. But that doesn't matter because today is Caleb's birthday.

"How are we getting into Bridgeville?" I ask him. It's not like we can order a rideshare or get a taxi off campus. There are rules in place to keep us impressionable, saintlike minors safe. If this were back on the rez, I'd have asked my mom to borrow her car and accept whatever answer she gives.

"I requested a faculty driver for tonight," he answers.

"You can do that?" I am shocked.

"Yeah. You didn't know that?" he says.

"There's a lot of things I don't know," I respond. It's true. I haven't really pushed boundaries or figured out what types of limitations I have. Largely because I'm afraid that if I do, I could be kicked out of Sagefield or have my scholarship canceled.

"You don't know what you don't know," he says.

Three of his soccer pals and Xavier are waiting by the first-floor door.

"Happy birthday!" they shout.

"Thanks, everyone," Caleb says. "Save the celebrations for the restaurant."

Caleb leads us out the front door, and in the parking lot is a large luxury SUV. A language teacher who instructs in the classroom next to my Latin class waves at us.

Because of my size, they make me sit in the front while they file into the back. Caleb and his soccer buddies are talking about what varsity is going to be like next year.

"I didn't know that teachers can drive students to town," I say to the language teacher.

"Only on special occasions," he says. "Buckle up!" After several clickings of seat belts, the language teacher drives forward.

"What's in it for you?" I bluntly ask. Only when I've said it do I realize how rude it sounded.

"I wanted to go into town to grab some things, and the school SUV has a much larger trunk space than my tiny car." He turns the steering as we leave the campus.

The guys in back are still in their own world. I ask the language teacher, "So, can I request a teacher driver on my hypothetical birthday night?"

"Yes, you may. You'll probably get approval if you do it at least a week before."

"Gotcha," I say. "What other things can I request?"

"A whole lot of things." The language teacher smiles. "It's

probably best just to ask your floor faculty to see if anything you want to do is appropriate and can be handled by school volunteers. But let's say you want to change classes, say change your language class to my German class, because mine is the best, then you'll have to go through administration."

"I can change my language class?" Another shocking revelation. "I thought I was committed to Latin until I graduated."

"You can change any of your classes should they still meet your requirements. Like, say you want to take biology instead of chemistry. Both will satisfy the science requirement. For language, if the teacher is certified to teach that language, you can request to take another language."

Things are connecting in my head. As long as a teacher is certified to teach that language. Can I change my language class to something a little more personal, like Diné Bizaad? "So if I wanted to take a language that isn't taught at Sagefield but found a teacher who is certified to teach it, I could in theory take that teacher's language class for my requirement?"

"Yes. Happens all the time because students from underrepresented communities often take their mother language for credit. But let's be honest. You want to transfer to German because it's the best language in the world!"

I smile. I'll never get over the fact that almost all the teachers here are extremely passionate about their subject and genuinely love to teach. There are some great teachers on my rez, but often, I got the teachers who just sit behind their desks, surfing the web, waiting for the bell to ring. Some of the teachers have long lost their passion and are simply showing up to work to cash a check until they retire.

At the sushi restaurant, the six of us sit in a large room with a translucent-paper sliding door. After taking a picture, I put my phone back in my pocket, which would be easier if we weren't sitting so close to the floor.

Just then, a huge replica of a wooden ship, easily four feet long and two feet tall, complete with sails and oars sticking out of the sides, arrives at our table. On the ship are rows upon rows of colorful sushi. Toward the front are the traditional rolls of cucumber, eel, and salmon, and various sashimi. There are rolls with tempura shrimp, dark shiny sauces on avocado, and choice cuts of fish. My eyes and stomach spin with giddiness.

I lean in and whisper to Caleb, "Dude, thank your parents for me."

Caleb simply smiles. "Dig in!"

There is ravenous devouring of sushi for the next twenty minutes as we all stuff our faces. Even the low-key cucumber rolls are phenomenal! The pickled ginger has this deliciousness that coats my entire tongue. And it lingers!

When we finish all the sushi, the translucent-paper sliding door slides open and there is a large green cake with a single candle. Several of the staff sing "Happy Birthday."

We all join in, and after Caleb blows out the candle, we dig into the cake.

"Six more days of classes," Caleb says after he takes the first bite.

His friends chat while I eat mine. It's sweet and has a grassy taste that I'm not too fond of. Yeah, I'm not going to go out of my way for this cake.

"Then Thanksgiving," Xavier says. "Which, I'm curious to know, Derrick. Do your people celebrate Thanksgiving?"

"My people?" I ask.

"Natives?" Xavier clarifies.

Everyone's eyes are on me. I wasn't expecting to be put in this teaching position again. It takes me a moment to think through how to answer. Then I say, "I mean, not really. For Thanksgiving, my family still has a big lunch, but we don't do the whole Pilgrims-and-Indians myth. There's a growing movement with a bunch of Native peoples to change it to the Day of Mourning."

"Why's that?" Caleb asks.

I quickly scan everyone. They are attentive and quiet. They want to learn. I ease a little more and open up. "Because for the Wampanoag and many East Coast tribal Nations, there was rampant death from all the diseases that the Pilgrims brought with them."

"So Natives don't like to do anything for Thanksgiving Day?" a soccer friend of Caleb's asks.

"I'm not going to speak for all Natives. We're not just one big group that thinks the same. There may be Native people who truly celebrate Thanksgiving, and that's their choice. But it's kind of hard to not participate in Thanksgiving activities, like having days off work, when the US observes it as a holiday."

I remember previous Thanksgivings when Másání Mildred

and Grandma Rosie wished me a happy Thanksgiving, but it wasn't to celebrate the mass death of the East Coast tribal Nations.

"That's interesting," Xavier says.

"Speaking of holidays, I'm surprised Headmaster hasn't called a holiday," says the soccer friend.

Xavier explains, "He doesn't normally call one until after Thanksgiving."

I ask, "What's a holiday?"

"It's a random day when the headmaster cancels all the classes," Caleb says. "And we're about due for one."

"Dude, don't jinx it!" one of his friends says. "If you talk out loud about it, then it'll get pushed back!"

"I hope it's between Thanksgiving and Christmas," Caleb says.

"Why's that?" I ask.

"Because it's so brutal during that time," explains Xavier. "Everything is due, and you got to get ready for finals."

"Oh, yeah."

My adrenaline spikes. I have barely started writing my final paper on the boarding schools. "I second Caleb's hope."

"We're in November, Derrick," his friend says. "It's going to just pop up in your face. November and December, they fly by so fast. Then it's a whole new semester."

"Enjoy this peace while it lasts," Caleb says. "This is the quiet before the storm. And the maelstrom of finals is going to kick all our asses."

I pretend not to have heard him. Even though the words are registering in my brain, I try to unremember them, to unhear them. My history paper is going to be due sooner rather than later. I haven't even talked with Másání Mildred about her experiences. Tonight. I have to do it.

Later that night, I sit in my stiff chair. The back support digs into my lower spine. I have been staring at my contact information for Másání Mildred for the past few minutes.

I'm terrified of asking her questions. It could upset her and stress her fragile heart. Any elevation in stress could lead to a serious medical situation. Worst-case scenario, she ends up in the hospital. That's a real possibility.

But I have to talk to her. It's more than just a history paper. It's family history. Who knows what could be uncovered? I inhale deeply. I call. A few rings and then she answers.

"Hello?" Másání Mildred answers.

"Yá'át'ééh, Másání!" I say loudly so that she can hear.

"Oh, Derrick, sha'awéé'! How are you?" she asks. Her soft voice wobbles. I put the phone against my ear so that I can hear her more clearly.

"Shił nizhoní." I tell her I'm okay. "I'm just getting ready to do some homework. How do I say homework in Diné, Másání?"

"Homework?" she slowly repeats. Then, "Naanish."

"That's just 'work' in Diné."

"'Aoo'. Homework is work."

I can't argue with that logic.

I ask her, "Are you taking your medicines?"

"Yes, I am."

Without being there in person, I have to take her at her word. I hope she is. There is a moment of silence. I don't know how to continue the conversation, so I try to pivot. "Másání, I was actually hoping to ask you about when you were a young girl."

"Huh?"

I try to be coy and let her talk about her experiences. "You know. What was the world like when you were young?"

"More water and rain on Diné Bikéyah," she says.

"What did you do during that time?"

"Me? I was living with my aunt," she says.

"Your aunt? Why is that?" I immediately open my laptop and the Word software to type notes. I can ask for her permission later.

"My mom and dad got sick when I was little. I don't remember because I was too young. I don't even remember their faces. I have no pictures of them. But when they were sick, I was sent to live with my aunt until they got better," she says. I frantically type on the keyboard. "But they never got better, so I stayed with my aunt. She told me every day that I should be grateful for what she did."

I can't imagine anyone saying that to family. "That's horrible."

"It happened a lot back then," Másání Mildred says. "Why are you asking me about my childhood?"

She can see right through me. Best to be upfront. "I'm actually writing a paper for my history class. I have to use firsthand documentations for this paper, and I was hoping to interview you."

"Me?"

"Yes, because you have lived a very interesting life," I say to butter her up. It feels a little like I am taking advantage of her. "I was hoping to hear about your time at the boarding school you went to. That's what my paper is about.'"

"Doo 'ajínída'. You're not supposed to talk about that stuff," she flatly says. There's no emotion in her voice, and she declares it like it's a fact.

I decide to leave it at that for today. I'll give her time to absorb the topic of my paper, and in the meantime, I can write a few more pages of my final history paper with the research I've done so far. Hopefully, Másání Mildred will open up later.

"Hágoshį́į́, Másání," I say to her. "But just think about it."

"No."

"Okay," I say. I'm not sure what to tell her next. I was hoping to have other avenues of conversation. Wait! "I'm excited to come back for Thanksgiving in a week!"

"Is it?"

"'Aoo'," I excitedly answer.

"Are you going to come by and chop wood for me?"

"I will," I say. "How's your wood supply right now?"

"I can last until you come by. No one chops wood for me."

The thought of her running out of firewood doesn't sit well with me. Moments like this really test my desire to be here at this school. I realize it was always my mom, Demi, and I who'd chop wood for Másání Mildred. Now that I'm here, it's only going to be my mom, whose day job always tires her out. And Demi's stationed in Alaska. "I'll chop all your wood when I get back." That's a promise.

"Hágoshį́į́, sha'awéé'. I'll see you."

"Seven days!"

"Oh yeah, huh!" There's joy in her voice.

"Okay, Másání, I'm going to go to sleep now. I love you and miss you," I say.

"Me too, sha'awéé'. Thank you for calling and thinking of me. It makes me feel good," she says. Then she hangs up.

I sit in my chair and stare out the window. The rain has stopped, and the wind has slowed. I wish all this rain could come back with me to the rez. I imagine all the greenery that would grow from this moisture.

I think about the conversation I just had. I asked Másání about her boarding school years. She automatically shut me down. I'll call this progress for now. Hopefully, when I am home for Thanksgiving break, she'll open up and talk.

What if I am successful? She will tell me about the abuse she endured. The physical kind. The emotional kind. Even the kind that should never happen to anyone. My throat clogs with fear. If I am successful, am I even prepared to listen?

18

THANKSGIVING BREAK

Dimóo, Níłch'ih Ts'ósí 24

Sunday, November 24

I land in Albuquerque on a bright, sunny Sunday morning. I double-check my phone to make sure my mom knows where to pick me up. After that, I quickly text Chris and Jayden that I have landed and ask them what they are up to the next few days. I don't get an immediate response. Should I be concerned? They haven't been responding to my texts recently. Are they ghosting me?

I search the end of the driveway, where the cars enter, and spot our rez ride, a mid-2000s Dodge Neon that my mom has been keeping together with willpower, cedar smoke, and her experience as a mechanic. The sides of the tires are caked with mud. Washing the car was one of my chores.

She idles the car in the passenger pickup zone. The trunk pops open. We quickly hug as an airport worker yells at nearby vehicles to keep on moving.

"I missed you, Mama," I say.

"I missed you, too, shiyáázh. Hurry," she says as I carry my stuff to the trunk.

Before I carelessly toss my luggage in, I notice three huge packages of bottled water, a big bag of white rice, so many packages of SPAM, and other dried goods.

"Here, let's organize," my mom says, stepping out of the car. She wears her favorite black shirt that has a picture of Selena, Aaliyah, and Left Eye underneath the phrase *Forever Queens*. She dives into the trunk to sort and stack the items.

"All this for Másání, huh?" I ask even though I know it is.

"Two birds, one stone," she says.

She doesn't need to elaborate on that. Picking me up in Albuquerque, a three-hour drive away from home, was a good enough reason to also do a stockpile run at Costco for Másání Mildred.

"There," my mom says. The trunk has just barely enough space to squeeze in my luggage.

We stop by Laguna Burger near Route 66 Casino, half an hour west of Albuquerque, to grab some green chili cheeseburgers for a quick lunch. Then we're back on I-40 heading toward Gallup as I stuff the amazing meal into my mouth.

I soak up the dry landscape outside, marveling at the clear blue skies and wide expanse. I've missed this sight. But I still feel the pressures of Sagefield, even though I'm two thousand miles away. My head is clouded with thoughts and busy trying to figure out a schedule that will allow me to finish my history essay and study for my finals. Mr. Henderson even thought it was a great idea to assign a five-page paper over Thanksgiving break. Geez, he needs to loosen up.

"I never knew how beautiful the landscape is," I say.

"This? Really?" My mom smirks.

"Yeah, there are so many trees and hills on campus that I can't see beyond them." I don't tell her that the campus feels claustrophobic. The dense forest feels like a fence, one that is meant to prevent escape. Here, the baby-blue skies and the open desert make me feel like I can breathe.

"I guess so," my mom says.

"Thanks again for picking me up," I say to her.

She smiles. "Your grandma pitched in for gas since we're doing a stockpile run for Másání Mildred."

She does that sometimes. She'll downplay her excitement or shrug off a compliment. I don't know if she's aware she's doing it.

"By the way," she says, "I'm making a quick trip to Sawmill to deliver this stuff. You can come, but I understand if you want me to drop you off at home first."

I say, "I want to see Másání Mildred. I also promised I'd chop wood for her."

"Easy there," my mom says. "She has enough wood to last another week or so. Rest up first. Don't wear yourself out."

"You're one to talk," I say. I mean it. There were times when she was working three jobs and was getting only four hours of sleep. When Demi was eleven and I was six, we had to cook and keep the house clean while she kept a roof over our heads.

"I know what I'm talking about," she says. She sips her dark cola and eats some fries.

When we get to the outskirts of Grants, New Mexico, my mom points to Tsoodził with her lips. "Got your tádídíín?"

Her question is more a command that we are going to stop to

pray to the sacred mountain. Every time we head to Albuquerque, we stop outside of Grants to pray to Tsoodził.

"Yeah," I answer, and reach into the top pocket of my backpack.

My mom takes an exit off I-40. She drives a little farther south to avoid the traffic and potential drivers who may question what we are doing. She parks on a dirt road that veers away from the pavement.

My mom and I stand facing the southern sacred mountain and quickly say our thanks while standing on Mother Earth. I take this time to ask the sacred mountain for help to get Másání Mildred's story out of her.

We sprinkle our corn pollen and get back into the car.

When we're on the highway, my mom says, "Ms. Thomas called me again."

My entire body tenses up. Should I be scared? This could go any way. So I ask as coolly as I can, "What did she say?"

"You can relax," my mom says. "She was just checking in to see how I was doing. I was surprised, honestly."

"She was worried about you?" I ask. "Wow." Ms. Thomas truly is an incredible and kind woman.

"That woman," my mom says with admiration. "We owe her so much. She's literally changing your future." She drives for a few seconds before saying, "So are you."

I nod. "It's hard at times."

"Then get stronger. Face those challenges. There are so many people sacrificing so you can go to that school."

I feel ashamed that my mom has to sacrifice things. "Thank

you for all that you're doing so I can go."

My mom says, "It's my job. And my privilege. You're going to be someone special when you grow up. It's every parent's dream to see their children succeed. All these challenges you are going through right now, I know it's tough, but when you graduate from Sagefield, you're going to see that the difficulties weren't meaningless. You struggle because you don't know how to exist there. Now imagine next year, when you know how to exist and how best to study, you're going to be an unstoppable force."

She said *when you graduate from Sagefield*, as if it was fact and not some impossible dream. I think of Bryan, the alumnus I spoke with. Graduating really is something I can do. I smile and nod.

We don't even bother stopping by our hometown of Navajo and head straight to Sawmill. I'm glad we do, because my energy levels are dropping. It's one o'clock in the afternoon, and yeah, I'd have a cup of coffee about now back at Sagefield before wrestling practice, but I promised myself no coffee during the break, to reset my tolerance, per Markus's suggestion.

In Sawmill, we veer off the paved road and drive on meandering dirt roads that are in desperate need of grading. There are houses on the side of the road that have fallen into disrepair. Their roofs have caved in. Graffiti decorates their broken windows. The log walls have the color of rotten bananas and probably have the same squishy texture.

I've been told that a long time ago, there used to be an actual sawmill in Sawmill. Lumber was huge business here and created many jobs. For a while, Sawmill was an amazing place to be. There was an old log building that was the post office and trading post. But when the sawmill shut down, the entire economy of the town collapsed. Now the only source of jobs is the newish laundromat/gas station/store, the chapter house, and the elementary school.

A few minutes of driving later, my mom pulls up to Másání Mildred's house. It's less of a house and more four walls plastered with cracked clay and a roof of aluminum panels. One of the two windows at the front is shattered. Silver straps of masking tape hold the glass shards together. Some forty or so yards away stands her hogan, where we have our family ceremonies. Before her house was built, that's where she raised Grandma Rosie and Grandpa Dominic.

Grandma Rosie keeps asking her to move in with her in Fort Defiance. If she were to move, then she wouldn't be lonely and would also be just down the road from the hospital. But Másání Mildred doesn't want to leave her own home. I didn't understand before. Having spent a few months at Sagefield, I now understand how hard it can be to leave your home. I understand how much heartache it causes someone to sleep in an unfamiliar bed.

Másání Mildred has lived here her entire life. It would be the hardest thing to do at her age, to leave the place where she has tons of happy memories with my great-grandpa and their children, my grandparents. I can't say for sure that if I were in her shoes, I'd have the strength to leave this place. So the best thing I can do for her in this moment is respect her desire to live here.

We step out of the car and stretch. My head goes fuzzy for a second. This far up in the mountains it is so cold that we can see our breath as we exhale. We knock on the door before entering.

Másání Mildred sits in front of her woodstove by her windowless wall. She's wrapped in a faded and patched quilt, sitting at her table examining puzzle pieces.

"Who's that?" she asks, then looks up. It takes a moment for her to recognize my mom. "Oh! Shiyázhí!" She opens up her arms for a hug.

"Hi, Másání!" my mom says to her, and kisses her forehead as they hug. My mom sniffs her head. "When was the last time you had a bath, Grandma?"

"Last time you were here," she says.

My mom shakes her head. I see concern in her eyes. "Let's pretty you up, then."

"I was born pretty," Másání Mildred jokes. She smiles and pats my mom's arm. When she sees me, a wide, warm smile spreads across her face. "Sha'awéé'!"

She is the only one who calls me sha'awéé', which translates to "my baby." No matter how old I get, no matter how long the time spent apart, whenever she calls me sha'awéé' I feel like everything is going to be fine because this wonderful woman loves me for who I am. I feel protected.

I hug her, and she holds my arm. Her hand gently squeezes. "Yá'át'ééh, Másání."

"Thank you!" she sings.

"For what?"

"For visiting me." She smiles at me.

"Of course," I say, and release her. I notice how low her pile of chopped wood is. It'll only last a week, max. "I'll make sure that you have a full stack of wood before I head back."

"'Ahxéhee'," she says.

"Son," my mom says to me, "go grab the stuff from the trunk. When you're done with that, cook some tóshchíín for her."

"Yeah. How much should I make?"

"Make a big batch. But don't put any sugar in it. There are plastic containers that you can put it into. If we aren't done by the time you finish, start dicing some of her potatoes and any veggies she has."

She tosses me her car keys. Then she rolls up her sleeves and pushes Másání Mildred toward the bathroom connected to the living room. "Txį'." My mom helps Másání Mildred stand and walk into the bathroom. She closes the door behind them. In the kitchen, I pour some water into a large measuring cup to begin cooking the tóshchíín.

After I bring all the food items into her kitchen, I pour the ground blue corn mixture into the boiling water and attentively stir to make sure that it comes out smooth. I sneak some sugar in, despite what my mom told me. I think Másání Mildred should enjoy the remaining months of her life. The last six words of my previous thought hit my heart.

I try to ignore it and focus on making sure that the tóshchíín doesn't burn or overcook. This could very well be the last time that I cook for her. This could be the last time I see her alive. I reassure myself that while that is a possibility, it's not a certainty.

By the time I finish washing and dicing half of a five-pound bag of potatoes, my mom and Másání Mildred emerge from the bathroom. A cloud of steam pours out of the bathroom and dissipates in the living room area. My mom helps her into her wheelchair and then pushes her to the kitchen table, where I have left a bowl of tóshchíín and some decaffeinated black tea.

"The blue corn mush has probably cooled off," I say to them.

My mom blows her nose and bites her lower lip. Is she sad?

"That's fine," Másání Mildred says. "I like my tóshchíín like me: cool."

I laugh at that. Her mood always becomes playful when people visit her in her home.

After my mom turns on the oven, she opens the fridge and begins to toss outdated and spoiled foods into a large white trash bag. "Son, bake those potatoes with a little bit of vegetable oil."

"Got it." I immediately get to work.

"Másání," my mom says. She sounds weary and worried. "You need to move in with my mom."

"Yáa!" she says, and spoons more blue corn mush into her mouth. "I'm fine right here."

"What if you get hurt? And you can't reach your phone? It takes the ambulance thirty minutes to get to you out here. That's if there isn't a storm that makes the road impassable."

"I'm fine." Másání Mildred sips her tea loudly.

My mom shoots me a look that means *Back me up*. So I chime in, "Másání, please. You're all alone out here."

"I'm just fine here. Safer than living with your mom, shich'é'é," she says to my mom. "There's all those gangs in Fort."

"There's gangs here, too," my mom counters. "Think about it some more."

"It does get lonely here at night," Másání Mildred admits.

"If you live with Grandma Rosie, you won't have to be alone all the time," I say.

"I'll think about it," she relents.

For my mom and me, that's all we want to hear. The first step in getting her to move where we can keep a better eye on her.

An hour later, my mom and I sit in her car. She turns it on and drives away from the house. There's something odd in her energy. She's quiet and calm. Not in a relaxed way, but in a tensed, forced way. Like she's fighting an urge to yell.

When we leave Másání Mildred's driving path, my mom pulls to the side, and I notice that there are tears forming in the corners of her eyes.

"Mom?" I say, and hold her hand.

She wills herself together and drives a little farther.

I worry for her. "Are you okay?"

"I want to be sure she can't see us out her window," she says.

A heaviness develops in the small interior of her car. It weighs this silence with discomfort and uneasy anticipation as she pulls off again to the side of the dirt road in the shade of a leafless tree.

"Your great-grandma said something," she tells me. "She told me she's been having dreams about your great-grandpa." She covers her mouth and sniffles.

I grasp her hand and interlace our fingers. I don't know if she needs it more than I because it pains me to see her sad and to think of what this means for Másání Mildred.

"In the Diné way, when you reach są, old age, people in your life who have passed away begin to visit you in your dreams. It's their way of welcoming you to the land of our ancestors. Sometimes, people close to those who are about to pass dream about them, too. Before your great-grandpa passed away, he used to say that his mom would visit him in his dreams. Then, during the last days of his life, he would talk as if his mom was in the room with him. The morning he passed, I had a dream about him."

My mom struggles to tell me the last part. I know why she's telling me this. I know why she's scared now. Másání Mildred is getting ready to go to the land of our ancestors, and Great-Grandpa is visiting her in her dreams. Her time with us truly is ending.

"I don't know how much time she has left with us," my mom says. "But it might be a good idea to say goodbye to her before you head back to Sagefield."

My heart breaks.

We need to prepare for the real possibility that Másání Mildred might pass away before I return. I rest my head on my mom's shoulder. I'm scared and need my mom.

I say, "She's going to be okay when I return, Mom." It comes out more like a question.

"We can pray for that, shiyáázh," she tells me. "We can hope." She pulls a tissue from her purse and blows her nose. "I'm going to call your grandma and tell her this. Preparations in the land of our ancestors are beginning. We still have time with her here.

You should spend as much time as you can with her. She's so very proud of you, shiyáázh."

My heart warms. Hearing that Másání Mildred is proud of me soothes the lump of sadness in my throat.

"She's always asking about you when I visit her. None of her other great-grandkids visit her or cook or chop wood for her like you do."

I'm suddenly very thankful my mom forced me to go with her to visit Másání Mildred when I was younger and didn't want to.

"She tells me that she burns cedar for you every morning. She prays that you are happy and succeeding over in Sagefield."

All the struggles I'm going through with my assignments seem so small now. Every time I smelled a whiff of cedar, that was Másání Mildred's blessings and prayers; that was her guidance and support. She was there with me through the tough times when I felt alone. Even though we were almost a continent apart, we were never separated. But now these dreams she's been having, I have to face the fact that we inevitably will be separated soon. And I can't change that.

"Mom, do you think I can spend the night with her?" I ask. "Like later in the week?"

"I'm sure she'll love it," my mom says.

My mom drives forward, and the heaviness hangs over us the entire journey back to Navajo. Because we both know every minute that passes from here on out is a minute that we'll never get to be with her again. There's nothing we can do but let our hearts ache.

19

Dimóo dóó naakijį́, Níłch'ih Ts'ósí 26

Tuesday, November 26

I spend all of Monday sleeping. I barely had enough energy to get up and eat. I was so tempted to make myself some coffee but rode through the caffeine withdrawal instead.

This morning, I'm feeling a little better. I have a headache, but it's tolerable. I turn in my twin-sized bed. The hand-me-down mattress is stiffer than the one at Sagefield. But I love it anyway. I grab my phone and text Chris and Jayden again to see if they want to hang out. Neither has responded to my previous four texts.

I yawn and start to get my day going. Today, I plan on chopping the rest of the wood my mom has. Even though I'm on break this week, I don't have the luxury of completely vegging out. Plus, it's a good workout.

My phone vibrates. It's Chris. Finally! Yo! Let's hang tonight. Let's meet up at That's-A-Burger after my shift!

I quickly respond, For sure!

That works! After I hang with Chris, and hopefully Jayden, he can drop me off at Grandma Rosie's. Tomorrow, she's going to pick up Másání Mildred for her hospital visit so I can tag along.

I make my way to the kitchen, where my mom has left several dishes. It's nine. Yeah, she already took off to work. After I make myself some boiled eggs and oatmeal, I sit down and devour my breakfast. I didn't expect to feel so happy to cook for myself. I've missed it. Don't get me wrong: Having the kitchen staff at Sagefield prepare delicious meals for me and wash my dishes for me is awesome. But an ingredient called independence makes this meal taste absolutely delicious.

A brief thought crosses my mind. I should finalize the quotes I'm going to use from my PDFs and *Boarding School Seasons* for my final paper. I should start on that five-pager for Mr. Henderson. There are also assigned readings for English and some translation sets for Latin.

I fill the kettle with water and put it on the electric stove. I go to the fridge. Mom must have recently gone to the grocery store in Gallup to pick up food for me. There are tons of fruits and veggies. In the freezer there are three boxes of Philly Cheesesteak Hot Pockets, my favorite. I'll have some of those after I chop wood.

I investigate further around the kitchen and discover bags of snacks like chips and salted peanuts and a twenty-four-count box of microwavable popcorn. I wonder how she paid for all of this. This is a splurge for her.

Then I realize that since she didn't have to pay for my food while I was at Sagefield, eating that fancy, organic, non-GMO crap, she wasn't spending too much to feed herself.

The kettle whistles. I pour steaming hot water into the kitchen sink with some cooler tap water and a generous dab of dish soap. I get to washing my dishes and my mom's that she left on the counter.

All right, time to get some studying done.

No, not today. Today is for resting and relaxing. Tomorrow I can get some hardcore studying done. Suddenly, I remember the file that contains all the current final exams. I could use it to help me study. As I wash the dishes, I digest both my breakfast and that thought.

Later that afternoon, when my mom comes home from work, she looks exhausted. Her hair is frizzy and her shirt has grime on the sleeves.

I open the door for her, and she smiles. "Hi, son."

"Mom, can you drop me off at That's-A-Burger to hang out with Chris and Jayden?"

"Not a chance in hell. I'm so tired."

"But, Mom! I haven't seen them in months."

"I haven't seen you in months," she says. She raises an eyebrow.

"You've been seeing me all day."

"You've been sleeping all day and I've been at work," she says. She pushes past me and sees the clean living room. "I sure do miss having you at home."

I knew she'd appreciate coming home to a vacuumed and dusted living room. "I even did some prep work for dinner. All you have to do is cook. Please, Mom."

"I said no," she says.

I know better than to disobey her. I pout. "Okay."

"When you get your license, you can borrow the car when I'm not using it," my mom explains.

I don't want to suggest that I just drive the car. I mean, I got my driver's permit before I left for Sagefield. It's unfair that Chris's and Jayden's parents have been letting them drive around since they were fourteen.

"I actually was gonna ask Chris to drop me off at Grandma Rosie's so I can go with her to Másání's doctor's appointment tomorrow morning," I admit.

Before she can respond, she pulls out her phone and texts someone. A weird, girlish smile appears on her face.

"Who's that?" I ask. There's something going on here. She's acting all coy and flustered.

"Fine, I'll drop you off in Fort," my mom relents.

I notice that she's redirecting my attention. I'll let her have this so that I can hang. But I'm definitely going to revisit this weirdness later. "Okay!"

I quickly text Chris to see if he can drop me off at Grandma Rosie's after we hang. My palms sweat while I wait for his response. My phone nearly slips out of my hand when I receive his No prob!

"Thank you, Mom!" I say, and wrap her in a hug.

"Let's go. The sooner I drop you off, the sooner I can relax," she says.

"Relax, huh? Not going to have someone over?" I ask. I waggle my eyebrows to pick on her some.

"Do you want a ride or not?"

"I'm sorry. Yes, love you, Mom. Thank you for everything you do!"

I hold my tongue as we enter her car. I have an inkling of what she's up to. I smile. She deserves to have fun.

My mom drops me off at That's-A-Burger by the car wash in Fort. I watch some clips on my phone while I wait in the dining area. Then I see Chris's beat-up rez truck pull into a parking space. I can barely contain my excitement as I zip up my jacket.

"Dude!" Chris jumps out of the driver's side. I wonder why Jayden isn't with him. We rush toward each other. We hug it out for a good minute or so.

Chris says, "You're so pale! You turning white on me?"

I show him my forearms, and we compare our color. It's true. I have become pale, for a Diné. His arm is much darker than mine.

His joke stings a little. But I have to ignore the jab or I'll get more crap from him. I joke to disarm my emotions and say, "Just all colonized, huh!"

We both laugh. Then Chris says, "Missed ya, buddy. You kind of just made like a newborn and headed out so quick."

"How long were you waiting to say that golden dad joke?" I ask Chris.

"Too long." Chris smiles.

We make our way to his truck.

"Where's Jayden?" I ask while I jump into the passenger seat. It was always the three of us. It feels weird that he's not sitting next to me.

"We had a falling-out," Chris explains as he buckles his seat belt.

"What?" I say, completely surprised. "What happened?"

"Earlier this month, Starletta got arrested for selling drugs. Jayden's taking it really hard because no one in his family is helping her," Chris explains. "I tried being supportive and everything. But he just became this huge ass."

"What?" I shout. "He didn't tell me. Where is he now?"

Chris drives out of the parking lot and takes the road that runs by Black Rock and leads to Window Rock.

"He's been dodging me. Hasn't been coming to school," Chris explains. "So, yeah. There's a rumor going around that he's been hanging with the meth heads."

The air leaves my lungs. I'm devastated. "You're kidding," I say. My chest feels like it's collapsing and compressing my heart. "No. Jayden wouldn't do that. He can't."

I'm too shocked to absorb all of this. Was it my fault that Jayden succumbed to meth because I wasn't here? I can't shake the guilt. "You should have told me," I say.

"It wouldn't have mattered," Chris says glumly. I sense that Chris is a little angry at something. At me?

"I'm sorry I wasn't here," I say.

Chris responds, "It would have played out the same if you were around."

"I can't believe it," I say. I sit back.

"Two months and some change is a long time, man," Chris says.

"What else happened while I was gone?" I ask.

"Orien and Chester got in a drunk driving accident," Chris says. "They didn't make it."

"No way!" I react. I'm not that surprised because there were several times where they were buzzed during practice. I wasn't exactly close with them. The sad truth is that things like this are common enough on the rez that I have to just roll with it.

But it's still a lot to process.

While I was at Sagefield, life here kept on going. While I was so focused on doing well, Chris was dealing with the harsh realities of rez life. He doesn't have the opportunities or resources that my friends at Sagefield have. Orien and Chester, while not the greatest humans in the world, were decent enough guys. Would they all have different outcomes if they were as rich as the kids at Sagefield?

Jayden. Chris and I have to save him. I can't stand losing Jayden. But how do we even begin if he's not responding? "How are you holding up, with all this?"

"It's life," Chris replies. He says it so hard-heartedly that it scares me. This isn't the same Chris that I had hung out with at Window Rock. "Friendships break. People die. You can't do anything about it. So why stress? Sorry to just dump it all on you like that. But that's how it is."

I can't respond. Has Chris changed to the point that losing a good friend means nothing to him? If I change too much for him, will he be this apathetic if our friendship ends?

20

Dimóo dóó tágíjį̨́, Níłch'ih Ts'ósí 27

Wednesday, November 27

After hanging out with Chris, I spend the night at Grandma Rosie's in Fort Defiance. She lives in Black Rock Acres, whose streets are in desperate need of repair. When driving through, my mom has to zigzag across both lanes to avoid deep potholes that keep getting bigger and bigger.

Grandma Rosie is very certain that the house four doors down, the one with plywood nailed onto the windows, is a meth house. Small blades of light escape through the cracked wooden panels during the night. When it is winter, smoke billows out of the chimney. She told me once that she counted twenty cars coming and going on a Friday night, staying no more than five minutes each.

I help her put breakfast on the kitchen table for the two of us. It's very early. Even though it's still dark outside, Pubby and Yáadilá whimper and wag their tails as they stare inside through the sliding glass door. They press their wet noses through the steel security door that she installed with Grandpa Greg years ago. A pang of grief and longing stabs into my chest. It's been three years since he passed. And now I feel like we have to get ready for Másání Mildred's passing.

"Are you still working on that essay about boarding schools, shiyáázh?" she asks me.

"Yeah. I'm hoping to get Másání Mildred's story," I tell her. If there is anyone who could help me get it, Grandma Rosie would be that person. Part of the reason I spent the night here is that Grandma Rosie is picking Másání Mildred up to take her to her doctor's appointment at the Tséhootsooí Medical Center. Maybe it'll give me time to talk with Másání Mildred about her boarding school experience.

She scoops some fried potatoes and bacon from her cast-iron pan with a freshly made tortilla. We both eat like this.

"What do you know about her childhood?" I ask her.

"When she was a toddler, there was a disease spreading across the rez. We think it was tuberculosis, but we didn't have hospitals on the rez then, so we just weathered the sicknesses. Both her parents caught it. She was given to her auntie on her dad's side. It was supposed to be temporary, but both her parents passed away. So Mildred's aunt raised her along with her own kids," Grandma Rosie says.

"How many cousins did she have?" I ask.

"There used to be two of them. Parker passed away. Now it's just Mildred and Gertrude," Grandma Rosie says.

"Másání Gertrude," I say.

"Mm-hmm. During my kinaaldá, shimáyázhí Gertrude tied my hair." Grandma Rosie squeezes her hair.

"Did she also go to boarding school? Maybe she and Másání Mildred went together," I suggest.

Grandma Rosie says, "Doo 'ajínída'!"

"We can't just ignore all that trauma and hurt," I say.

"That's Diné philosophy. It's our culture," Grandma Rosie says.

I want to say more to her. I want to say that not talking about this stuff is causing great harm to our Elders. It's causing harm to all of us. But this is as far as I can push the conversation today. If I go further, Grandma Rosie might not take me to see Másání Mildred. So I join her in "Doo 'ajínída'."

"Though, I am curious about her time as a young girl. I don't know much about that part of her life. Finish your breakfast, then get ready. We'll head out in thirty minutes." She drinks some of her light brown coffee. "She keeps asking about you. You visiting her will be good for her.

"When she heard you say that you were happy over there, she stopped yelling at me. Now she's curious. Asking how you're doing. She always asks who's going to chop wood for her." Grandma Rosie smiles. "I think she just wants that gesture of someone taking care of her," she says. "She wants someone to show that they care about her. It means a lot when your grandchildren do things for you. It shows that you love us. Even if you just call, it makes our day. We think we're so special that you made time in your day to think of us."

I'm so glad that I got into the habit of calling them while I was at Sagefield.

* * *

When we get to Sawmill to pick up Másání Mildred, there are dark clouds overhead. A thick sheet of tiny specks of snow fall to the ground. The snow doesn't stick and just melts. In-law snow.

Grandma Rosie says, "When I was young, it used to snow so much. During the winter, the snow would be up to my waist, and I'd still have to walk to the bus station by the old post office."

I reply, "I've been waiting for it to snow at Sagefield. They keep saying it's going to be a lot."

"Don't forget to take a snow bath when it does," she tells me.

"I won't." Every first snowfall, Diné are supposed to jump into the snow and rub it against our bare skin. One, it thanks the Holy Beings for the snow. Two, it toughens you up physically by waking up your immune system, jiní!

She parks the car in front of Másání Mildred's crumbling house and turns it off. I follow her up the makeshift ramp that Grandpa Dominic constructed. She knocks on the door and lets herself in.

There is a small fire in the stove that blasts out waves of heat in all directions. Másání Mildred sits directly in front of the woodstove wearing a thick jacket and earmuffs.

"Txį', shimá! 'Azee' 'áłį́ góó!"

"Huh?" Másání Mildred says. Her eyes land on me, and immediately she smiles. "Sha'awéé'!" She waves me over.

I hurry over and kneel to hug her.

She begins to cry. "Sha'awéé', I missed you with all my heart."

"I was just here three days ago."

Másání Mildred says, "I know. I still missed you."

My heart melts. Grandparents have such medicine and power.

"Mom, come on, we have to go if we're going to make your appointment," Grandma Rosie says.

"Oh, okay! What about my fire?" Másání Mildred asks.

Grandma Rosie looks at it. "It'll burn out. Your house will be fine."

I disengage Másání Mildred's wheelchair brakes and take her to the car outside. Meanwhile, Grandma Rosie grabs her aluminum walker as well as her purse.

Both Grandma Rosie and I help Másání Mildred into the passenger seat and turn the heater on full blast.

"Shiyáázh," Grandma Rosie says, "can you double-check and turn off the lights and lock the door?"

"No problem," I say, and quickly run into her home. In her room in the back, Másání Mildred left her radio on. I turn off various lights here and there, then lock the front door. I notice a huge hole in the side panel. This house really is falling apart. Másání Mildred can't live here much longer. I lock her front door and then jump in the back of the car. We all head to Fort Defiance.

The three of us sit in an exam room, waiting for Dr. Platero. The results of tests Másání Mildred took are complete, and we are here to discuss next steps.

"Derrick, shiyáázh, do you have something you want to ask?" Grandma Rosie says.

"Oh yeah! Shimásání, what was it like when you were a little girl?" I begin.

"There were no cars. We had to travel by horse to get anywhere," she says.

"Where was your favorite place?" I ask.

"Shibízhí bidá'ák'eh," she answers.

"Her aunt's cornfield," Grandma Rosie translates.

"Before my kinaaldá," Másání Mildred says, "she started to teach me how to care for the crops. How to plant certain things next to each other."

"What was your favorite food to eat back then?" I ask her.

"Peaches. We used to plant these small peach trees. Shibízhí traded with a family in Canyon de Chelly and got some pits from them. After we harvested the peach trees, we dried the peaches and would eat them during the winter."

"How old were you?"

"I was nine."

"Did Másání Gertrude also help?" I ask her.

She looks a little confused. "No. Jerome did."

"Jerome? Who's that?" Grandma Rosie asks.

Fear flashes in her eyes. Then she explains, "Gertrude. I said Gertrude."

That was weird. I let it go for now. "Where was she at this time?" I ask.

Másání Mildred massages her temples. "Gertrude wasn't there."

"She wasn't born at the time?" I ask.

"No," Másání Mildred answers.

Grandma Rosie looks a little confused at her response. "Wait. Isn't she two years younger than you?"

"Oh! Gertrude! Yeah, she was around," Másání Mildred says. This sounds off to me.

Just then, Dr. Platero comes into the room. She wears a turquoise necklace and has her hair in a tsiiyéél. "Yá'át'ééh, shimá!"

"Shich'é'é, how are you?" Másání Mildred asks the doctor. They hug.

The doctor turns to look at me and says, "Derrick! So good to see you again. How's your first semester going?"

"It's weird, man," I say to her.

Dr. Platero laughs. "It is! I grew up hearing that all our problems on the rez—the lack of jobs, infrastructure, and opportunities—all of them were caused by rich white people. Then I go out there and suddenly I'm surrounded by rich white people." She turns to face Másání Mildred. "All right, ready to talk results?"

She opens a manila folder. With a warm yet concerned expression, Dr. Platero says, "Your heart is operating at twenty-five percent capacity. Meaning that twenty-five percent of the oxygenated blood that is pumped into your aortic valve is traveling to your limbs and your brain. This is why you get dizzy and confused."

"Does that qualify her for the TAVR procedure?" Grandma Rosie questions.

"It does. I can put in a request to Flagstaff to see if they can schedule a consultation. She'll have to be examined by their specialists to see if she can withstand the surgery. While it's not open-heart surgery, it's still a major operation at her age. Any operation is major at her age and in her state of health."

I'm a little lost at what's going on. "What's that procedure?"

Dr. Platero smiles at me and explains, "The TAVR procedure is a minimally invasive surgery. Essentially, we would be sending a very tiny balloon through her veins into her heart valve, where there is extensive blockage. The balloon inflates and creates more space in that valve. From there, we could see an increase of oxygen intake anywhere from five percent to twenty-five percent."

My own heart shakes from the description of this procedure, and I hate imagining this being done to Másání Mildred.

"Okay," Grandma Rosie says.

"So, that is a potential way to get higher percentages," Dr. Platero says. "With those results, shimá here will have a higher quality of life and this could possibly give her more time with us."

My heart swells with hope. I want this.

Grandma Rosie asks, "Mom, is this something you want to do?"

"'Aoo', shich'é'é," Másání Mildred says to Dr. Platero. "I don't like being dizzy all the time."

"Hágoshį́į́, shimá," Dr. Platero says. "We'll move forward and schedule a consultation for the TAVR procedure. You'll have to go to Flagstaff in person. We'll aim for the earliest that they can schedule."

"Hágoshį́į́," Másání Mildred says.

Dr. Platero closes the manila folder and shakes our hands before she exits.

"That's my doctor daughter," Másání Mildred says.

I walk behind her and begin to wheel her back to Grandma Rosie's car.

"Grandma Rosie," I say, "can we stop by your house for supplies? I want to fix Másání Mildred's wall. There's a huge hole."

"Oh yes, I keep forgetting! Mom, we're going to Window Rock for lunch."

We navigate the hospital hallways, slowly making our way to the parking lot. Something doesn't leave my mind. Másání Mildred had forgotten that her younger sister, Gertrude, was around when she was little. What about that name, Jerome? Forgetfulness isn't one of her symptoms. And her memory is still sharp, given her age. She was able to recognize Dr. Platero. She couldn't have forgotten about her sister. I'm missing something. Did Másání Mildred just lie about her childhood?

21

Késhmish Yázhí
Thanksgiving

Thanksgiving morning, I wake up early to help Mom in the kitchen. She brews herself a big pot of coffee. While I am tempted to have a cup, I will myself to ignore its smell. Not that it's hard, as the entire kitchen smells like pumpkin pie spices, too. No complaints here.

"Hey, Mom," I say.

"What's up?" She carefully guides the pumpkin puree into the four graham cracker crusts.

"I was thinking of asking Másání Gertrude about her boarding school experience instead of Másání Mildred."

We both carry the four fresh pies and place them inside the warmed oven. All the hard work is done. Now we just have to hang out and make sure the pies don't burn.

"That's a better idea. She talks a little more about things that Mildred would say 'Doo 'ajínída" to. All this talk is getting me curious. I wouldn't mind knowing about their time in boarding school." I don't tell her that Másání Mildred might be hiding something from us. Something that happened during that time. "I can ask after lunch."

"That sounds good," my mom says. Then she squares her stance and faces me directly. "I need to tell you something."

There's that weird tone again. I spot the beginnings of a coy smile, despite her efforts to be serious. "Yeah?"

"I was thinking of bringing someone to Christmas dinner." She looks down, avoiding my gaze.

"Someone like a coworker?" It's so funny to see her so uncomfortable! I love the idea that she's nervous talking about her snag.

"No." She tucks her hair behind her ear.

"Like a friend from middle school?" I say, mocking her with a smarmy voice.

"Shut up," she says. But she can't help blushing.

"So, what's his name?"

"He's got no name," she quickly says.

"So, there is a 'he'?" God, I wish I could pick on her until the end of time. "Does he wear skinny Wranglers?"

"If you must know"—she mumbles her words—"he wears Carhartt."

"Is that a big deal or something?" I ask.

"Listen." She stops and looks me in the eye. "Are you okay with this? Me seeing someone?"

"Mom, are you really asking for my permission to see someone?"

"No. I don't know!"

She's super conflicted. It's gone beyond teasing and into serious territory. I sit next to her and rest my head on her shoulder. "I think it's cool, Mom. Demi and I have seen you give so much of your life to us. Now that I'm out of the house—" I say.

She interrupts me. "It's so damn quiet at night." She wraps her arms around me.

"Demi and I used to plan who we'd set you up with," I admit to her.

"Who?" She laughs.

"We thought our second-grade teacher, Mr. Dahozy, would be best," I tell her.

"Ugly!" She lets me go. "Why?"

"Because he was single, and as far as we could tell the same age as you. Plus, he was like the best teacher in Navajo Elementary. So is it Mr. Dahozy?"

"Sick." She shakes her head. "He works at Jiffy Lube in Gallup."

"Which one?"

"I'm not telling you. You might go and scope him out. I'm still thinking about it. Inviting your snag to a family dinner is a big step, you know."

"So, when I meet him, should I call him step-zhé'é?" I laugh.

My mom huffs and walks into the living room.

"Mom! It's an honest question. I don't know what to call him."

"Fine, I'm not inviting him. You won't have to call him anything."

"I could just call him snag-daddy."

She stops and turns to look at me with a horrified look. "Don't you dare, you little twerp!"

I get out of the chair. This is her last nerve. I choke out through my laughter, "Sorry! Sorry!"

"Get your ass over here!" She makes for me, but I keep the table between us.

"Don't unmake me!" I yell.

She reaches for me. There's a crazed look in her eyes, but her mouth is in a smile. We both missed messing with each other.

"I made you. I can do whatever I want with you!"

"Snag-daddy gets a say, too, you know!"

"That's it. I'm canceling your phone!"

Right for the jugular! "That's not fair!"

"It's either your phone or your life."

I consider both options. "I've lived a good life." I stay stationary and let her approach me.

She bonks the back of my head, softer than her disciplinary smacks. Then she wraps me in another hug. "I'll text him to see if he's available for Christmas."

"He make you happy?"

"So far, yes."

"That's all I care about."

We stand in the kitchen, holding each other. Our hearts pump loudly from running around the kitchen table. The warmth of the oven fills the entire kitchen. Each of us tries to get our fill of this moment.

After the pies cool and the two of us take showers, we make our way over to Grandma Rosie's in Fort. My mom lets me drive so I can practice for the driver's test I'll take next year during spring break.

As I navigate the nearly destroyed pavement of Black Rock Acres in my mom's car, she gets a text that she blocks from my side view with her hands.

"Who's that?" I bug her.

"Pay attention to the road!" she commands. Her thumbs loudly tap against her phone. Then, after a whoosh: "He says he already has plans with his kids for Christmas."

I don't sense any disappointment in her voice. But she does loudly exhale.

"Were you nervous?" I ask her.

"Yes." She puts her phone into her purse. "Maybe it was a little too soon for him to meet everyone."

"Probably better to hold off," I reassure her.

Minutes later, my mom and I walk into Grandma Rosie's kitchen. She's dicing up some vegetables that she will eventually toss into the big pot on the stove. I notice that there are slices of sheep neck already boiling, releasing all the delicious marrow into the broth.

"Need help, Mom?" my mom asks.

"Take over this here. I need to get the dough ready." Grandma Rosie hands my mom the paring knife. My mom then takes over peeling carrots.

After Grandma Rosie rinses off her hands, she measures flour, salt, and baking powder with various parts of her palm into a large aluminum bowl.

"What about me?" I ask.

"Set up the tables, will you, yáázh?"

"On it." I hurry to her garage and quickly find her white folding tables. I carry them into the living area and, before setting them up, begin pushing chairs around to make enough room for everyone to sit. I've been told that Grandpa Dominic, Másání Mildred, and Másání Gertrude are coming. Demi will video call us later. Some distant family members from Ganado said they'd stop by, but we don't know if they'll come for sure. I honestly have no idea how many people will arrive. I'll just set up as many places as I can and will adjust as lunch gets started.

"Mom," my mom says from the kitchen, "Derrick is going to ask Grandma Gertrude about the boarding school."

"What? You are?" Grandma Rosie says.

"What do you think about it?" I ask.

"We should honor your great-grandma's wish of doo 'ajínída'."

"He's going to ask her, Mom," my mom firmly says. Then, a little softer, "It would be good for that generation to let it out."

"Holding it all in isn't good for anyone," I add.

Grandma Rosie resists. "You shouldn't be exposing your heart to the entire world."

"But we have to have these talks about stuff like boarding schools," I argue. "Or else it'll be forgotten."

My mom stands by Grandma Rosie. "Mom."

"What?" Grandma Rosie grumpily responds.

"I know she told you 'Doo 'ajínída'' all the time. Look at what it has done to her. And look what holding all this negativity in has done to you."

"It's what women do," Grandma Rosie says loudly. She drops the large wad of dough. It lands in her bowl and creates a sound similar to a punch.

My mom crosses her arms. Making them fight is the last thing I wanted to do. To my surprise, my mom says, "We don't have to anymore."

Grandma Rosie is silent for a moment and then relents. "You can ask."

"We weren't asking for permission," my mom says. She must still be wound up. Grandma Rosie tenses.

This is how their arguing usually escalates; both want to have the last word. I step in quickly and say, "If Másání Gertrude says 'Doo 'ajínída',' I'll respect it."

Both look at me. Slowly, they nod in agreement.

"After lunch," Grandma Rosie says. "You can drive her back to Gallup, then."

"Deal," I say.

Two hours later, Thanksgiving lunch begins. Másání Mildred and Másání Gertrude sit next to each other. They both wear a rose-patterned scarf over their thin gray hair. That's about the only thing that signifies their relationship. Gertrude's cheeks are a little bigger and her eyebrows are a little thicker. Their noses also appear a bit different. Everything about them is slightly different.

I take my gaze off them and continue to wait for Grandma Rosie to finish her blessing over the food. Grandpa Dominic leans back in his chair. His dusty cowboy hat casts a dark shadow over his face. To my left sits my mom, who crosses her arms and stretches her neck.

For a moment, my mind wanders, and I imagine the Thanksgiving my white friends from Sagefield are having. Are they perpetuating the myth of Pilgrims and Indians?

A stack of fresh hot tortillas sits in the middle of the table. The stew rests on the stove, its delicious aroma filling the entire house.

Finally, after what feels like an hour, Grandma Rosie says "Hozhó Nahasdlį́į́" four times.

Grandpa Dominic pretends to snore. "Oh, what? You're done?"

Grandma Rosie playfully swats a dishcloth at his shoulder. "You eat last!"

"Let's go," my mom says to me.

We both stand up and begin to plate food for my two great-grandmas. As I head over to Másání Mildred and Másání Gertrude, Grandpa Dominic holds his hands out to me. "Are these both mine?"

Grandma Rosie says, "Get your own food."

I give the plates to them while my mom follows behind me with bowls of stew.

"Hey, I'm an Elder now. I'm supposed to be served," Grandpa Dominic jokes.

"Fine, since I'm older, you can serve me." Grandma Rosie sits down.

Grandpa Dominic chuckles and leans toward Másání Mildred. "Mom, remember when Rosie was served papers for speeding?"

Grandma Rosie shushes him. "Remember when I bailed you out of jail for public indecency?"

"Hey," Grandpa Dominic says, in a mocking serious voice. "It was the seventies."

"If I give you food, will you tell me about her getting served?" my mom asks Grandpa Dominic as she holds a plate of food in front of him.

"Deal," he says, grabbing at the plate. My mom sits next to him. "You doing okey dokey, shitsi?" he asks.

My mom nods as Grandpa Dominic wraps an arm around her. "Thank you for helping with your grandma."

Másání Mildred sips the broth and smiles. She asks me, "Did you cook all this, sha'awéé'?"

"Yup. Just me," I say.

"Bull crap," my mom says.

"Yáa!" Grandma Rosie shouts at my mom. "Don't use that language."

"Oh, you used to cuss, too!" Grandpa Dominic steps in. "Would make a sailor blush how much you would bad-mouth everything."

I feel the sides of my cheeks aching from smiling so much. There's laughter in the back of my throat. Good food and loving family have a way of soothing heartache.

The rest of the Thanksgiving lunch continues much in this way. I push away the thought that when I go back to Sagefield, meals like this will be another thing that I have to give up.

* * *

After lunch, my mom and I help Másání Gertrude walk toward my mom's car.

"You okay with driving me all the way to Gallup? I'm sure Dominic can drop me off," she tells my mom and me. She walks using her cane more as though to test the firmness of the ground as opposed to fully leaning on it. Despite being only two years younger than Másání Mildred, Gertrude has way more mobility and stability. It's a surprise that Gertrude doesn't have as many health concerns as Mildred.

"It's fine, Auntie," my mom answers. She uses her keys to unlock the doors to her car.

"I'll sit in back," I offer them.

"Thank you, shiyáázh," Másání Gertrude says.

Ten minutes later, we are on the main road out of Fort Defiance, heading toward Window Rock. It will take about forty minutes to get to her house.

"Hey, Másání?" I begin.

My mom lowers the radio.

"I was wondering if you could talk to me about Másání Mildred."

"What about?" she asks. I hear apprehension in her voice.

I don't know if I should mention the essay just yet. This information is bigger than my paper and my grades. It's family history. "I was curious about when both of you were young. She was in a boarding school, and I'm assuming it was Chinle."

"Yes. It was Chinle. We both went. Against our will," she says.

"I'm sorry to bring it up. Are you okay talking about it?" I ask. I have to be gentle and respectful as it may be too painful for her.

"It's okay if you don't want to talk about it," my mom offers. She turns on the headlights. The sun lowers behind the western horizon, and the deep red colors of sunset turn to the early night colors of purple.

"I'm not sure how much I can tell, but I will," she says.

"Thank you," I say, trying to hold in my excitement. Through sheer will, I keep myself calm. "First things first. I'm writing an essay for my history class. May I reference you as a resource?"

She folds her arms across her chest. "Change my name."

I quickly open my recording app and say, "I can do that. Uh, first question." I pause. I realize how blunt these questions are. I try to think of ways to ask them tactfully. "Where did you grow up?"

"We all grew up in T'iis Yázhí, between Sawmill and Nazlini in the mountains. Way back where the power lines are these days. Mildred came to live with us after her parents died."

"What year was this?"

Her eyebrows scrunch, and she squeezes her eyes. "I don't know for sure. I was told she came to live with us around the first thunderstorm after winter. So could be anywhere from March to April. I must have been about five when she arrived."

"How did you both end up at Chinle Boarding School?" I ask now that we are a little warmed up.

"I volunteered to go at first. I wanted to learn to read."

"Really?" This completely shocks me.

"'Aoo'. Our family at the time, there were three of us kids. The oldest, Parker, was going to become a medicine man and was sent to work with one. The second, Mildred, was supposed to stay home and help with the sheep and learn to weave. They told me that I could choose what I wanted to do. Around that time, there were soldiers riding about, telling their parents that they needed to send their children to school 'éí biniinaa the treaty agreements.

"One day, some soldiers came to our hogan and saw me, my mom, and my dad. Parker was out helping a hataałii with a ceremony and Mildred was herding sheep. So they thought it was only me. I almost went with them right then and there, but they said school was starting in a week and that I should report then."

"Did you know what they were doing at the boarding school?" I ask her. I can't believe that she wanted to go.

"There were rumors. That's about all we heard. News and rumors spread slowly, much slower than today. But our grandparents, our parents, feared breaking the treaty. If we didn't honor it and send our children to school, the US could say we broke the treaty and would be able to relocate us again to Hwéeldi. That was the mindset of my parents. So I volunteered and told everyone I wanted to go."

I am absorbed by what she is saying. Fear of breaking the treaty contracts! In all my research, this wasn't a reason that was mentioned why parents sent their kids to boarding schools. I already know that I want to quote this part of her interview.

She keeps talking. "Mildred walked with me to the school. That was a mistake. We thought it was just going to be me, like one child from one family would be enough. So when Mildred and I showed up, they also took her."

"Did they cut your hair?"

"Yes. But it wasn't violent like other boarding schools I've heard about. As long as you didn't resist, it was quick. One of the first girls I remember screaming and crying. The scissors snipped off a tip of her left ear. The rest of us remained calm and didn't resist.

"We learned quickly that punishment was cruel and painful. We weren't allowed to speak to each other unless it was in English. We were forced to pray to their god. But most of us were still praying to Diyin Dine'é in our hearts."

I take this moment to say, "I've read that a lot of Native kids resisted indoctrination with little things like praying to their tribal Nation's deities instead of the biblical God."

"We were survivors. We were forbidden to speak our language, to practice our beliefs, but we still did. Sometimes we got caught and were punished. But we got smarter and found ways to do it without getting caught. That's one thing I don't like about how white people talk about that era. It's always 'Poor Native children were abused.' White guilt. But we are tough. We found ways to be ourselves despite their efforts. White people glorify our abuse and ignore our resourcefulness and our will to survive those conditions."

"Actually, Másání Mildred says that you guys performed a kinaaldá after she had her first period."

Másání Gertrude rubs her temples. She's trying to remember details. "It was dangerous, but worth it. A lot of us females had our first cycle in boarding schools. Man, those religious jerks would beat us senseless and tell us that it was Eve's first sin. That's another thing, all their Bible teachings, I've completely forgotten them. But the traditional teachings survived.

"So, Mildred's kinaaldá. When a young girl has her first period, it's a celebratory event. It's sacred. And you're supposed to have a kinaaldá before the next full moon."

I know that much. My older sister, Demi, had her kinaaldá at Másání Mildred's hogan. She stretched me and blessed my brains, saying that I was going to grow up tall and smart.

"We weren't allowed to perform that in the boarding school. But there were two older girls with us. We all had the same clan. In that way, we were sisters. Anyway, the oldest of us was Zelda. She had attended and helped with many kinaaldá before boarding school. So she knew some of the songs and the general structure. During the day, we would sneak and gather materials. I got some corn kernels, and Berta, the other older girl, she got two rocks that Mildred could use to grind them. For gifts, in normal kinaaldá, you're supposed to gift blankets and fabrics. But in the boarding school, Mildred cut pieces of her school uniform and gave them as gifts. Little things like that. Little gestures that represented what happens in real kinaaldá.

"Then, one night, a bunch of us waited for the nuns to fall asleep. It was late, and Zelda sang what she knew while Berta tied Mildred's hair, or what remained of her hair anyway. Instead of stretching us to grow tall, Mildred squeezed our muscles so that we would grow strong enough to run away from that place. We knew the risks. We knew it was dangerous. But we wanted to hear those songs. We missed them and our families, too. But like how our ancestors at Hwéeldi forged new families, we, too, forged sisterhood through the clan system."

I'm simply amazed beyond words at this. They were kids, but

they possessed a bravery I'll never know. "That's . . . I can't think of a word."

Másání Gertrude continues, "We heard that the school was going to reduce its student population because it was too expensive. Most of us were going to be transferred to Phoenix. Some of the more challenging girls, like Zelda, were going to be sent to Pennsylvania. But we all knew that once we were transferred, we weren't going to see our families for years. So we waited and waited. All four of us listened patiently for any opportunity. Then it happened. There were rows of wagons that came to pick us up to take us to the different schools. But those wagons already had kids in them. There was some confusion. The soldiers thought they were dropping off some of the kids there. While they discussed it with the nuns, the four of us knew it was our only opportunity, and we snuck away.

"Berta knew Canyon de Chelly pretty well because it was one of her sheep-herding routes. She navigated the canyons and led us to caves when we thought soldiers were catching up with us. It took us a few days. We were always brushing our footprints with yucca leaves. Then Mildred and I returned to my parents. They were happy. We told them what happened while they cooked to feed all four of us. And after a few days of rest, Zelda and Berta took off to their own families."

I ask her, "Do you know what happened to Zelda and Berta?"

"I don't know. I never heard from them again. I hope they made it back."

"'Ahxéhee', shimásání, for all this information."

"No problem at all, shiyáázh," she says. She turns to my mom and says, "Now you know where you get your headstrong, no-nonsense attitude. A long line of warrior women. Including your mom."

My mom sniffles. "She's a tough person to have as a mom."

"Now that you're a parent, you know how difficult it is to raise strong kids. You punish them too much? Not enough? You don't know. You always regret yelling too loudly at them. You hurt when you don't hold them when they are crying, because they have to be tough in this world."

My mom wipes away a tear.

Másání Gertrude holds my mom's hand. "You do these things because you love your babies."

I know that Grandma Rosie was tough on my mom. Extra tough when she was barely out of high school and got pregnant. I turn off my recording app.

I think of all the times my mom yelled at me. When she told me she couldn't afford things, even though we could have asked Grandma Rosie for help. I think of all the times she punished me by taking away my phone, forbidding me from seeing friends. There are small scars on my mom's left shoulder from a whipping branch that she tries to hide. I've never asked about it because Demi told me not to. But hearing this last part, of how Grandma Rosie was a tough mother to grow up with, all I can focus on are those discolored lines on her left shoulder.

22

Nida'iiníísh, Níłch'ih Ts'ósí 29

Friday, November 29

I mix the spackle and apply it evenly across the hole in Másání Mildred's wall the evening I stay with her. Másání Mildred is in the kitchen using her microwave to warm up leftovers from yesterday's lunch for dinner. She's very happy I'm staying the night.

"Are you excited about the surgery?" I ask her.

"I am. It'll get rid of the dizzies that I have in the mornings," she answers.

"You've been taking your medications, right?" I ask her. "They're also supposed to help."

"I do. But sometimes I want to eat first."

The directions on her pill container say that her medicines have to be taken on an empty stomach. "Grandma, you have to be sure to take your medication the way it says on the bottle. Your heart is stronger because of it."

"Okay," she says.

"This is why you should stay with Grandma Rosie; she can monitor your medication and food intake."

"I'm happy you're here, sha'awéé'." She rubs my knuckle with her wrinkled palm. She eats in front of her heater, listening to the radio. After she finishes, we watch some episodes of *Golden Girls* until 8:30.

Then she says, "Help me to my bed, sha'awéé'."

I stand up and push her wheelchair to her room toward the back. In her room, there is a table covered with crossword books and boxes of jigsaw puzzles. I make a mental note to look for puzzles in Connecticut for her.

I act as an anchor for her to lie down on her bed. She's yawning. There's an oxygen machine on the floor next to the front of the bed. I grab the plastic tubing and help her put it around her neck and into her nostrils. I quickly check to make sure that there is water in the machine. It's full. I turn it on, and it hums to life.

"I'm sorry I don't stay up late." She looks into my eyes. Her own droop. She's falling asleep fast.

"Don't worry about me. I need to do some schoolwork," I assure her.

"Thank you for spending the night with me," she chokes out. "No one visits me anymore."

My heart and throat constrict. I hate the idea of her being all alone out here. It's a very volatile situation. If she trips, that could be it.

"I'm here, Másání," I tell her. I lean in and kiss her forehead as she slips into a peaceful sleep. I turn around to walk out of her room and notice a picture of the two of us on the back of her door. It was taken when I was probably three or four. She was using a cane at that time. We are holding hands. She has a huge smile, and I look entranced by her cane. This is the first thing she sees in the morning. I'm the first person she sees every day. I walk out and gently close the door behind me.

23

Dimóo yázhí, Níłch'ih Ts'ósí 30

Saturday, November 30

The next morning around six, I sit in the living room, typing out the conversation I had in the car with Másání Gertrude. Eventually, I have to mention to Másání Mildred that I heard about her past from her younger sister. It doesn't sit well with me to treat this like some embarrassing secret.

I have a lot to do today. After Grandma Rosie picks me up, I need to start packing because I go back to Sagefield tomorrow. I wish I had done more at home. I wanted to check in with Jayden, but I just got so busy. I'm not even near where I need to be on my assigned readings and homework. Damn, I didn't even start on my five-page essay for history!

I knead the growing knot in my lower back. I didn't have a great time sleeping in the living room. The sofa cushions kept caving in on themselves. When I awoke at five, I couldn't go back to sleep, so I decided to build a fire for Másání Mildred.

In this quiet hour, I hear her stirring in her bedroom. There's some scuffling that's slightly louder than the crackling of the fire. She probably could use some help. I put my laptop on the sofa cushion next to me and make my way to her room.

It's still dark but in the predawn, I'm able to navigate to her bedroom with some ease. When I open the door, I gasp at what I see.

Másání Mildred is standing in the middle of the room in just her nightgown, with no wheelchair, no cane, staring out her window. The curtains are wide open, and it looks like she's looking for something. Even at this distance, I'm chilled by the cold air. She must be freezing!

"Come back, shahastiin," she says. "Don't leave me."

I rush to her side and gently touch her bony shoulders. "Másání, come. Sit down, please." I squeeze her hand, and she looks at me.

"Jerome?"

It's that name again! I force myself to focus on making sure she doesn't fall. As calmly as I can, I say, "Másání, it's me, Derrick. Come sit down; you shouldn't be standing like this."

"Jerome," Másání Mildred says to me again. Her body sways back and forth. There are some blunt edges near her, like her dresser and the desk with her puzzle. If she were to fall, she could break something. "Why? Why did you let her do that?"

I calmly pull her wheelchair behind her and gently lower her down. After she is secured, I quickly grab a blanket and wrap her in it. I place my hand on her cheek, and it's like touching the inside of a refrigerator.

"What did I do?" I ask her. I mainly want her to keep talking and snap out of whatever trance she is in. But I can't ignore the name Jerome. Is this a real person?

It takes me a few seconds to remember that Másání Mildred's health is far more important than figuring out who Jerome is. Her medication! She's having a dizzy spell. She needs her pills. I carefully wheel her to the living room to place her in front of the fire. "Please sit here, Másání."

I rush to the kitchen and grab the medication that Grandma Rosie organizes for her every Sunday. Then I realize that the previous day's medicine is still there. She hasn't taken her medication for two days!

I return to her with her pills and a glass of water. "Drink this, Másání. Please."

She's crying. "Why didn't she want me? I did everything she asked."

"Másání, please take your medicine. You'll feel better."

"Jerome. How did you find me?"

I decide to play along. "I found you, remember? So that I could tell you to take your medicine."

"You found me? No. You didn't know I survived."

I'm totally dumbstruck by this. I can't help but ask, "What do you mean?"

She doesn't answer.

"I'm sorry, Mildred," I tell her. Hopefully, if she thinks I'm Jerome, my apologizing to her might give her peace and comfort. "Take these pills. You'll feel better."

She looks at them as I place them in her palm.

"Medicine?"

"For your heart."

"No," she says, tossing them to the floor.

"Mildred!" I nearly shout. I drop to the floor and quickly pick them up.

"I don't need pills!" Her voice has changed. Even her expression has changed. She is no longer the scared woman who was confessing. She's now enraged.

After I gather the last pill, I grab her landline phone and call Grandma Rosie.

"Yes," Grandma Rosie answers after the first ring.

"Grandma," I say, some fear slipping through my voice. "Get here quick. Másání Mildred is having a dizzy spell."

"Watch over her. I just passed Dajizį́į́." She hangs up.

My muscles relax slightly, knowing that Grandma Rosie is a few minutes away. The pills rattle in my palm. I have no idea how to get her to take her medication.

I slowly approach her. She's staring into the fire. Fresh tears collect at the corners of her eyes. "Másání, it's me. Your great-grandson Derrick."

"Derrick?" she questions, staring at me.

"It's me. You need to take your pills," I remind her. I show them to her in my palm.

She shakes her head. Then she rubs her eyes. When she looks at me, I see that face from earlier. She's back in her memories. "Jerome."

"Mildred." I resume the role again. "Please, take your pills. They are for your heart."

"My heart? Yes. My heart. That surgery."

"Yes, you're going to have the surgery for your heart," I say to ground her in the present.

"How do you know about my heart, Jerome? Who told you?" she asks.

I desperately think of ways to respond. But I'm coming up zero. "You told me. Remember? You found me."

"I never went back to Kaibeto," she discloses.

"For me, you did," I say to her. She seems to accept that. I sense that she still has some love for this Jerome. Kaibeto. I have to remember that. "Now, please, take these pills. They'll help you." If I say it enough, maybe I'll reach her.

She grabs them and holds them in her palm. All she needs to do is swallow them. "Take them with this." I hand her the cup of water.

She stares at the pills and the water. There's a hint of recognition. Like her body knows and remembers what to do. But her mind struggles to understand what is happening and why she's doing it. She's almost there.

The picture! I quietly walk to her room so as not to startle her. I gently pull the picture of the two of us off the door. Then I hold it in front of her eyes. "This is me, remember? I'm Derrick."

She examines it. "That's me. And that's Derrick."

"That's me," I tell her.

"He looks just like you, Jerome," she says, still locked in her confusion. "One of the reasons he's my favorite."

Just then, Grandma Rosie rushes inside. "Mom!" Grandma Rosie scans the situation and immediately says, "Mom, your pills."

"Rosie?" Másání Mildred is confused again.

"Your pills, Mom," Grandma Rosie repeats. She grabs Másání Mildred's hand and gently places it in front of her eyes. "Right here."

"Oh, right. Medicine." Másání Mildred puts one pill at a time in her mouth and swallows them individually with sips of water.

My heart rate slows. My fear retreats. Grandma Rosie sees the terror in my eyes.

A dense cloud of static envelops my head and rushes through my nerves. I sit down. Jerome. Kaibeto. I can't help but think that there's more to her story. I know for sure that she's hiding something.

An hour later, Grandma Rosie and I sit in the kitchen while Másání Mildred is in the bathroom. I told her everything that happened.

"There could really be a Jerome?" she questions. She's utterly shocked and confused.

"If there is, he might be in Kaibeto," I confirm.

She shakes her head. "One thing at a time, shiyáázh. I'm sorry that you had to see what you saw. It isn't the first time I've caught her in a spell. But the way you're describing it makes it sound like she's getting worse."

The toilet flushes. Grandma Rosie stands up and helps wheel Másání Mildred to the kitchen table. She ravenously eats the blue corn mush that I warmed up for her.

"Mom," Grandma Rosie starts. "You're moving in with me. I'm going to bring Derrick back down with me to help me set up a bedroom for you at my house."

"No, I'm staying here," she says.

"You're going," Grandma Rosie interjects. "Staying here all by yourself is dangerous! If I have to physically lift you into my car I will."

Másání Mildred doesn't look happy to hear this. "This is my home. You can't just take me away from here."

"She's right, Grandma Rosie," I say to her. "She was taken from her home before, when she was young."

Grandma Rosie doesn't respond.

I turn to Másání Mildred and plead, "But you can't stay here by yourself, Másání." I just release all the fear that has accumulated in my spirit. From hearing that I only have a few months left with her. From hearing that she's dreaming of ancestors. I'm very near tears but hold myself together to be strong for the two of them. "I want to see you when I return from school for the Christmas break. I want you to be here for many more months. If you stay in your home, I don't know how long you'll live."

"Doo 'ajínída'!" Másání Mildred commands.

"Not for this," I say to her. "Not when your life is on the line. I love you, Másání. I know it's going to hurt not living in your old home." I remember my first few weeks at Sagefield. "I know the homesickness can feel suffocating at times, but you'll get through it. You'll have a new home with Grandma Rosie. You won't be lonely. You'll be with family."

Something I say gets through. She pats my hand. "Fine."

I hug her. I pray and wish and hope and yearn and want and need and beg that this isn't the last time I hug Másání Mildred.

24

Dimóo, Níłch'ih Tsoh 1
Sunday, December 1

I sit in one of the food courts at Dallas Fort Worth International Airport. Everything is so expensive at airports! Still, I permit myself to splurge a little for lunch on my layover.

There's this fancy burger joint called Shake Shack. It's all right. The only complaint I have is the price. I overheard from some students at Sagefield that they had the best burgers in the world, and no, they do not. That's-A-Burger does.

I unlock my phone and start a video chat with Chris. After a few rings, he answers. But he doesn't have his video on.

"Sup," he says. I sense some tension in his voice.

"How's it going, man?" I ask after swallowing a bite of my burger.

"What you need?"

He's not happy. Something's up. "You okay?"

He sighs. "Yeah. Just a bit tired. Did a late shift last night."

"Dude, check this out. Everyone at Sagefield says these are the best burgers in the world." I show him the thick slab of beef patty and fresh condiments.

"That's nice."

"For serious, That's-A-Burger is so much better."

"Cool."

"Yo, what is going on?" I'm not going to ignore that he's got attitude.

"Told you. Tired."

The last time I tried to pry information from him while he had this attitude, he became a jerk. This is something that will probably go away if I leave it alone. "All right. Just thought I'd share this with you."

"Where you at, anyway?" He seems to want to meet me halfway by changing the subject.

"At the airport in Dallas."

"You're in Texas?" His voice raises with excitement.

"It's only a layover." I play it down. Though I am hyped to be traveling on my own.

"Yo, show me the outside," he says.

"Mind if I send you a picture? I don't want to leave my table. Took me twenty minutes to get this one."

"That works," he says.

I want to thank him for being my friend. From what he told me, everyone we knew at Navajo Pine is changing. I'm grateful that he and I still are buddies. I start, "Hey, man. I just wanted to say—"

Before I can continue, he jumps in. "Yo, I gotta get ready for my shift."

"All right, I'll let you go," I say.

He doesn't say goodbye and leaves the conversation.

I shrug off his attitude. If something is wrong, he should just come out and say whatever is on his mind. I haven't done anything. I breathe and let my annoyance with him dim. He's my best friend. He probably has something else going on. I can check in on him later. He'll tell me then what's going on.

I send a quick text to Jayden. Hey man, I heard about Starletta. I'm so sorry. I'm here for you. I hope he responds.

I finish eating my lunch and make my way through the airport. There are so many different types of travelers. There are the businesspeople who are wearing fancy clothes and more comfortable travelers who wear sweats and flip-flops.

I need to find a window to take a picture for Chris. I got time to kill. My boarding time is in an hour, and my flight from Dallas to Bradley is going to be about four hours long.

The straps of my duffel bag dig into my shoulder, so I switch it to the other side. I was hoping that Chris would have wanted to talk a little longer. Despite being among all these people, I feel isolated. I wanted him to take my mind off Másání Mildred. I didn't want to think about the fact that I will have about a week of classes and the hardest part of the semester will start very soon—finals.

There are some flight attendants walking as a group in the direction opposite from me. Behind them, a vehicle carries three elderly people. It honks to get the flight attendants' attention.

I should have written more of my five-page history essay and done more work on the final essay. I should have studied some

Latin. There were so many things I could have done to get ahead of the schoolwork. But I had to help Másání Mildred. I wanted to spend time with her. Because I don't know if I'll see her after the surgery.

I gently squeeze my tongue with my teeth until a tinge of pain distracts me from my sadness. It only works for a second, and my dread wells right up.

I don't have anyone else to call.

I'm just here. Among strangers. I am sure as hell not going to cry among them. They'll think I'm a wimp.

I find a wide pane of glass that shows the open skies of Texas. Outside it's seventy degrees Fahrenheit. In Connecticut, it's currently in the mid-twenties. And we are due to get our first snowfall soon. So there's that to look forward to.

I look just like Jerome.

I open my camera app and take a few pictures.

I send them to Chris and anxiously wait for him to respond. I see the read receipt and nothing more.

Jerome thought Másání Mildred died.

Jerome could be in Kaibeto.

When I return to campus on the charter bus from the airport, I'm surprised I'm excited to be here. Did I miss Sagefield? Maybe not Sagefield itself, but my friends, my room?

I'm no longer a stranger here, and that's strange as hell. I open the door to my room and happiness erupts in me when I see my space. It feels safe. I can process all the emotions I was shoving down, all the fear for Másání Mildred, all my heartbreak for Jayden. I drop my luggage on the floor and flop onto my bed. I press my face into my pillows and release everything.

I didn't want to cry in front of my mom. It was hard enough holding it together when I told Másání Mildred that I wanted her to move in with Grandma Rosie. As the only male there, sometimes I feel like I have to be the rock. The source of stability.

"Derrick, you back?" I hear Caleb from the other side of my door.

Damn! I left the light on. "I'm here."

"My mom wanted me to give this to you." He turns the knob and walks in. And of course I didn't lock the door.

It's too late for me to do anything. I sit upright on my bed. I do my best to dry my tears and wipe snot from under my nose.

"Derrick?" Caleb says, looking at me as he enters.

I focus on my breath, trying to get it steady. But the look he has for me. It's like he's seeing me being weak, and I hate it. But I'm tired of fighting these emotions.

He closes the door behind him with his hip. He has a medium-sized box that he places on the floor, and then he sits next to me. "Hey."

"Stop," I command.

He raises his hands and asks, "You okay?"

"Yes," I nearly shout. "Everything's perfect!"

I stand and look anywhere but at his eyes. I want Chris and Jayden to be here. I would have told them everything, but things have changed so much. Only when my neck aches do I realize that my head is drooping. I squeeze my eyes shut. It's the only way to prevent them from tearing up.

I feel Caleb stand next to me and wrap an arm around my shoulder. "Hey."

That breaks me. Everything rushes out of me in a long wail. Snot leaks onto his shoulder. I manage to say to him, "My great-grandma is dying, and I can't do anything about it!"

"That sucks," Caleb says.

I push out of his hug and sit on my bed. He pulls the chair from my desk and sits near me.

I pour my heart out to Caleb. I feel a whole range of emotions: angry at Chris, terrified for Jayden, sad about my remaining time with Másání Mildred, scared that she will leave us, happy my mom is dating again, pissed off that I didn't get any schoolwork done. By the time I finish telling him everything, his eyes are wide. I'm not sure he can handle what I just told him. But my lungs feel clearer, my head less clouded. My sobs aren't causing my entire body to shake. I see a dried glob of snot on his shoulder. "Sorry about your shirt."

"Don't worry about it," he says. He looks like he's searching for something to say.

"You don't have to say anything," I tell him. "I just needed to vent."

"I had no idea you were going through all that," Caleb finally says.

"I don't know if I'll see my great-grandma again."

"I'm sure you will. You helped her move back into your

grandma's house. That'll ensure that she won't—what's the word?—endanger herself. She's in a safer space."

No one said that to me. No one acknowledged me for helping move Másání Mildred. I wasn't doing it for the attention or gratitude. But no one thanked me. Not even Grandma Rosie. I hate that I'm selfish enough to be bothered by that fact.

"Dude, you're carrying so much."

That sends an ache throughout my nervous system, from the base of my skull to the ends of my toes. I still need to finish my translation of this contemporary story that was written entirely in Latin. I haven't even started on my geometry. Physics I was able to finish, but I need to review it. For history, that stupid five-pager! My head aches. "I should get started on work . . ."

"No, man. What we're going to do is hang out and watch something funny."

"What are you talking about?"

"The homework is always going to be there. And you are, like, the hardest-working person I've ever met. You're always pushing and driving yourself. You hardly ever relax. You need to find some time to just breathe. And from the sounds of it, you didn't get much over the break."

"If I don't get good grades, I'll get kicked out."

"It's hard to get kicked out of here. You'd have to be a complete idiot and actively try to fail. Or do something stupid like get caught selling drugs."

Selling drugs. Harris and Mancini. They offered me something stronger than coffee. I can relax tonight and then tomorrow get caught up with the work I didn't do. I might need that extra help. I know it's wrong, but I'm desperate.

"Sure," I say. I ignore the churning in my gut that erupted when I thought about getting "extra help." Tonight, though, I'm just going to decompress. I doubt I'd even be able to study.

"Mind coming to my room? I have all the streaming accounts on my computer. Oh, my mom sent you a care package."

"What's that?"

"You don't know what they are? Wait, so you haven't gotten one? They're, like, just a big box of snacks and treats. She even sent one for Xavier. I have mine in my room that we can open. Should I invite Xavier over if he's back?"

I'm not in the mood to be around anyone other than Caleb. "Nothing against him, but I'm still feeling raw."

"Understood. Come on."

In his room, Caleb pulls up his streaming account on his thirty-two-inch OLED monitor while I sit in his wicker chair. And geez. If I ever get rich, this is going to be the first thing I buy.

Caleb pulls up an adult animated show. We spend the rest of the night laughing our butts off. I allow myself to fully enjoy this time because I'm going to work extra hard tomorrow. I can do this. Tonight, I need to decompress. If I have to, I can use the cheat sheets. At this point, I don't care if I cross that line. I just want to get through finals. I just want to finish my papers and be back home.

25

Dimóo biiskání, Nílch'ih Tsoh 2

Monday, December 2

I walk into my history class and sit down next to Ife. She holds a small dictionary in front of her. She's not fully fluent in English and will occasionally flip through her dictionary when she hears an unfamiliar word. I don't think I'd be able to go to another country, whose language I'm not fluent in, and take a class as hard as this.

I take a swig of coffee from my bottle. I was counting on lowering my tolerance level by not drinking coffee over the break. But it barely did a thing. I still need to drink a huge amount just for it to work. I even had to place another order for powdered coffee.

"Good morning, Derrick," Ife says, breaking me out of my thoughts.

"Hi, Ife. Did you have a good break?" I ask her.

"It was amicable. I mean adequate. I stayed on campus with a teacher and just slept a whole lot."

"I'm so jealous that you were able to sleep a whole lot," I say to her. I still feel raw emotionally. Better because I talked with Caleb but still exhausted.

"I'm jealous of past me, too," she says with a bright smile. "I read a bit forward in the syllabus."

Just then, James hustles in with a few other classmates. They settle down.

"Nice," I say, a little annoyed that I didn't get a chance to read ahead.

"How do you feel about the Trail of Tears?" she asks, catching me off guard.

"The Trail of Tears?" I say in a questioning voice to figure out how she wants me to respond.

"The forced relocation of so many Indigenous Nations."

"I know that part."

"Then how do you as a Diné person feel about that?" she asks me.

"Yeah, how do you feel?" James asks me.

I blurt out, "It's a genocide that isn't recognized."

"No, I mean, but like, what's your family story?" James asks me. All the other students look at me. The room grows quiet.

"What do you mean my family story?" I grow angry. What is he implying?

"Weren't your ancestors on the Trail of Tears?" Brandon asks.

"No," I hotly respond. Yeah. They think that Diné people were on the Trail of Tears.

"So, did they like hide? What did they do during the Trail of Tears?" James presses.

I sigh. I'm not in the mood to teach, as Bryan would say. But this is something I can't overlook. I summon as much patience as I can. "The Trail of Tears wasn't the only forced genocidal relocation. For my people, the Diné, we were forced out of the boundaries of the four sacred mountains on the Long Walk. And it wasn't like the Native people of the relocation era were simply bullied to leave. They were starved and murdered along with countless other inhumane atrocities." I stop because I don't want to get any angrier.

Ife takes out her iPad and quickly scribbles a note on it.

"Wait, there was more than one relocation?" James asks.

"Yes," I say.

"I didn't know that there was more than one," Ife says. "I'm so sorry. It just seems so horrible."

Brandon then says, "But the history book doesn't mention anything about murders and starvation."

Thankfully, Mr. Henderson walks into the room and sits at the oval table. He pulls out his laptop. Then he looks at me. "Mr. Hoskie. Mr. Williams. Ms. Fern. You three didn't email me your paper."

"I forgot," I say. Cold beads of sweat collect on the sides of my face. I was so caught up in Másání Mildred's condition. I am so pissed at myself. My cheeks turn cold while my forehead burns with resentment toward myself. "I'll email you tonight."

"I will have to deduct a few points," he says to the three of us. I'm more disappointed in myself than his tone conveys. "Email me by midnight tonight. After that, you'll have to accept a ten-point deduction each day your paper is late. Now that that's out of the way . . ." Mr. Henderson opens his laptop and adjusts his glasses. "Western expansion will be the topic of this week. Does anyone know what Manifest Destiny is?"

I want to say it's a lie that caused massive genocide across the continent.

Ife raises her hand.

"Ms. Achebe, you will have to allow your peers to answer from time to time," Mr. Henderson says. Does he ever smile?

I raise my hand. He points at me. "Good. Go right ahead, Mr. Hoskie."

I do my best to be calm and say, "Manifest Destiny is the belief that the United States was ordained by the biblical God to expand toward the western coast of North America. It is through that belief that they were able to justify the forced relocations and genocide of the Indigenous Nations."

There. I said it. Genocide.

"Exactly," Mr. Henderson says. I wasn't expecting that. I thought he was going to push back against my use of the word *genocide*. "Manifest Destiny is a belief. It's not a fact, though at the time it was treated as a fact. What other factors feed into Manifest Destiny being treated as fact?"

"Race," I contribute.

"Good," Mr. Henderson says. "Elaborate."

I take a deep breath and say, "Manifest Destiny applied largely to white males."

Mr. Henderson says, "I'd say it applied only to white males. And unfortunately, the Indigenous populations suffered for this mindset."

"Indigenous Nations," I correct him. He leans forward like he wants me to continue talking. Speaking up when you're the only Native student in class takes a lot of bravery and energy. "If you say 'Indigenous *populations*,' you neglect to acknowledge that we had our own forms of government, commerce, trade, and stewardship of land."

He smiles at me. "Very good, Mr. Hoskie. Excuse my previous error. Indigenous *Nations* suffered for this mindset." He searches for another quiet student to request to speak. It may be the last week of this semester, but I think I finally figured him out. He doesn't pick on students. He challenges us. He expects us to work hard. And that is something I can totally respect.

By the time I get to the dining hall for dinner, I take only seven minutes to grab food that I'll eat back in my dorm room. I need to finish that history paper. So I quickly squish cheesy pastries, chicken breast, and some fruit into a large wad of napkins and shove everything into my backpack. When I have enough food, I rush out to the soda fountain and fill my bottle.

After I close my bottle, I spot Mancini sitting in a far corner of the dining hall. He waves at me. Before I realize what is happening, my feet are already walking toward him. I smell a whiff of cedar and ignore it. It feels like my heart and mind have split. I dread the steps I'm taking but am powerless to turn around.

"Sup, Mancini?" I say to him.

"Hoskie," he says, and we do a bro handshake. "How's it going in wrestling? Love manhandling other guys?"

I ignore his homophobic remark. Do a "your mom" joke and it'll be cool. "Your mom puts up less of a fight."

Mancini laughs. "Always about moms, this guy!"

"Hey," I start. I can't stop myself from saying the rest. "I was wondering about procuring some extra help."

"Oh yeah?" Mancini says. He pulls out the chair next to him.

The words flow out of my throat like fire racing across oil. "I'm pulling an all-nighter. I have to write a five-page history paper by midnight. And I got all this other work that needs to get done."

Mancini responds, "Listen. We've all been in your position. That's why we got to do everything we can to graduate, right?"

"It feels like that," I say. Just hearing that he understands my position cools my freak-out a bit.

"I got your back," Mancini says. He reaches into his pocket and then drops the tiniest of things into my palm. "Here." Before I can look at what he placed in my palm, he closes my hand. "Be smooth, Hoskie. Don't show the entire dining hall."

It's a pill. I covertly slip it into my pocket. "I got you."

"That's ten milligrams of Vyvanse. You can take it all, but I think for you, being your first time, you shouldn't. It's pretty strong stuff for the uninitiated. Instead, open the pill and pour all the powder into your bottle there. Sip on it throughout the night. You'll get your work done. Easy."

"How much do I owe you?" I ask him.

"Don't worry about it."

My body tenses up. There's a catch. There always is. But I'm not in a position to say no. "I really, really appreciate this."

"I got your back, Hoskie," Mancini says.

"I should get going," I say. "You know, got that essay."

"Get on top of homework, homie. Like me on your mom."

I snort. "Got me at my own game."

I leave the dining hall and walk outside into the cold. When I'm sure no one can see what I'm doing, I examine the pill he gave me. It looks so ordinary. It's white. Its exterior feels like plastic. *Vyvanse* is written in bright blue letters on it.

This feels wrong. I know I shouldn't be doing this. I'll do it just once. Only this once.

After Mandatory Study Hall, I open my bottle filled with the soda that has gone flat. I hold the Vyvanse pill in between my fingers. This is my first time. I should do what he told me. I twist the pill in my fingers, pull apart the plastic portions, and pour the powder into my soda. For good measure, I toss in the plastic coverings and then close the lid to shake up my drink.

I take a large swig. That should be it for now. I place my bottle aside and look at the cheat sheet folder. No. History paper first. I locate the assignment on my syllabus. I read the essay topic: *Describe in detail how Northern Mexico (current-day Arizona, New Mexico, Utah, Nevada, and Colorado) as well as California came to be a part of the United States. Include dates and significant events. Be expansive.*

Half an hour later, the medicine starts to work. My fingers fly across my keyboard. Words flow out of my mind, through my hands, and onto the Word document like a rushing torrent. Everything I'm writing down has this amazing quality. Like, I'm making some really solid and valid points. My head is so clear and focused that it takes me only one hour to type out a first draft. I just need a little bit of time to tighten up the sentences and work on some typos. For extra measure, I double-check my resources. And when midnight is five minutes away, I click send on my assignment. Now on to the rest of the work. I've never been this excited to do homework!

26

Dimóo dóó naakijį̨́, Níłch'ih Tsoh 3

Tuesday, December 3

I take another swig of my Vyvanse-laced cola around 12:40 a.m.

All right, time for some English. I open my copy of *Bless Me, Ultima* by Rudolfo Anaya. The paragraphs and sentences fly by my eyes. This story is so great. It's, like, the closest thing I've ever read to Diné culture. It takes place in New Mexico and is about a young boy named Antonio who is studying to become a curandera underneath Ultima. There are some crazy similarities to Diné culture, too. I highlight passages so that it feels like I'm absorbing the information. Done with the reading assignment, I create a Word document to write down my thoughts, which continue to rush out of my head like a river. This is amazing. I'm making so much progress.

Whoa, it's two in the morning, and for the first time, I'm feeling the sting of tiredness in the back of my eyes and the hollowness of yawning in the back of my throat. I drink the last bits of my Vyvanse cola and push through some physics and geometry homework.

When four in the morning rolls around, I crawl into my bed feeling super accomplished. I have done all my homework and have even gotten ahead in studying for my Latin exams. I should have asked for help earlier, I think. After wrestling practice, I'm going to hit up Harris and Mancini. I close my eyes ready to go to sleep. But the loud thumping of my heart keeps me awake a little while longer.

I wake up a little later and can't go back to sleep. I'm groggy, and tiredness has become a blanket of sludge that covers me from head to toe. My head is in a thick, dense cloud of blandness. I can't go back to sleep, so I just lie in my bed. I exist, and that's all I can manage. The medication has worn off, and I am experiencing an exhaustion that drenches my bones and limbs in weariness. And now the happiness I was experiencing while on Vyvanse is replaced with guilt.

I stare at the dark ceiling, hearing the thump and bump of my heart still beating fast. I really don't want to know what time it is. But when I get enough gumption to do simple tasks, I reach for my phone and discover that it's five in the morning.

My mouth and throat are dry. My tongue aches for water. I quietly moan and get out of my bed to make my way to the bathroom for some water.

The automatic lights aggressively flare into my corneas when I walk in. A second later, my eyes adjust, and the headache sets in. It stings and burns. There's pressure just above my temples that feels like my brain is actively pushing against my skull to be released.

I fill my entire bottle with cold tap water. In seconds, I down the entire thing and refill it. My throat wants more, so I down another full bottle.

I lean against the sink to let things settle. I stare at my expression. Red veins cover my eyes so much that there is very little white at the edges. My jaw slacks. I see the back of my head from the reflection of the mirror behind me. There is a hallway that expands into infinity of my face and the back of my head. I grow dizzy from the sight and splash my face with cold water.

My body yearns for more Vyvanse. It's like my brain and my body have separated and are at war with each other. My brain argues that this is the consequence of abusing medication, while my body wants to feel that energetic high again. My body tries to communicate to my brain that it also feels magically great. But my brain says that this is what the come-down is going to feel like again and again.

I remember my dad in this moment. His eyes often looked like mine. He had the same sunken cheeks. I wonder if he had this same argument with himself when he was trying to battle his addictions.

"I can't do this," I say to my reflection. I nod. The back-and-forth and up-and-down motion sends a dizziness into my stomach, and I feel everything coming back up.

I toss my head over a toilet and vomit all the water I just drank. I do my best to keep my groans quiet. No one should see me in this position. No one should see me weak.

When I feel like all the water has come out, the nausea is still ravaging my stomach. I begin to dry heave, and my head pounds in agony with every cough. The nerves along my spine spasm with every tightening of my stomach. I feel electric torment from my skull to my toes.

I've been kneeling on the tile for so long that my kneecaps ache. When it finally feels like I'm done vomiting, I crumple into myself. Everything feels sore. My muscles. My joints. My tendons. My ears. My brain. I flush and push myself back up. Is Sagefield truly worth this?

After suffering through my morning classes, I walk through the hallway toward the dining hall. I feel as though I just got out of a war zone. It wasn't until second-period physics that someone pointed out to me that there was a huge stain on my shirt.

At lunch, I grab some food and some cola and sit down with two of my wrestling teammates. I zone out and don't even notice what they are talking about. I slowly push food in my mouth, tell my jaws to chew, remind myself to swallow.

"Yo, Derrick," Gabriel says, scaring me alert.

When did he sit down? I look around at the table and discover that two more wrestlers joined us. Man, I am out of it.

"What's up?" I ask. The words are slow like wet concrete sliding down an incline.

"You look like someone beat you with an ugly stick," Gabriel jokes. I hear concern underneath his humor.

"I still look better than you," I clap back playfully. There are *ooo*s and laughter from the table. Gabriel smiles and gently punches my shoulder. "Easy, I just pulled an all-nighter."

"Those are rough!" Gabriel says. "I pulled three last semester."

"I've had to pull two already this semester!" I hear a freshman wrestler say.

Their voices blur together.

"I pulled two in a row!"

"I have to do one tonight!"

There's this weird competitiveness underneath it all. I can't believe everyone's bragging about not sleeping. It's like all-nighters are this badge of honor that everyone wants to wear. This ain't healthy. No one should revere all-nighters like this.

I eat as much as I can, which is a small peanut butter–jam sandwich. I crave my soft, warm bed. So I say to them all, "I'm going to get some sleep before practice."

I walk into the main hallway and out onto the grounds. The coldness pricks my senses awake. I exhale and see the mist. It feels so delicious out here. Up above, there's a mass of beautiful dark gray clouds lazily traveling across the sky. We're supposed to be getting some snow. I'm so tired that I can't even get excited for it. I might have to get more Vyvanse. The come-down sucks, but I can't go to practice this exhausted.

I pull out my phone and text Mancini. Within minutes, he responds and tells me to meet in his room.

Ten minutes later, I sit on Mancini's bed. This room is larger than my room by a few feet in width and length. There are posters of Pink Floyd albums and Quentin Tarantino films. There is a pile of dirty clothes in the corner of his room. It smells strongly of air freshener, which is a big giveaway that he smokes.

Harris sits on a large beanbag chair in his school uniform. He reads a thick book of poetry from Thoreau. I assume it's his English homework. We are all always doing homework. Mancini went to the bathroom and should be back soon.

"How was your first time?" Harris asks me, flipping a page.

"It made staying up a lot easier," I answer.

"Be careful with it," Harris says. He closes the book and looks at me. "It can be addictive."

"I get that. Thanks for the warning," I say.

Just then, Mancini walks in with a large smile. "Hoskie!"

We bump our fists, and then he sits on the edge of his bed.

"Thanks for the quick response," I tell Mancini.

"Not a problem at all," Mancini says.

"So, how much do I owe you?" I ask him. I don't have a lot of time to fiddle around. If I can get back to my dorm by 1:15, then I can have about thirty minutes of sleep before I have to make my way to wrestling practice.

"Aren't we an eager beaver?" Mancini chides.

Harris chuckles. "Eager beaver, that's what I call your mom."

I resist yawning and force myself to laugh. "Sorry, I don't have a lot of time. I want to try and get some sleep before wrestling practice."

"Understandable," Mancini says. "And yeah, I got a sixth-period class coming up. So let's get to business."

"Mancini and I run a pretty lucrative distribution operation," Harris contributes from the beanbag.

"Very lucrative. What I gave you I normally ask for ten a pop," Mancini says.

"Sometimes twenty for the completely oblivious," Harris says.

"He's talking about the Asians," Mancini says.

God, these guys are jerks.

"So, we have a proposition for you," Harris says. "Mancini and I could use a third partner for the demand we got coming in."

This sounds like nothing I want to be involved with. I just want an extra pill, so I humor them. "What are you thinking?"

"Have you heard of Dr. Demise?" Mancini starts.

My face contorts, and they understand from my expression that I haven't.

Mancini laughs. "He's the school's on-call doctor. It's hilarious! He's on trial for medical malpractice in several states. But his crimes are just below extradition, so they can't do anything. And he's just working here."

How much of what he's telling me is true, and how much of it is people tossing gossip with large amounts of exaggeration?

"He's the literal worst doctor in the world," Harris says. "He's only here because he went to the same university as the headmaster or something like that. I went in to get a few vaccinations and examinations done for my summer abroad program, and he shows me my blood results and says, 'Good news, you don't have HIV.'"

Both bust out laughing.

"I had to remind him that I was there for vaccines, and he looked so confused!" Harris says.

"Anyway, there's another name that he goes by. Candyman," Mancini says.

There's only one reason why a doctor would be called Candyman: he prescribes medications freely and loosely. Then my mind connects the dots. "You want me to get prescribed Vyvanse so you can sell it."

"There's that good old Sagefield brain at work," Mancini answers.

Harris says, "I know where you come from because my family doesn't make that much money. It's a real drag being here seeing all this wealth while you are barely scraping by. This can be an extra source of income and access to Vyvanse for your own studying. It's a win-win scenario."

I grimace and my brows scrunch. I fold my arms across my chest. This is wrong and illegal.

Mancini clarifies, "Once you get the prescription, put away half for yourself and then the two of us can sell the other half. Dr. Demise always refills our prescriptions, no question."

"I have to think about it," I say. If I were to outright say no to them right now, would they still sell me the pill?

"It's super easy. Good old Dr. Demise is required to ask several questions before prescribing Vyvanse. Honestly, I'd be willing to bet that he'd prescribe it to you if you just said that you were having trouble studying. But just in case, we have the answers he needs to hear in order to be able to prescribe it. All you do is show up, tell him the answers in your own words, of course, and get that prescription."

They're quiet. They probably waiting for my answer. "I'm good," I finally say after a moment of silence. They look slightly disappointed, but I don't care. I'm only here to get through the next few hours.

"Mull over our offer," Harris says. "But to give you an idea of the profits, if you were to get the full prescription dose of fifty milligrams, which shouldn't be too hard an acquisition, we can sell *those* for forty bucks easy. You can easily get a ninety-day supply from Dr. Demise. So forty-five times forty? That's eighteen hundred dollars. I'm considering that we already combine and divide Mancini's and my share. It'll still be eighteen hundred dollars for you for one prescription. But, dude, last year's spring exam seasons. Guess how much we made?"

I toss out a random number. "Two thousand dollars?"

"We netted five thousand dollars. Each."

My jaw drops. That's more money than I've ever seen in my life.

"You see"—Mancini takes over explaining—"we started setting aside our prescriptions since last May and had ourselves a nice little bank of Vyvanse. Even with our stores, we still had students aching for more. And if we add your prescription, I'm hella certain we can push an easy ten thousand dollars each."

"It's ambitious," Harris says. "But you're new to the medication. So you won't need the full strength of it. You can easily use a fourth of a fifty-milligram pill, and the other three-fourths will be pure profit."

I grow dizzy. This is a lot to process. Ten grand in my pocket! That's a laptop, an iPad, a new iPhone, an Apple Watch. Books. That's a whole year of rent for my mom. My mom. She would be so disappointed in me if I did this. So why haven't I said no yet?

"I don't know."

Mancini says, "Here." He reaches into his desk and pulls out a pill bottle. He hands me another tiny pill. This one says *5 milligrams.*

"Thanks, man," I say. "How much?"

Harris tells me five, and I hand it over to him. Then he says, "Mancini will be graduating next year. So when he leaves, I'm going to need a business partner."

Despite my heart absolutely wanting to decline and cut these guys off for good, I say. "I'll get back to you on the offer."

Both of them smile, like fishermen who know they've snagged a fish. "We got your back, brother," Harris says.

I close the door behind me and quickly make my way to my dorm room. All I can think about it is the $10,000. That amount of money could change my entire life. I force myself to remember that if I get caught, it's jail for me.

Back in my dorm room, I sit in front of my brick of a laptop looking at the newest laptop model on the Apple website. The thought of thousands of dollars in my bank account revved me up, and I wasn't able to take a nap. It's all right; the pill I got should help me with wrestling practice. I'll deal with the come-down later. But, man, this new laptop is so sleek, slim, and powerful! Unlike the chunky dinosaur I'm using right now. My fingertips ache to type on that gorgeous backlit keyboard.

I texted Chris a few minutes earlier to call me as soon as possible because I wanted to get his opinion. If he thinks it's a solid idea, I might hit Harris and Mancini back up. What if there is a way to get him involved? He would also be able to benefit from a few extra thousand dollars. He wouldn't have to wash dishes, and he could focus on sports.

My heart tells me this is wrong. But listening to my heart isn't going to buy me textbooks or help pay for my food when I go out to eat with friends. I'm sick and tired of people paying for me! It's so embarrassing to have to rely on others like this. Listening to my heart isn't going to help me stay up to finish all this work and begin studying for the upcoming finals.

While I wait for Chris to respond to my text, I pull the pill out of my pocket, ready to swallow it so that I can go to wrestling practice and not be miserable.

My phone vibrates. It's Chris.

"What's going on, man?" I say, excited to talk to him.

"Sup?" he says. There's some concern in his voice. I guess I should have told him it wasn't, like, a life-or-death scenario.

"Hey." I'm not entirely sure how to break the ice and decide to just go for it. "Yo, so I just had this talk with some of the kids here, and they offered me this interesting opportunity." Why did I say *opportunity*?

"Oh? What is it?" he asks.

"It's—it's . . ." I stammer. "It's selling Vyvanse to other kids here."

"Vyvanse? The ADHD medication?"

"Yeah. I could make up to ten thousand dollars if I join."

"If you join? What the hell, man? Seriously?" There's anger in his voice.

"What?" Why's he coming at me like this?

"You can't be that stupid," Chris says.

He just called me stupid! "The hell?"

"You're talking about becoming a drug dealer. Did you forget what happened to Starletta? What happens when you get caught? You don't have rich parents to bail you out. Once you mess up, that's it. You don't get second chances like those rich brats. Out of everyone I know, I never thought you would disappoint me."

Ouch.

"You don't know what's going on over here," I argue.

"The hell I don't! That's all you talk about. You, you, you! You never ask about us or what's going on with us. Even so, the old you would have walked out of that room the moment those jerk wads offered it to you."

I nearly yell into the phone, "So there's an old me now?"

"I guess so. I mean, I don't know this version of you."

"You're right, you don't know me anymore. You don't know the stress I'm under. You don't know how hard it is."

"So, the moment it becomes too hard you become a bitch ass and take shortcuts?"

Anger rises to my chest. Who the hell is he calling a bitch ass? I want to punch a wall. I want to punch him. I say, "You're just jealous I got into Sagefield and you didn't, because you're not good enough."

"Do whatever the hell you want to do. Just don't get in touch with me," he says, and then hangs up before I can say another word. I toss my phone onto my bed.

The hell does Chris know? He's not here! He's not struggling to keep up with the schoolwork. So where the hell does he get off saying he's disappointed in me? He couldn't even get into Sagefield! You know who's proud of me? My mom! My grandma! My great-grandma! They are proud of me, and that's all that matters.

But would they be if I were to sell prescription medication?

It all comes crashing down on me. He's right. The old me would have walked out of Mancini's room the moment he mentioned selling medication for a profit. The old me would have never reached out to them in the first place.

Chris's words hurt so much because they are true. And I hurt him real bad. What I said was spiteful. I wouldn't be surprised if Chris never talked to me again. I think I broke our friendship.

I go to the bathroom to splash some water on my face. The cold moisture stings, but not as much as the knowledge that I really hurt one of my best friends, who has always had my back.

I dry my face with a paper towel and toss it into the trash can. It's not until I'm holding the pill against my lip that I realize I'm about to take Vyvanse again.

I desperately want to ingest it. My lips part, and my fingers place it on my tongue. It moves toward the back of my throat. Saliva collects and wraps around it, getting ready to slide it into my stomach and work its magic.

I look at my reflection and don't recognize my eyes. The

mirror behind me shows the back of my head and the infinite hallway. There's a crack at the bottom corner that reflects a million times. I stare at it so that I don't have to look at myself swallowing the pill.

Then I smell the waft of cedar smoke. Másání Mildred.

I spit the pill into the sink. If feels like something is helping me to turn on the faucet so the pill is washed beyond my reach and disappears into the drain. I leave the bathroom and make my way to my room to get ready for wrestling practice. I open my laptop and see the folder for the cheat sheet. I drag the entire folder to my trash. Then I empty the trash.

This is going to be a long day.

27

Dimóo dóó tágíįį́, Níłch'ih Tsoh 4

Wednesday, December 4

The moment I wake up, my heart rate instantly shoots up and I am anxious and feel nauseous. Adrenaline floods my veins. It feels like the world is going to end and I'm powerless to stop it. Everything that I've struggled for, everything I've sacrificed, is going to crumble. My breathing increases. I'm not getting enough oxygen. Dizziness builds in the center of my skull and expands throughout my brain. I can't go back to sleep, so I sit up and massage my head. My phone says it's 5:00 a.m. I'm nowhere near done with my physics and geometry sets.

I feel like I royally screwed up everything and I'm going to fail finals. I'm a loser who got to go to Sagefield for only one semester. Everyone back on the rez is going to say I couldn't cut it. I don't think I can face my friends, my old classmates. But on the other hand, I'll be closer to Másání Mildred. That's a positive. I can spend as much time with her before . . . I gasp. I have to face this. I can't escape it. I can spend more time with her before she passes away.

It's still dark outside. But I see something beautiful falling from the sky. It's snow, the first snowfall. My stress, my worries, and my grief start to dissolve. I've been waiting for this.

Moments later, I walk out in my boxers and sleeping shirt. The sky is dark. The streetlights create domes of light, the falling snow reflecting their yellow beams. They look like shaken snow globes. I step out of my shoes and take off my shirt.

My bare feet step into a tall mound of snow. The cold stabs at the space in between my toes. My arms reach out to my sides, and I fall backward and let my body disappear into the fresh, clean snow.

My senses are all afire. The sweetness of the snowflakes coats the insides of my nostrils. Beyond the streetlights, the clouds swirl in the sky. Wind blows across my skin and further chills my body temperature. I hear myself laughing.

I remember my first snow bath back home. Demi picked me up and tossed me into the snow. I cried because I didn't like the sensation of falling. But then she jumped in with me and began to rub the fresh snow on her skin. My mom came up behind me and scrubbed my skin with cold whiteness. She explained that the first Diné to do this were the Hero Twins; they snow-bathed for strength of body and mind.

I rub the large flakes of snow against my bare chest and arms. I gather another clump of snow and rub it against my back. The coldness counteracts the poison in me, and my heart pumps fresh blood through my veins. Finally, I scoop up more snow with both hands and rub my face. The dizziness and nausea are dispelled.

My teeth chatter and I hurry back inside. I dry myself off and then put my shirt and shoes back on.

I'm not a loser. I have my family. I have my friends. I have my culture. And they all want me to succeed. I want to succeed.

On my way to my room, I send a quick text to Chris saying that I'm sorry for what I said. There's an unread text from my mom. Before I read hers, I send another text to Jayden telling him that I'm here whenever he needs to talk.

One thing at a time, I think. Give them space. Now I have to finish these sets as best I can.

I text Harris and Mancini after I return to my room from my morning shower. I say that I don't think I'd be a good fit for their "opportunity." They are more than likely still asleep.

Then I read from my mom that Másání Mildred's surgery is scheduled for this Monday, December 9. I'm equally excited and scared for the outcome.

It's 6:45 now and still dark outside, though the snow has stopped. I put on a thermal layer underneath my white button-down shirt. I don't want to mess with a tie, so I put on a bolo tie with a singular chunk of turquoise in the center of a sterling silver squash blossom design. I throw on a heavy coat and make my way outside.

Toward the east beyond the bull sculpture, I see the predawn. Hayoołkaał. I pass by my snow bath area, and a thick carpet of snow has already filled in most areas. Each of my steps crunches as I trudge through the walkway that is now more like a hallway with walls of frozen snow on either side of me.

I get a text when I'm halfway to the dining hall.

It's from Harris. If you change your mind, hit me up. I consider deleting Harris's and Mancini's phone numbers. I'm more than done with them at this point. But something prevents me from doing so.

I enter the building and shake off the snow that crusts the bottom of my boots.

The dining hall is almost empty. I grab my bottle and stand in front of the coffee machine. This time, I fill it halfway. I need to work on getting through this school without relying on substances. After I gather some food, I find an empty table where I can eat and work on my Latin flash cards.

A group of students is madly tapping away on their laptops. Their fingers race and the keyboards click loudly, almost to the point of annoyance.

I'm about halfway through my words when there's a loud, joyful scream behind me.

"Holiday! There's a holiday!" a girl from the Upper-Mid class shouts.

I open my email and see a brand-new message from the school dean. I click on it and graphics of confetti fly across my screen. A group of girls in the main hallway all scream with joy.

I read the email:

Dearest Sagefield students,

We, the administration, have declared today an academic HOLIDAY! Please note that classes for today are canceled. There will be an all-school meeting in the Gertrude Claasen

Auditorium at 10:00 a.m. and athletic commitments will occur at 1:00 p.m.

Please enjoy your day off, as you have worked so hard!

I can't believe it. My classes have been canceled! I'm near tears. This couldn't have come at a better time. Now I stand a chance of finishing some late assignments. I smell some cedar and think of Sawmill. I smile. Thank you, Másání Mildred.

Suddenly, a senior from the swimming and diving team runs in from the outside wearing only his Speedos and goggles. His shins are covered in a thin layer of snow. He dashes through the dining hall, hoisting up a flag with the Sagefield emblem. He runs through the dining hall and into the main building.

At ten in the morning, I sit in the school auditorium, where we have all-school meetings and the school plays are performed. It's pandemonium all around me. No one is in school uniform, and instead everyone wears festive and silly clothing. It feels like a party. Madonna's "Holiday" blares out of the speakers in the ceiling of the auditorium.

Wendy dances with her friends on the racquetball team. They all wear goofy, brightly colored sunglasses. They take selfies.

Caleb sits down next to me with the largest smile I've ever seen. Several other wrestlers in our class join us. Most of them wear thick cotton robes. We make silly faces and flex for some selfies. As we let loose, stress melts away and endorphins flood my heart.

Headmaster Wordsworth, our version of a school principal, walks toward the center stage from behind the curtain. Normally he wears a royal-blue suit with a silver tie, but today he also has on a silly rainbow propeller hat that covers the few strands of silver hair on his balding scalp. He shakes his arms and shoulders to the music.

All at once, the entire study body chants, "Wordsworth! Wordsworth! Wordsworth!" I join in, shouting with my teammates at the top of our lungs. It's absolutely glorious!

One minute passes as he stands at the podium with a microphone, smiling at everyone. He raises his hand, and everyone quiets.

"It is my honor to inform you all that today is an academic holiday!"

Everyone screams! To my right, I see a student absolutely crying her eyes out. I feel that.

"Please enjoy this day off to do as you will. Might I suggest two school-sponsored activities to further your enjoyment of this holiday. First is sledding on golf hole nine. Sleds and inner tubes will be provided. All you need to bring is laughter and thrills! Or mayhap you'd prefer a sweet option. In the dining hall, local Merewell bakery Strokos will generously cater a hot-chocolate-and-cinnamon-bun afternoon treat. Both activities will begin at three o'clock. If you have athletic commitments, please refer to the email sent this morning for further details. Now, please relax and enjoy!"

Several students toss their hats and sunglasses into the air.

The guy in the Speedo jumps onto the stage and then somersaults into the seniors in the front row. Reese, Gabriel, and others catch him with ease and lower him to the floor.

* * *

After wrestling practice, Reese, Gabriel, Caleb, and I make our way to golf hole nine in our winter gear. They dragged me out of my dorm room to enjoy this special day, even though I wanted to stay indoors and focus on my schoolwork.

Caleb and I walk a few steps behind Reese and Gabriel. We have to lift our knees high to step forward in all this snow. Caleb quietly says, "Dude, just tell your teachers what's going on with your great-grandma and that you need some extra time to turn in assignments."

That feels too much like asking for pity, in my opinion. Also, with extra time today, I truly feel like I can get this done on my own. "I got it."

We hear laughter over the hill. Reese and Gabriel rush over and disappear from the bend of the land. When Caleb and I stand on top of the hill, I see the long tubing track. There is a line of students waiting to pick up sleds and to race down the snow-covered golf course.

It's easy to spot Esme, who of course is wearing all black, standing next to Reese. She smiles and gives him a little kiss on his cheek. Gabriel meets up with Julia, and they hold gloved hands.

"Hi, Derrick," Esme says to me.

"Hey," I say, and smile at her.

She leaves Reese's side and comes over to me. "How's the semester been for you?"

I laugh. "What are my options for answers?"

She smiles. "There's lying and saying it was a breeze. There's being somewhat honest and saying you just got rammed. There's being completely honest and saying you are wondering if you're going to be kicked out because of how behind you are with schoolwork."

"On the nail. Completely honest."

"Be easy on yourself, young Padawan," Esme says. "We're all behind. Just get the work done when you can."

"Last year," Caleb says, "I thought I was going to fail Spanish because I didn't turn in five translations. Ended up getting a B."

"So, it's normal to be behind?" I ask.

"Not really," Reese jumps in. "What's considered normal is the absolutely daunting amount of homework. But there's more to Sagefield than just academics. It'd be a shame to miss out on something like this because you feel that schoolwork overrides everything." Reese holds his arms out to the side like he's displaying the sledding event.

"You'll get it done eventually," Esme says, and pats my back.

"Thanks," I say. I really do want to enjoy the freshly fallen snow. Now I'm hoping I can enjoy sledding without worrying about my schoolwork.

When we get to the line, I notice Wendy and Markus holding hands. I wave at them and smile. Wendy notices me, smiles back, and waves. Markus motions for me to come over.

"Hey, guys," I say, approaching them.

"Darren, right?" Markus asks.

"Close," I say. "Derrick."

Markus says, "We never heard back from you about the study group. We're planning one for after dinner, if you're free."

That's right. I had completely forgotten about their offer. And that does sound like a good idea. "Mind if I bring my friend Caleb?"

"The more the merrier," Wendy says. "As long as he doesn't fall asleep like this guy."

"Hey, it only happened once," Markus says.

Wendy continues, "We have this master Google file where we all share notes. Super helpful."

"Really? Is that like cheating?"

"No!" Wendy says. "We're sharing notes and helping each other with the work. And Markus here is in calculus. He helps me with all the stuff I can't quite get."

"Which is pretty much everything," Markus adds.

That actually sounds amazing. "Yeah, count me in. No pun intended."

They both chuckle.

"Yeah, you'll fit right in," Markus says.

"Derrick!" Caleb yells near the front of the line.

"See you this evening," Wendy says.

"Yeah, looking forward to it. I definitely need help with geometry."

I take off and join my friends. I'm so glad I am hanging out today.

Then, as I'm walking to my friends, I feel a tap on my shoulder. When I turn, I vaguely remember the girl who is standing in front of me. She's the pretty Black girl. She has her hair in a natural curly style. I smile, but I'm struggling to remember her name.

"Hi . . ." I trail off.

"Andrea," she supplies. "I just wanted to say sorry again."

"For what?" I ask.

"For trying to touch your hair without permission," she answers.

Then it all floods back, and I smile. I haven't thought about that in so long. "It's good. I actually forgot about it."

"Do you shave your hair because of me?" she shyly asks.

"Oh, no. Not you specifically. But I was getting a lot of stupid questions about why I don't have long hair. So it was kind of my middle finger to all those questions."

"That sucks. Sorry you had to go through that. I like your hair better this way," she says.

"Thanks." I feel myself blush.

"Well, I'll see you." She turns and heads to her group of friends. I don't notice that I'm staring until she turns to wave at me.

"Yeah, see ya." I walk back to my own friends with the widest smile I have ever had.

28

Nida'iiníísh, Níłch'ih Tsoh 6

Friday, December 6

I focus on finishing up the first draft of my final history paper in Mandatory Study Hall. I am on page fifteen of twenty. I have already pretty much typed out everything I want to say and now am just extending sentences to meet the minimum requirements.

I'm not as distracted as I thought I would be, considering that Másání Mildred's TAVR procedure is going to be in three days. I'm trying not to overdramatize things and imagine the worst. So far, I've been more focused on this essay.

"First five-minute break," Ms. Laramie says. The other students take this moment to stretch and move about.

Caleb and Xavier, who sit next to me, stand and groan loudly. I keep on writing. But my thoughts jumble. One phrase haunts me while I write my essay. *You look like Jerome.*

I review the facts I know. Both Mildred and Gertrude were forced into the Chinle Boarding School, which closed in 1976. It was then relocated to Many Farms, Arizona. Students were distributed to other boarding schools, some as far as the Carlisle Indian boarding school in Pennsylvania. But, somehow, Mildred, Gertrude, and two other girls were able to escape during the 1930s. Would Jerome have been in the boarding school with them? I doubt this theory is true because it seems like the girls and boys were kept separate.

As I reread my quotes and research, the horrible treatment those children, who are now my Elders, endured becomes tangible and real. I think about the fact that boarding schools in the United States were breeding grounds for communicable diseases. Pink eye and tuberculosis were common ailments that ravaged the student population. These stories are no longer just words. They are physical scars on the bodies of Native Elders. They are the emotional traumas that our Native Elders are afraid to talk about. Doo 'ajínída'.

When I look at the pictures, especially the ones taken in Phoenix, I want to cry. The more I read, the more I understand Másání Mildred's fear when I said I wanted to attend Sagefield. My coming here must have been the hardest thing for her to understand. I'm sorry for what I put her through.

"All right, students," Ms. Laramie says. I tune out what she says because I already know it's about getting back to work.

I stare at my paper. It's now sixteen pages, and I have extended every sentence I can.

"Everything well with you?" Ms. Laramie whispers. She sits in the chair next to me.

"I don't know," I say.

She quietly says, "How may I help you?"

"I'm not sure you can help. I need four more pages at least to finish my history paper. I've already said what I wanted to say. It feels like I can't say any more."

"That's sounds like a conundrum and a half," she says.

"More like two conundrums," I admit, though not entirely sure if this is right.

"When I hit a stumbling block, I write down with pen and paper what is immediately on my mind to figure out what is preventing me from finishing what I need to get done. Want to try that?"

"Couldn't hurt." I reach into my backpack and pull out a pencil and my notebook.

"Okay, five minutes, brain vomit. And go!"

The pencil in my hand scribbles. The first thought I write is that Másání Mildred is hiding something from me, and I want to know what it is. I know there's something missing in Másání Gertrude's story. If I don't get it out of her, it will disappear forever.

"Would you like to share your thoughts?" she asks.

"Sure." I show her my paper.

Her eyes widen when she finishes reading what I've written. She takes a moment to process it. I imagine she's also thinking of the best way to voice her opinion. She scratches her head and finally says, "This is very important to you."

"Very."

"I can see why you're experiencing writer's block on your essay."

"Is it because I need to know who this Jerome is and who he was to my great-grandma?" I keep my voice low to avoid distracting the other students.

"Our brains have a mind of their own," she says. I see a cheeky smirk appear.

"That's food for thought," I add.

She presses two fingers to her lips to stop herself from laughing.

After a deep breath, she says, "Clever. Now, for the immediate response, I think you have enough research to supplement your statements. But correct me if I'm wrong: you want to know your great-grandma's boarding school story."

Her simply stating that makes it clear. I don't want her story just for a grade. I want her story because it's a part of my family. I want her story because I feel like if she told us, she could have some peace. There's a hole in her heart. Its name is Jerome. And every time we get close, she retreats and summons "Doo 'ajínída'." I don't know my great-grandma fully yet. "I want her story."

"Is there someone who might know who this Jerome is?"

"Not that I can think of."

"Let's retrace our steps."

My mind thinks back to my research. Then Másání Gertrude pops into my thoughts. She told me this version. "Másání Gertrude might know. If she does, then it means she lied to me." It makes perfect sense. If I mention Jerome, will she finally tell me everything? "I think I know what I have to do to get over this writer's block."

"I would love to read your paper when you're done," she says.

She stands up and checks in with one of the other students. I look at my paper. I just might be able to figure out the full story of Másání Mildred's time in Chinle Boarding School. How will Másání Mildred react when that part of her life is known? And am I ready to hear what happened?

I make my way back to my dorm room. Caleb and Xavier decided to hit up the Grillery for some late-night food. I declined their offer because I have something to do. A chilly breeze forces its way into my jacket. The cold feels so amazing. My cheeks prick and tingle.

The moment I'm back inside my dorm, I tap my mom's contact info. My mom immediately answers, "Hi, son."

"Hi, Mom. How are you doing?" I ask her.

"Fine. I'm just dropping off more of Másání's stuff at your grandma's."

"How's Másání doing?" I ask.

"Is that Derrick?" I hear Grandma Rosie say in the background.

"Are you able to do video?" I ask my mom. I would love to see all of them.

"Sure," my mom says. Then, a few seconds later, my mom's face covers the entire screen. They are in Grandma Rosie's guest room, which I used to sleep in when I'd spend the night there. My mom flips the camera, and I see Grandma Rosie fluffing up the pillows behind Másání Mildred, who sits on the bed looking a little sad.

"Derrick, are you eating and keeping warm? The Weather Channel says you're having a snowstorm," Grandma Rosie says. She turns and grabs the phone from my mom. Even though it's not even been a week since I was with them, I already miss them.

"Yes, Grandma," I say.

"We are all so proud of you. Keep working hard and doing your best," Grandma Rosie says to me. She then takes a large lump of Másání's skirts from a box that is labeled "clothes."

"I will."

"Take pictures! I want to see how much snow Connecticut gets!" Grandma Rosie says.

"Will do. Can I talk with Másání Mildred?" I quickly ask.

"Okay," Grandma Rosie says.

"Mom," my mom says to Grandma Rosie. "There are still some more boxes in my trunk. I'll be right back."

"Let me help you," Grandma Rosie said. "Mom. Mom! Derrick kǫ́ǫ́. Na'!"

"Yes?" Másání Mildred nearly shouts into the phone. She holds the phone against her face, and my screen goes dark.

"Yá'át'ééh, Másání! This is a video call!"

"Yá'át'ééh, sha'awéé'! Oh!" She holds the phone underneath her face. "I miss you!"

A wide smile crosses my face.

"Másání! It's good to see you. Are you ready for your surgery on Monday?"

"'Aoo'. I just want it done so I won't be dizzy all the time."

"I think that's a good idea," I say. Outside, the wind howls. I quickly grab my sweatshirt from the nearby dirty laundry pile and toss it on.

"What's that?"

"I'm cold. Kǫ́ǫ́ tł'óodi deesk'aaz." I struggle to think of ways to pivot the conversation to her childhood. I decide to just go for it. "Másání, how cold was it when you were a little girl?"

"Huh? Oh, it was really cold. My auntie would make me chop wood even if it was snowing."

That surprises me. I was told that her aunt who raised her was a kind woman. Is she letting bits of the truth slip? I press for more. "Can you tell me about your auntie?"

"Mean lady. She made me do all the chores. She knew. She knew that there were soldiers around taking children. That's why she made me herd the sheep." Her eyebrows scrunch.

I quickly make a mental note to write this down in my notes app as soon as I hang up. There's something that doesn't sit right with the information that she's providing me. Grandma Rosie said that Másání Mildred's auntie was kind and patient. "What do you mean, made you herd the sheep?"

"What?" she asks. There's genuine confusion in her voice.

I fear pushing for more information, especially with the surgery so close. I decide to drop it. But this mention of her own aunt being mean contradicts what I've been told before. I hear someone in the room.

"Hágoshį́į́, sha'awéé'. Thanks for talking with me. I miss you! Rosie!"

In a few seconds, Grandma Rosie holds the phone and asks, "Did you ask your questions?" She walks through her hallway and into the living room.

"Yeah, actually I wanted to follow up with you. What was Másání's auntie who raised her like?"

"She was an amazing woman. She was a medicine woman. She knew how to heal almost everything with plants."

"Was she ever mean?" I ask.

"Moms have to be mean when raising their children."

That makes sense. I think of all the times my mom had to take a stern voice with Demi and me.

Still, none of this is adding up. Either Gertrude or Mildred isn't telling the truth. And I think it's Másání Mildred. I think she slipped in her story. There is a Jerome. Her aunt was mean. Could be another aunt. We Diné have tons of aunties, uncles, and relatives everywhere.

"Hey, Grandma, I have to head out now."

"Hágoshį́į́. I love you and miss you, shiyáázh."

We say *Goodbye* and *I love you* back and forth before she hangs up.

I look at my contact info for Másání Gertrude. I wonder how I'm going to get that information from her. I'm so close to piecing together what happened back then.

Ten minutes later, I stand in my dorm room, waiting for Másání Gertrude to answer my call. After the fourth ring, she asks, "Yes? Hello?"

"Yá'át'ééh, shimásání, this is Derrick."

"Oh!" Her voice changes immediately. "Hi, shiyáázh. How are you?"

"I'm doing okay. I'm just about done with my first semester at this new school."

"Yéego ni'ołta', shiyáázh. It's the ladder to success," she says.

"It is. Listen. I'm actually calling about Másání Mildred."

"Oh, how's she's doing?" I can hear some nervousness in her voice.

"She's . . ." I start, not sure how to explain. "She moved in with my grandma in Fort. She's getting her surgery soon."

"I know that much," she says.

"Well, back during Thanksgiving break, I spent the night at her place. And in the morning, she kept calling me Jerome." Másání Gertrude gasps at that name. "Can you tell me who he is? She also mentioned Kaibeto. Is that where Jerome is?"

There is an uncomfortable silence that lasts fifteen seconds but feels like minutes. "Shiyáázh, are you sure you want to know this?"

"Yes. Másání Mildred has been dreaming about Great-Grandpa, err, the ancestors, my mom calls it. Sometimes she's happy to see him. And other times she's sad."

"She's dreaming about the ancestors? No one told me that." I can hear the heartbreak in her voice. "Not shádí."

"Can you tell me, please?"

"It might be too late to change a thing, if she's having dreams." There's a brief pause. I am ablaze with anticipation. This is the moment. She will either tell the truth or keep it hidden.

I chance a push. "If there's anything that I can do to help her find peace, I'd like to know."

She exhales loudly into her phone. "Mildred and I aren't blood-related."

"What?"

"We met at the Chinle Boarding School. I was dropped off by my mom, not Mildred. I was scared and crying, and Mildred took care of me because by clans she's my older sister. She'd give me some of her lunch, and we grew close. I know very little of her life before Chinle Boarding School. But I do know she lived in Kaibeto. Both her mom and dad died from a pandemic that was spreading across the United States. Tuberculosis. She was sent to her aunt's, who hated Mildred's father and, by extension, her. So the aunt sent Mildred to herd sheep in the path of the soldiers who were looking for children to send to boarding schools.

"After we escaped from the school, the four of us ran north

toward Kaibeto, not through Canyon de Chelly. It made the most sense to run northward because the wagons were traveling east to west. When we arrived, her aunt told Mildred that she didn't know her, and that Mildred had died in the boarding school. Her aunt wanted nothing to do with her. But Mildred wanted to talk to this young boy, her cousin, Jerome. Her aunt wouldn't allow it.

"I convinced her to keep moving and that my family would take her in. She cried and cried the entire walk to my home in T'iis Yázhí. I convinced my family to take care of her because she treated me as her younger sister in the boarding school. And we loved her with all our hearts."

I can't speak. I can't even think.

"When your grandma little Rosie was born, she told me never to tell any of you that she was adopted. She didn't want any of you to feel like you weren't loved or didn't belong to a family, like she did when she was young. Shiyáázh, you are all family regardless of blood."

Of course my love for Másání Gertrude hasn't changed with this information. And I'm sure Grandma Rosie as well as my mom will feel the same way, too. Adoption doesn't change the fact that we are family. It never will. This must be a lot for Másání Mildred to carry. "'Ahxéhee', shimásání, for telling me. I love you."

"I love you, too. You and your family are still my children, shiyáázh."

I'm near tears. "You should probably visit Másání Mildred. We're not sure how much time we have left with her."

"I'll visit her when she gets back from the hospital."

"I don't want to keep you if you've got other things to do. But I'll visit when I come back."

"Hágoshįį. I'll leave it to you if you want to tell her what I told you. All these secrets don't do anyone any good."

We hang up after a few back-and-forth goodbyes.

I need a moment to process all this information. I have a clearer, fuller, broader understanding of the woman my great-grandma is. And I'm so proud to be her great-grandson. I just hope that I can see her in person at least one more time.

And I am so angry at "Doo 'ajínída'" for all the harm that it is doing to generations of Diné. How it stole the voices from my Elders and how it eroded our ability to heal. But how can I be mad at my culture, at this important part of myself?

No, I'm not mad at "Doo 'ajínída'." That philosophy didn't abuse my great-grandma's generation. "Doo 'ajínída'" at its core is about cultivating positivity and strength. It was colonization. It was the abuse from boarding school priests and nuns. All those decades of colonization have warped our philosophy into a rigid mindset of suppression and erasure. Like how poison can invisibly contaminate clean water. If we are to heal, we are going to have to identify where the philosophy of positivity and the effects of colonization have intermingled and become indistinguishable.

Before I get back into study mode, with a firm stop time at midnight, I quickly open PicsPress and begin to search for *Jerome* and *Kaibeto.*

29

Dimóo biiskání, Níłch'ih Tsoh 9
Monday, December 9

The moment I open my eyes, I know something is off. I'm sitting in Másání Mildred's hogan in Sawmill. Outside, there's a sea of grass billowing. The green blades reflect the dazzling sun as they bend to the whims of wind. But above them, there are bright stars, as well. Both sun and stars? I'm dreaming.

There's someone standing behind me, but I'm not scared of her. How do I know it's a woman? Her hand reaches around my shoulders and wraps me in a comforting hug. I smell cedar.

I try to look behind me, but my neck won't move despite my efforts. In fact, my whole body can't move. My eyes scan downward, and I see that I'm wrapped up in a cradleboard. I now see the wooden arch above my head that is supposed to represent a rainbow. My back feels stiff from the two wooden boards that are tied together by deer hide string.

The woman behind me sings. The song mentions the four sacred mountains and the colors associated with them. My confusion and stress are soothed away. I'm safe. I'm warm. I'm loved.

"I'm so proud of you, sha'awéé'," a female voice says to me.

I'm lifted and placed on her back. She walks out of the hogan, eastward. I know that this woman is human, like me. She's not a Holy Being. Who is she? She called me sha'awéé'. There's only one person who calls me that.

My heart knows it's Másání Mildred.

My mind fights against that realization. It's someone else. Másání Mildred doesn't visit me in my dreams.

I can't turn to see her face. I see the hogan growing smaller and smaller. She turns around so that I'm facing east. In front of me are the skyscrapers of downtown Manhattan. She walks forward, and we navigate the ant-like movement of people. My heart knows that Másání Mildred is wearing her black hair in a tsiiyéél, her rug dress, and her wrap-up moccasins. She's young, happy, and not dizzy. We meander through the streets, presenting ourselves in this fashion to everyone. And I don't care that they are staring at us.

"Through you, I'm able to visit these faraway places that I never imagined," Másání Mildred says.

I try to speak, try to ask her what's happening, but my mouth won't open.

She turns again, and we are on the Sagefield campus.

"Not many people can do what you are doing, sha'awéé'. Living among them. In that way, you are a warrior. My brave warrior."

I'm equal parts honored and ashamed. I know it's a big deal. But I'm not proud of what I got into, what I did when I was confused and desperate, what I was thinking of doing.

She seems to sense my unease and says, "We all make mistakes. We are human. But we grow. We learn. We move forward."

I don't feel the need to cry. The growing sense of acceptance of this moment warms my soul. There's a reason this dream is happening. And I know the reason. I don't want to say it or acknowledge it. It's too painful.

She takes me off her back and holds me facing the entrance of the main building. She walks forward, and we are in the hogan.

"Sha'awéé', today there's going to be someone who approaches you to say you can come back. That's not what I want. I want you there, doing your best to succeed."

She bends over to look me in the face, and that's when I wake up at four in the morning, cold and saddened. I just had a dream of Másání Mildred, and that means only one thing.

Later that morning, I walk down the main hallway away from the dining hall. I'm doing my best to not be haunted by my dream. I have this heaviness in me, this dark cloud above me. I can't shake either off. I could barely eat a thing at breakfast.

I don't want to call my mom. If I do, she'll confirm that things aren't okay with Másání Mildred. Today is the day of her surgery. Something must have gone wrong. The longer I postpone calling, the more time I'll be able to avoid hearing that she has passed.

Just then, a flustered Ms. Thomas spots me down the hallway. I freeze because she is staring right at me and rushing toward me.

When she's close enough to me, I sputter out, "Good morning,

Ms. Thomas." I feel a hollowness in my throat. I will myself to not cry.

She holds my arm and whispers, "I need you to come to my office." There's fear in her voice. My heart drops. There's only one thing that would cause Ms. Thomas to seek me out like this. Ms. Thomas keeps talking, but there's a sharp ringing in my ears that muffles everything.

Suddenly, I'm being guided down the hallway. My breathing becomes loud. My heartbeat slows but becomes loud and strong. I'm remembering odd things that I would otherwise ignore. Ife from history sits with her friends and sips on some soda. There's a fray in the carpeting in the corner. These details, I realize, I'm always going to remember, because this is when I am told that Másání Mildred has passed away.

I snap to and shake off the dread. I think of Caleb. I think of Jayden and Chris. I think of my mom. The memories I have with them ground me and prevent me from slipping into despair.

Minutes later, I sit in a chair in Ms. Thomas's office. I have no idea how I got here. It feels like I just blinked and appeared here. She closes the door behind me. I hold my breath and wait for the glass floor I feel like I'm standing on to shatter. I can only brace myself for the fall.

Ms. Thomas rubs my shoulders. "I have something to tell you."

"My great-grandma," I say.

"Yes."

It's all but confirmed. She's passed. And I didn't get a chance to see her again. I didn't get to tell her what I found out.

"Your mom has been calling you," she starts.

I quickly grab my phone and see several missed calls and some texts from my mom. I forgot that I put it on focus mode during my two morning classes. My eyes sting, and my tears are ready to fall.

"Your great-grandma is in the ICU," she explains carefully. "Currently, she is stable."

"What?" My dread thins. I can breathe somewhat. But now I'm heaving. I can't help myself. I was ready to hear the worst. Adrenaline rushes through my body. My lungs inflate. There's a clarity to everything around me. I hear D'Angelo's typing in the hallway. There's a phone ringing in the next room. I breathe. Beyond Ms. Thomas's window, a strong gust of wind blows across Lake Lavender, creating shivers across its dark body. I manage to ask, "She's alive?"

"Yes. But at her age . . ." Ms. Thomas stops.

I don't need to hear the rest to understand that no one knows if she'll recover. All those signs rush back into my head. Her dreaming of the ancestors. Her episode that I witnessed. My own dream of her last night.

"Do you want to fly to Flagstaff? Your grandma and your mom are staying there. Sagefield has a fund set aside for family emergencies such as this. You can be on the next plane out of Hartford. I can reach out to your teachers to help with rescheduling your finals."

Ms. Thomas's words circle in my head.

I recall Másání Mildred's words from my dream. I have to

honor her wishes. "She doesn't want me to go back. She wants me to stay here and focus on my education."

"If you change your mind, I can personally buy your tickets and have the school reimburse me. Derrick, is this what you want? To stay here?"

No! I want to go home! I want to see my másání and be with my mom and Grandma Rosie. But she told me to stay. "Yes."

I'm finally alone in my dorm room that afternoon. I lie on my bed and give in to the sadness that has been constantly growing and gnawing at my strength throughout the day.

It feels as though since we heard that she might not have much time left, every moment with her has been pregnant with fear and absolute precious happiness. There's always the lingering thought in the back of my mind that this is going to be the last time I see her. Every one of her smiles is a million times more valuable. Every laugh is golden sunshine. Every hug is warm enough to melt an iceberg.

And then I visit her and go through the entire process all over again. I cherish the new last memories with her. I never want to leave her because what if this truly is the last time?

My backpack falls off the edge of my bed to the floor with a loud thud, and I don't move. I can't move. I just stare at the dark ceiling. I have turned off focus mode on my phone so if my mom calls, I won't miss it. I don't have the strength to call my family. I just need a few moments to deal.

When I can't take the silence anymore, I call my mom.

"Son?" my mom asks. I can hear exhaustion in her voice.

"Mom. How's Másání?" I ask, my voice wobbly.

"It's up to her at this point. The doctors have done all they can."

"I dreamed about her last night," I tell her.

"Huh? What happened?"

I don't want to share the entire dream because it feels too personal and too sacred. "She told me someone was going to ask me if I wanted to go back home today and that she wanted me to stay here and focus on school."

"That sounds like her. She never wants to be in anyone's way," my mom says.

"How are you holding up?" I ask her. I bet she's taking this pretty hard.

"I'm holding."

"Where are you?" I ask.

"I'm in the ICU with your great-grandma. I was just telling her about you."

"Can you put the phone against her ear for me?"

"Yeah, hold on," she says, then blows her nose. "Okay, you're on speaker."

I hear some beeping and the gentle exhale of a breathing machine.

"Másání Mildred," I start. I have no idea what I want to say. I just want her to hear my voice. "Thank you for visiting my dream. What happens now is up to you. If you want to go, we can't ask you to stay with us. I know you must be excited to finally see your own mom and dad. But I've been doing some research and reaching out through social media. I think I found Jerome. Your cousin Jerome, in Kaibeto. Well, I found one of his sons, Randall. I sent a message to him. He hasn't responded yet. I hope he does. There's a side of the family that you haven't met yet. If you decide to stay, you might be able to see them."

I didn't tell anyone about the message because I sent it two days ago. I'm not confident I'll get a response. When Másání Gertrude told me about Jerome in Kaibeto, I began to search. Kaibeto isn't that big, so I called the chapter house there and they were able to confirm that there were two Jeromes enrolled at that chapter. Jerome Atcitty and Jerome Becenti. After I explained that I was trying to reunite Másání Mildred with her family, the chapter house official told me the names of their sons. I thought it was for sure Jerome Atcitty, who was still living in Kaibeto. But his son who I reached out to on social media said they didn't have a long-lost grandma named Mildred. I sent a message to Jerome Becenti's son Randall who lives in Page, but he hasn't responded. It could be him. I don't know if I'm too optimistic, but I want Másání Mildred to know there's the potential for her to see Jerome again—if he is still alive, that is.

"There really is a Jerome?" my mom asks me.

"Yeah. I'm sorry I didn't tell you. I can tell you everything later. But Jerome's family hasn't responded, and I'm not sure they will."

"Let me know if they do," my mom says. "And don't make that a habit. Keeping things from me."

"Sorry."

"Your heart's in the right place. But this is a delicate matter," she says.

I agree. It's a pretty big thing, as well. It could have blown up in my face. But there's the possibility that we will reconnect after all these years.

"I have to leave the ICU, son; call me later. I'll give you an update," she says.

"Will do, Mom."

We say our goodbyes and hang up. Then I realize that I have an unread text. It's from Chris. I was never going to talk to you again.

That's all I need. I text him, I'm sorry for everything.

Suddenly, this isolation is suffocating me. I don't want to be alone. Before I realize what I'm doing, I text him, My great-grandma is in the hospital.

Immediately, my phone rings and it's him.

My heart swells to know that he still cares for me. I answer.

"Are you okay?"

"No."

"Dude, let it out."

And I do. Chris listens to me cry and reassures me that everything is going to be okay. I thank whatever Holy Being allowed this to happen, because I don't see how I could have gotten through the next half hour without someone to talk to.

30

Dimóo yázhí, Níłch'ih Tsoh 14

Saturday, December 14

Másání Mildred pulled through. About two days after she was admitted to the ICU, she regained consciousness.

I didn't do as badly as I was expecting on my finals. I was able to confidently answer most of the questions and sets. Now I have one more task, and my first semester at Sagefield will officially be complete—one more round of quick edits to my final history paper. It's due in nine hours, at midnight.

I stand up and stretch in the middle of the library. A handful of other students have their eyes laser-focused on their books and computers. Caleb was picked up by his parents this morning, and it was great to see them. Of course, they invited me to stay with them in Manhattan for spring break, and I might just do that. Right now, my head tingles and my vision becomes staticky for a moment. The head rush passes, and I gather my laptop to get ready to return to my dorm room.

I enter my dorm and walk up the stairs. There's a box on every floor where students can donate clothes they don't want.

I've already gone through every floor and picked out some nice designer clothes from brands like Prada. I even grabbed a Gucci sweater for Chris and a leather jacket for Jayden. I enter my room. It's empty and feels very lifeless and cold. I can't wait for the charter bus tomorrow evening that will take the last of us students to the airport.

I sit at my desk and open my final history essay. It's currently twenty-two pages long, not including my resources. I start at page one and read it out loud—another one of Ms. Laramie's suggestions that makes editing more efficient.

This is probably the thirtieth time that I've read my essay aloud. I have to say that I'm super proud of it. It's the largest, most intensive school project I've ever done. It's also been the most personal.

Memories from the semester flood into my head. I immediately think of Harris and Mancini. Not my proudest moment. I'm not going to turn them in for their drug dealing. But I think I want to reach out to them next semester and help them realize that what they are doing is wrong. Jayden. I also have to step up for him. I'm not giving up on him.

I realize that my mind is darting off into different avenues of thought. I take a moment to focus on my breathing to keep my mind from wandering. Yet another trick from Ms. Laramie. She instructed us to be aware of when our minds wander. When we realize we are distracted, we have to take a moment to breathe and zone in on the sensations of breathing.

In two hours, I have found two misspelled words and even

double-checked the formatting of my references. It's five o'clock, and the last dinner of the semester starts.

I don't need the extra seven hours. I attach the file in an email, cc myself, and hit send. While the electronic file is due at midnight, I still have to print out the paper and leave a physical copy of it in front of Mr. Henderson's office by noon tomorrow.

I lock my room as I head out to print my final paper. Once I drop it off, I'll be done with my first semester. And I can't wait to feel the weight of this semester off my shoulders.

Later, I hold the stapled printouts and walk down the history wing. Light pours out of the teachers' office. I knock as I enter in case there's anyone here. Five teachers look at me. Mr. Henderson sees me and waves me over.

As I approach, he removes some books off a stack of essays on his desk.

"Mr. Hoskie," he says.

This is the first time I've seen him without his tie, and it's a little unnerving. I've always thought of him as uptight and rigid. Now he leans back. He smells lightly of cigarettes.

"Hi, Mr. Henderson. I'm dropping off my final paper."

He smiles as he grabs it from my hand. The first thing he checks is the references. Satisfied, he places it on his desk amid a huge stack of other papers that's easily eight inches tall.

"Are those all final papers?"

"Yes. Thankfully, they're all double-spaced and single-sided. Students aren't the only ones stressed out by the end of the year," he jokes.

"Best of luck," I say.

"I have to say, Mr. Hoskie, I highly valued your voice when you spoke up. You have an incredibly important perspective. And it'll be a shame if you keep quiet. Speaking up is something I can't teach."

I smile. "Thanks."

"I've honestly never been more excited to read an essay," he says.

I'm taken aback. It's hard for me to imagine Mr. Henderson excited. Does he know how to be excited?

"I hope that next semester you share your opinions and facts that you know. It's been an honor and privilege to teach you these past few months, Mr. Hoskie." He reaches out a hand. "Now rest up, because you are going to have another essay to write next semester."

I shake his hand, the first physical contact I've had with him. And damn! His grip is rough and strong. This is the first handshake I've had here that I genuinely respect.

"Thank you, sir." I nod and turn to leave. It's weird. I used to hate history. But now it isn't my least favorite subject anymore. I think I might actually like it.

After dinner, I pack my clothes and the rest of my stuff. The bare walls feel cold. The room feels bigger.

My phone vibrates. It could be my mom.

It's a message from PicsPress. My mouth drops when I realize who has responded. It's Jerome Becenti's son, Randall. He has also accepted my friend request.

My eyes devour the next words.

Hi. Sorry for the late response. I didn't know who you were. Yes! My dad, Jerome, actually used to talk about an older cousin named Mildred who died at Chinle Boarding School! I don't know what to say. Can we talk soon? I'm sure my dad wants to see Mildred!

I'm ready to scream for joy. Másání Mildred is going to be so happy to see Jerome.

I quickly respond, Yes! Let's talk. My family and I live in Navajo, New Mexico. But Great-Grandma Mildred lives with her daughter, my grandma Rosie, in Fort Defiance. Mildred just had surgery and is recovering.

I send my message. This is so amazing. My fingers tingle with electricity and excitement. This is something that I can give to Másání Mildred.

I grow curious about Randall and open his profile. He lives in Page, Arizona, and is a retired car mechanic. I'm sure he and my mom are going to get along. He looks to be around the same age as Grandma Rosie.

Then I notice someone strange in his friends list. Chris. How does he know Chris? There's nothing on his profile that indicates how or why they would know each other.

I click on Randall's family list and see Chris's profile under *grandson*! I can't believe this. This can't be real. No way!

Chris is my blood cousin.

It hits me all at once. The happiness. The sadness. The frustration.

It's like I'm standing in front of the bathroom mirrors looking into the infinite hallway. Each reflection is a generation. My face is a future generation. The back of my head is a past generation. And there are cracks on one mirror, one generation, that echo through the past and future, beyond what I can see. The shards of glass, created by the violence we have survived, are further fractured by our own silence. Yet, the full image of my face is held together. By the strength of past generations and the wisdom they share with us, future generations aren't completely shattered. All generations have important work to do the healing so that, one day, this mirror can be made whole again. The cracks will always be there. But it will not fall apart.

The boarding school era destroyed so many Native lives and families. It nearly broke mine. It has prevented me from loving Chris as my cousin. I wonder at the immensity of the damage that still exists because of the "Kill the Indian, Save the Man" policy. How many families are still broken. How much healing there is left to complete. How much grieving must be shed. I wonder when the US government will start meaningful actions to return the remains of our great-grandparents home.

But for now, this is enough. This is a start toward healing the pain of the past. I open my texts and write to Chris, Dude, I have something to tell you. Call me when you get a chance.

Thirty minutes later when I pack my last school jacket, Chris calls me, and I answer with a wide smile.

31

Dimóo yázhí, Níłch'ih Tsoh 28

Saturday, December 28

Two weeks later, I peel potatoes for a huge family lunch at Grandma Rosie's. Grandma Rosie is busting out all her fancy recipes, including mutton stew, yeast bread rolls, and green chili chicken tamales.

Másání Mildred wheels herself into the kitchen. "Shich'é'é, give me a knife."

"What are you going to do, shimá?" Grandma Rosie asks.

"I'm going to peel potatoes," she answers.

I put my knife down and help her to a spot at the kitchen table while Grandma Rosie pushes some of the potatoes in front of her with a peeler instead of a knife. Másání Mildred reaches out with her skinny arms and cups a small potato in her palm. Slowly, she scrapes the dark skin, revealing the starchy white insides of the potato. She smiles, probably because Jerome is coming over for a late lunch. He's bringing three of his kids and one of his great-grandkids, Chris.

Through messages and phone calls, Jerome told me he thought

Másání Mildred had been murdered, like so many Native kids were in boarding schools across the United States. He had thought of her often and prayed to her in the mornings. He hated that his mom essentially used her as bait to keep him safe from the soldiers.

My phone vibrates in my pocket. It's a text from my mom. Just driving past the cemetery. Any last-minute requests from the gas station before I head back?

"Do we need anything from Speedway?" I ask.

"No, we are good," Grandma Rosie answers.

I text my mom, We be fine.

"Shiyáázh," Grandma Rosie says to me. "In an hour, start a fire in the back."

So, that would be at 1:30, I make a mental note. That should be plenty of time to create enough embers to grill the burger patties. Oh shoot, I don't think we started making those yet. "Grandma, I'm going to form the patties now."

"Do that when your mom gets back. Potatoes take longer. I should have started earlier," Grandma Rosie says. She huffs with frustration.

Másání Mildred drops her peeler to the floor. Before anyone says anything, I go to grab it. When my fingers wrap around it, I feel Másání Mildred's hand rest on my shoulder. As I stand, I notice that she's smiling with tears in her eyes.

"Sha'awéé', thank you," she says, looking into my eyes.

"No problem." I hug her, not entirely sure what she's thanking me for.

"If you stopped asking me about my childhood, I would never

have reconnected with Jerome. I wish I had told someone sooner, and maybe I could have had more time with Jerome."

I want to say that's the consequence of "Doo 'ajínída'" and not talking about past traumas like this. But I have to speak with love. "You were scared."

She pats my arm. "'Aoo'. I was scared that if you knew, you wouldn't feel like a family with each other. And I don't want any of my family members to feel like they don't belong."

I respond, "Family is more than blood. Másání Gertrude is still family. That will never change. But we have to find ways to talk about negative things. We can't just say 'Doo 'ajínída'' and expect all those experiences and emotions to disappear."

I don't think she fully understands what I'm trying to say to her. But when I look at Grandma Rosie, I see that she gets me. She realizes what I'm communicating.

"At my age, there're not many more conversations I can have left," Másání Mildred says to us. "I know my time in the Fourth World is coming to an end soon."

I see Grandma Rosie almost say something about Másání Mildred's acknowledgment of her impending death. I imagine she wants to say, "Doo 'ajínída'." But instead, she listens.

"I have lived a full life, and I have so much to be proud of. Sometimes, I get scared," Másání Mildred says. Her free hand covers her mouth.

This hurts so much to hear.

"But I miss my husband. I want to be with him. I want to see my mom and my dad. I have no memories of them. I don't know what they look like. So when I do go, feel your grief. But remember that I'm going to be with those that have passed on to the land of our ancestors. I'll be happy. I'll no longer have to worry about medicines. I'm ready. Death is no longer this final thing. It's my new adventure."

Grandma Rosie cries, "Mom!"

"I know, shich'é'é. Motherhood is a series of harder and bigger goodbyes, and this will be my final one to you. In this world, I've seen so many of my friends pass on without saying these things to their family members, and I want you to know them."

"We'll be fine, Mom," Grandma Rosie says. She blows her nose with a paper towel. "We're going to miss you so much, but your lessons will keep us strong."

I swallow the lump in my throat. We'll never be able to predict when her last day with us will be. The best thing we can do, the only thing we can do, is enjoy each and every moment with her. I'm not going to be stuck in this cycle of anticipation. It's exhausting living like that. You're stressing. You're sad. You're mad. You feel so many things in that time before a loved one's death. But I'm not going to live in fear, because that's not living. I'm not going to weigh every minute I spend with her as my last. Just as every day could be her last, every day could be filled with joy and beautiful memories.

My mom walks in the door with a large sheet cake smothered in colorful frosting. She sees us crying and comes to us after placing the cake on the table. Grandma Rosie pulls us into a large hug. And we breathe. We exist. We are. We are a family.

For now, that's enough to get us through these next few minutes, few hours, few days, few weeks.

An hour later, Grandma Rosie's house is filled with chatter and laughter. Great-Grandpa Jerome and Másání Mildred sit in their wheelchairs, their fingers laced together. They are speaking miles of Diné with each other. Grandma Rosie and Grandpa Dominic are talking with Grandpa Randall about their parents. My mom is busy chatting with one of my two new aunties.

Meanwhile, I'm at the firepit with Chris and his dad, who are now my cousin and my uncle. The weather right now is unseasonably warm for late December. We only need light jackets.

"I still can't believe we are actually blood-related," Chris comments.

His dad sips on a Diet Shasta. "It's unbelievable."

"I knew there was a reason we got along so well," I say to Chris.

"You know, I used to get so annoyed when people said we looked alike," Chris reminisces.

I laugh, remembering our third-grade class. Our white teacher would constantly mix us up. "That's probably why we started hanging out, to mess with Ms. Robertson."

"Oh yeah!" Chris laughs.

"Do you remember the time you two switched clothes?" Chris's dad says. "You tried to pass as Chris when I picked you up."

"Yeah! Totally got you," Chris says to his dad.

"Oh no. I knew from the start what you two had done. I was playing along."

"No, that's not how I remember it, Dad," Chris says. "You legit thought Derrick was me."

"Not even!"

"I'm with Chris on this," I say to Chris's dad. "You remember dropping him off at my mom's place?"

"I wanted to see how far you two would go," he says. "Pretty far, apparently. You broke down when we got to the stoplight. So I turned around, acting all surprised. Chris, you were crying your eyes out when I picked you back up."

"Yeah, because Derrick's mom wasn't home! I was stuck outside!"

We all laugh.

I finish grilling a batch of patties and place them on an aluminum-lined pan. Chris's dad grabs them and says, "I'll take this in."

"Do you mind bringing the buns out so we can toast them when you come back?" I ask him.

"Of course."

Chris's dad heads back inside. From what I see, he gets caught up in a conversation with my mom.

Chris grabs firewood and places the logs on the fire. "He's going to be a while."

"Thanks for coming," I say to him.

He doesn't answer and just sighs loudly. I sense that he wants to say something. So I wait.

But after a minute of sitting in silence, I decide to get him started. "Got something on your mind?"

"I almost cut you off. Forever."

I realize I never fully apologized for what I said to him, at least not face-to-face. "I was a complete jackass to you. I wouldn't want to talk with that version of me, either. I'm sorry."

"It felt like you were a completely different person. You were turning into someone I didn't get, but you didn't want us to change. You wanted everything to be the same when you came back."

"Maybe," I respond. I want to get defensive and fight. But I listen. I've done enough talking. I set aside my pride and let him talk.

Chris goes on, "Whenever you texted me and Jayden, it was always to talk about yourself and what you were doing. It was never to ask us what we were up to or how things were going. It was always about you."

I reflect on what he's saying. It's not easy to hear critical things about yourself from someone you care about. "You're right," I concede.

"Is that all you're going to say?" he asks.

"I had a tough time at Sagefield. There's all this schoolwork. Everyone is so competitive. I was constantly stressing out, and I'm certain I got addicted to coffee. I even resorted to trying Vyvanse just to get work done."

"You almost sold it, too."

"If it weren't for you, I don't know, I might have. It felt like if I admitted to using Vyvanse, I was also admitting that I wasn't cut out for Sagefield. Like I was a mistake and someone more deserving should be there and I messed up that person's chances."

"Oh," Chris says. "I mean, you did mess up my chance, you jerk."

He playfully punches my shoulder. Then an idea pops into my head. "Have you thought of applying to other boarding schools? Because Sagefield isn't the only one."

"Serious?"

"Yeah, if you got into Van Doren, we could even be rivals!" I say, half joking but also fully loving this idea. Chris is just as smart as I am. "Dude, do it!"

"I'll talk with my dad," he says.

"You could do your senior year!" I add. I really want Chris to have amazing teachers like I had and all the experiences of an elite high school education. "I can give you a heads-up on what to expect." We've avoided this long enough. I start by saying, "Jayden. We need to save him."

"Save him?" Chris asks. "When has Jayden ever needed saving?"

"Well then, what do we do? I've been texting him, and he hasn't been responding."

"Me too. I talked with my dad, and he says that's the best we can do at this moment. Just keep reaching out and reminding him we're here for him. He's our brother. We can't give up on him."

"Ain't a chance in hell," I say. We don't need to say it, but Jayden would never give up on us. So we can't give up on him.

"He needs support. When he's ready, he'll reach out. At least, that's what my dad said," Chris explains.

"Just waiting sucks," I say.

"I'm so worried about him," Chris says.

"He's strong. He'll pull through. Like you said, we'll be by his side the moment he reaches out."

"Damn." Chris laughs to hide a sob. "It's good to have you back."

We hug for a moment. Chris, my best friend since second grade. Now my long-lost cousin. We're both missing Jayden and worried about him. There's only so much we can do. But I know we're going to tear down mountains for Jayden. He's our brother. And we're not going to lose him.

All of us are crammed into Grandma Rosie's kitchen. Her table groans under the weight of so much food. Jerome's side of the family brought food, as well. My mom holds her phone up and shows Demi the entire room. I look around, seeing that my family has essentially doubled.

Both Másání Mildred and Jerome have not let go of their hands. I'm glad I pushed for the story and reached out to Randall. Because otherwise I would not have seen this joy, this happiness, on Másání Mildred's face. I'm so very glad she fought to live after her surgery.

Grandma Rosie stands up and says, "Thank you, Jerome, for coming down all the way from Page. Thank you, Randall, for driving your dad here. It's not every day that you find a long-lost branch of your family. Or that your best friend from elementary school is actually your blood cousin."

She looks at Chris and me.

"There are so many thanks to give, and I know you're all hungry. But real quick, I want to thank my grandson, Derrick.

Shiyáázh, none of this would have happened without you. You did the work to bring us all together."

Everyone looks at me and smiles.

"'Ahxéhee', sha'awéé'," Másání Mildred says to me.

Grandma Rosie continues, "Jerome, you and your family will always have a place to belong in Fort Defiance."

"'Aoo'," Jerome says. "And same goes to you, my beautiful niece."

"K'ad, da'ósą!" Grandma Rosie says as she lifts lids and plastic wrapping on the food.

Hours later, after Grandpa Dominic and Jerome's family have left, the three strong women in my life and I sit in the backyard watching the remains of the fire.

"Shimásání," I say to Másání Mildred. I hold her hand and ask, "Can you tell us about your time at Chinle Boarding School? I want to listen to you tell it."

"Hágoshį́į́. After I tell you, you need to tell me yours," she says.

I agree and scoot closer to her. She begins to talk about her years as a young girl living with her aunt.

I rest my ear on her shoulder and hear Másání Mildred's heart. Her heartbeat continues, quietly steady, as the embers perish and the stars above blink into life.

No matter what form your spirit takes, I'm forever going to love you, you wonderful warrior woman. In this world or in the land of our ancestors, you're always going to belong in my heart, shimásání.

A NOTE FROM THE AUTHOR

Yá'át'ééh, shikeh dóó shi dine'é. Hello, family and friends.

Thank you so very much for reading *Shards of Silence*.

This book is based on my last three years in high school at the Hotchkiss School in Lakeville, Connecticut. Transferring directly from Window Rock High School on my reservation was a difficult experience for many reasons. Culture shock was one of them. I was one of two Native students on campus. I don't want to reveal my friend, who was also from Window Rock High School, as their story is their own to tell and their experiences were much different than mine. There might have been other Native students who weren't "box checkers," people with faulty family narratives of a great-great-great-great-grandmother who was a "princess" of their tribe. But as far as I know, we were the only two Native students. We were certainly the only two who had come straight from a tribal reservation.

I had many beautiful experiences there that helped to shape who I am today. Upon reflection, my time at Hotchkiss was favorable and beneficial. I developed many wonderful lifelong friendships. I was taught by some amazing teachers whose passion for their subject was exceptional. I even had the incredible opportunity to play piano in Amalfi, Italy, as part of a school-sponsored summer activity.

On the other hand, I also dealt with stereotypes of Native peoples. Back in the early 2000s, there was almost no modern representation of Native peoples. There were a lot of incorrect assumptions of what a Native person should be, act, and look like. I was often asked if I grew up in a tepee. I kept my hair short and was often asked why I didn't have long braids and wear feathers in my hair. A few students even touched my hair without asking for permission.

I found that I had to be patient and teach the Hotchkiss community about the realities of current-day Native Americans. It was a responsibility that was forced upon me. I didn't ask for it or even want it. I felt resentment during some of my time at Hotchkiss. I was also weaning off antidepressants and navigating post-medication depression. I knew even then, however, that Hotchkiss was where I was going to graduate from. I knew that I had an amazing opportunity to do something that would set up my future for success.

During my first year as a Lower-Mid at Hotchkiss, my mom and my maternal grandma came to visit me on campus. Like Derrick, I had shaved my hair because I was frustrated with students asking me why I didn't have braids. I also had bruises on my forearms and shins because I was tackling as a defensive lineman on the JV football team. We went off campus to Millerton, New York, for some pizza. After we put in our order, my grandma started crying and asked if I was being hit by the teachers. I didn't know at the time of her own boarding school experience. I knew vaguely about the boarding school era and what the US government had done. But I never considered my grandma might have been a part of that history. She never talked about her time as a young girl. Then again, I never asked. Years later, an aunt of mine would tell me that my grandma was sent to a boarding school as a young girl.

Many more years later, as I sat down to write my next book, I was initially planning on writing another book in my middle grade Water Monster series, but I realized that if I were to ever hear my grandma's stories as a young girl, I would have to do it right then. Her health was failing, and we weren't sure how many years we had left with her. So I committed to writing about my time at Hotchkiss and was hoping to unearth her story. However, she passed away and never mentioned a word about her time at a boarding school. In the revision process, this book became my goodbye love letter to her, a strong and complicated woman, as well as a loving and protective grandmother.

Like Derrick, I set about researching and came across the book *Boarding School Seasons: American Indian Families 1900–1940* by Brenda J. Child and several important articles like "Boarding School Abuses, Human Rights, and Reparations" by Andrea Smith and "From Carlisle to Phoenix: The Rise and Fall of the Indian Outing System, 1878–1930" by Robert A. Trennert. Doing research for *Shards of Silence* was a challenging process, as I often envisioned my grandmother as a child in the scenarios that were depicted in these articles and the letters in the book. But reading these books and articles gave me a fuller understanding of what she may have gone through and the inner strength she must have had to survive such incredible ordeals.

As part of many treaty agreements, the United States had promised to provide free health care and free education to tribal Nations who surrendered. Part of that agreement meant that many Indigenous families would have to send their children to these boarding schools for the free education. But education was not the goal of these institutions. They were meant to assimilate as many generations as possible. The schools were run by priests, nuns, and clergy people from various denominations, such as Christianity, Catholicism, and Latter-Day Saints.

On March 3, 1819, the United States Congress passed the Civilization Fund Act, also known as the Indian Civilization Act, in which funds would be set aside and directed toward the "civilizing" of Native peoples. Through this fund, boarding schools would be built and financially supported. The education would be handled by Protestant and Catholic organizations. A total of 523 government-funded boarding schools were constructed from 1819 until the program ended in 1970. Most infamous is the Carlisle Indian Industrial School in Carlisle, Pennsylvania, which operated between 1879 and 1918. The Department of the Interior has documented nearly a thousand confirmed deaths at these institutions. The actual number is likely higher. These are our grandparents, our Elders, who need to be returned home.

Former president Joe Biden officially acknowledged the United States government's role in the boarding school era on October 25, 2024. Alongside US Interior Secretary Deb Haaland, a Pueblo woman, the first ever Native American to serve in a Cabinet position, he went to the Gila River Indian Community and apologized to all Native peoples for a century and a half of unjust policies. It's an important step toward healing many generations that suffered and continue to suffer from the policies of "Kill the Indian, Save the Man." But it can't be the last. An apology is only as meaningful as the actions that follow. The young bodies of our ancestors need to be returned home.

Thank you again for reading *Shards of Silence*. 'Ahxéhee'.

GLOSSARY

MONTHS

Bini’ Anit’ą́ą́ Ts’ósí	August
Bini’ Anit’ą́ą́ Tsoh	September
Ghąąjį’	October
Níłch’ih Ts’ósí	November
Níłch’ih Tsoh	December

DAYS OF THE WEEK

Dimóo biiskání	Monday
Dimóo dóó naakijį́	Tuesday
Dimóo dóó tágíjį́	Wednesday
Dimóo dóó dį́’íjį́	Thursday
Nida’iiníísh	Friday
Dimóo yázhí	Saturday
Dimóo	Sunday

WORDS AND PHRASES

'ahxéhee'	thank you
'aoo'	yes
'awéé'	baby
ché'é	colloquial shortened form of aché'é; daughter (mother to daughter)
cheii	Colloquial shortened form of acheii; maternal grandfather. It can also translate to "horned toad."
chizh	firewood
Dajizį́į́'	A place between Fort Defiance and Sawmill, Arizona. Literally translates to "Where they stand."
Dibé Nitsaa	northern sacred mountain, Hesperus Mountain, near Hesperus, Colorado
Diné	the people (how Navajos prefer to call themselves)
Diné Bikéyah	Diné homelands, which are within the boundaries of the four sacred mountains in the cardinal directions that extend beyond current-day reservation lands
Diné Bizaad	Diné language
Diyin Dine'é	Holy Beings
Dook'o'oosłííd	western sacred mountain, the San Francisco Peaks, near Flagstaff, Arizona
'éí biniinaa	because
hágoshį́į́	okay

hataałii	medicine man
hayoołkaał	predawn
hazhóó'ógo	careful
Hwéeldi	Literal translation is "Where they suffered." The name for Fort Sumner, New Mexico, where Diné were relocated and held in captivity.
Indígena	Indigenous (Spanish)
Jiní.	That's what I'm told / I heard.
jooł yitalí	football
Késhmish Yázhí	Literal translation is "Little Christmas." Thanksgiving.
kinaaldá	female puberty ceremony
kǫ́ǫ́	here (as in person/thing is in a place)
másání	colloquial shortened form of amásání; maternal grandmother
Na'.	Here, take this.
naanish	work
n'aye	an expression of joking
Ndáá-s	Colloquial shortened form of Ana'i Ndáá; Enemy Way Ceremony. The *-s* denotes an English pluralization of a Diné word.
są	old age
sha'awéé'	my baby
shádí	my older sister
shahastiin	my husband
shibízhí	my aunt (female to female)
shibízhí bidá'ák'eh	my aunt's cornfield

shich’é’é	my daughter (mother to daughter)
shideezhí	my younger sister
shimá	my mom
shimásání	my maternal grandmother
shitsi	my daughter (male to female)
shiyáázh	my son (female to male)
shiyázhí	my little one
Sis Naajiní	eastern sacred mountain, Blanca Peak, near Alamosa, Colorado
tádídíín	corn pollen
tóshchíín	blue corn mush
ts’í’ii-s	Mosquitoes. The *-s* denotes an English pluralization of a Diné word.
tsiiyééł	traditional Diné hair bun
Tsoodził	southern sacred mountain, Mount Taylor, near Grants, New Mexico
Txį’	Let’s go.
yáa	shortened form of yáadilá
yáadilá	Meaning can vary. With a lighter joking tone, it can mean “Good grief.” But in a heated disciplinary situation, it can take a harsher “What is the matter with you? / You should know better!” meaning.
yáázh	colloquial shortened form of ayáázh; son (female to male)
zhé’é	colloquial shortened form of azhé’é; father

SENTENCES

’Aoo’ yá’át’ééh, shimáyázhí. Ha’át’íishą’ baa naniná?	Depending on the speaker, shimáyázhí can mean maternal aunt or niece from a female relative. In this context, “Yes, hello, my niece. How are you doing?”
Doo ’ajínída’.	Don’t talk about that. / Don’t say that. Can also refer to the philosophy in which you shouldn’t talk about negativity in case you attract said negativity into your life.
Ha’at’iilah?	No literal English translation. Expression akin to “What in the world?” with some elements of anger and disappointment.
Hozhó Nahasdlį́į́.	There is beauty around me.
K’ad, da’ósą!	Now it’s time to eat!
Kǫ́ǫ́ tł’óodi deesk’aaz.	Here, it’s cold outside.
¿Saben como nalgas, no?	They taste like ass, no? (Spanish)
Shił nizhoní.	I’m good.
Soy Ramirez. ¿Cómo te llamas?	I’m Ramirez. What’s your name? (Spanish)
Txį’, shimá! ’Azee’ ’álį́ góó!	Let’s go, Mom! We’re going to the hospital!

Yá'át'ééh. Derrick Hoskie yiníshyé. Ts'ah Yiskidnii nishłį. K'aa' Dine'é báshishchíín. T'ó tsohnii dashicheii. Kinyaa'áanii dashinálí.	Hello. My name is Derrick Hoskie. I am Sage Brush Hill clan. Born for Arrow People clan. My maternal grandfather's clan is Big Water clan. My paternal grandfather's clan is Towering House clan.
Yá'át'ééh, Másání!	Hello, Grandma!
Yéego ni'ołta', shiyáázh.	Work hard at school, my son.
Yiiyah, yeenaldlooshi!	That's scary, skinwalker!
Yooweh.	Leave him/her/it alone.

ACKNOWLEDGMENTS

First off, I want to thank you, reader, again for reading *Shards of Silence*.

I'd love to thank my editor, Rosemary Brosnan, and the entire Heartdrum staff for their hard work in bringing stories like mine to life. Auntie Cynthia Leitich Smith, a huge thanks to you for everything you have done for me and for *Shards of Silence*! Carter Wilken, thank you so much for helping get the book across the finish line and for writing the amazing jacket copy. Thank you to the production editor and the copyeditor, Mikayla Lawrence and Jackie Hornberger, who no doubt had their work cut out for them, with all the *i*'s I forgot to dot and the *t*'s I forgot to cross. A huge thanks to the marketing and publicity teams, who do an amazing job at promoting this book! Thank you to my agent, Dan Mandel, for all your support!

I want to thank my friends who have helped me through many phases of my life. Michael Pabon, my best friend, I can't thank you enough for being by my side through everything. I'm not the best person in the world, but you've always reminded me that I can be a better person. Weslee, don't be jealous you weren't mentioned first, my best friend since grade school. I don't think I could have gotten through my teenage years without you and Steven. Thank you, Tiffany Tracy, for always pushing me to be more knowledgeable about Diné history and to take my role as an Elder seriously. To Danbi Lee, Pete Jacobs, Jennifer Lee, Anna Raithal, Molly Garvey, Angie Tse, Mike Chen, Dana Drost, William "Bob" Purinton, James Moore, Diane Gonzalez, Marguerita ten Houten, and all my many friends at Hotchkiss: thank you for helping me see that Hotchkiss was more than schoolwork. Big thanks to Andrea L. Rogers for helping with feedback!

'Ahxéhee', shicheii ye' dóó shimásání ye'. Thank you, Grandpa and Grandma, for your love and teachings. I am who I am because of your fierce support and gentle discipline. I can do the things I do because of your prayers and guiding grace. I miss you both so very much.

A Note from
CYNTHIA LEITICH SMITH,
Author-Curator of Heartdrum

Dear Reader,

Have you ever gone somewhere new that challenges, bolsters, or reframes your sense of self? Maybe, as with Derrick, it was an academically elite boarding school, or maybe it was a sleepaway camp or a faraway visit to family. Or maybe that kind of experience is still ahead at college or in the military or when you rent your first apartment. If you're an urban Native teen, perhaps you feel it when you return to your tribal lands, or if you're a rez kid, it might be the first time you fully experience life outside of your home community.

Derrick is grounded in his Diné (Navajo) identity and values, but even a strong person will struggle under intense pressure and in unfamiliar situations. His classmates' clueless questions and comments about his heritage cause ongoing frustration, but he responds by educating himself and his fellow students about the unspoken truths of Native history in the United States.

As in *Shards of Silence*, Elders in my family grew up in a US

Indian boarding school, and the trauma lingered for generations. I admire how author Brian Lee Young juxtaposes Derrick's college preparatory school with those historic schools designed to—in the words of Carlisle Indian school founder Captain Richard H. Pratt—"kill the Indian and save the man." Overall, the damage to those Native "students" was severe and, in a shocking number of cases, even fatal. But we must remember their courage, the ways they resisted, and that ultimately the attempt to stomp out Native cultures was a failure. We are still Indigenous—Diné, Mvskoke, and over a thousand more contemporary Native Nations. We are still here, and we always will be.

Have you read many stories by and about Diné (Navajo) or other Indigenous people? Hopefully, *Shards of Silence* will inspire you to read more. The novel is published by Heartdrum, a Native-centered imprint of HarperCollins, which focuses on books about young Native heroes by Indigenous authors and illustrators.

Mvto,

Cynthia Leitich Smith

Author and filmmaker **Brian Lee Young** is an enrolled member of the Navajo Nation. He grew up on the Navajo reservation in Arizona. Brian earned his BA in film studies at Yale University and his MFA in creative writing at Columbia University. His debut middle grade duology, *Healer of the Water Monster* and *Heroes of the Water Monster*, were American Indian Youth Literature Award winner and honor books respectively. Brian currently lives in Brooklyn, New York.

Cynthia Leitich Smith is the bestselling, acclaimed author of books for all ages, including *Firefly Season*, *Jingle Dancer*, *Indian Shoes*, *On a Wing and a Tear*, *Sisters of the Neversea*, the Blue Stars series, *Rain Is Not My Indian Name*, *Harvest House*, and *Hearts Unbroken*, which won the American Indian Youth Literature Award. Cynthia is also the anthologist of *Ancestor Approved: Intertribal Stories for Kids* and *Legendary Frybread Drive-In: Intertribal Stories*. She has been honored with the American Library Association's Children's Literature Lecture Award and has been named the NSK Neustadt Laureate. She is the author-curator of Heartdrum, a Native-focused imprint at HarperCollins Children's Books, and served as the Katherine Paterson Endowed Chair on the faculty of the MFA program in Writing for Children and Young Adults at Vermont College of Fine Arts. Cynthia is a citizen of the Muscogee Nation and lives in Denton, Texas.

In 2014, We Need Diverse Books (WNDB) began as a simple hashtag on Twitter. The social media campaign soon grew into a 501(c)(3) nonprofit with a team that spans the globe. WNDB is supported by a network of writers, illustrators, agents, editors, teachers, librarians, and book lovers, all united under the same goal—to create a world where every child can see themselves in the pages of a book. You can learn more about WNDB programs at www.diversebooks.org.